EAVES
DROP

# EAVES DROP

JAMES A. LANDRY

# CONTENTS



## YEAR 1991
## PART I: EQUITY

## PART IV: THE TRIAL

# PREFACE – INTERNET INTRODUCTION

Back in nineteen-ninety, the Internet was still all but a privately held Web accessible by the Services, the Government, Institutes and Universities. Luke L'Italian caught on quick, and it paid off quick, too.

Internet protocol suite (TCP/IP) links several billion devices worldwide. It is a network of networks that consists of millions of private, public, academic, business, and government networks, of local to global scope, that are linked by a broad array of electronic, wireless, and optical networking technologies. The Internet carries an extensive range of information resources and services, such as the inter-linked hypertext documents and applications of the World Wide Web (WWW), the infrastructure to support email, and peer-to-peer networks for file sharing and telephony.

## Overview

Origins of the Internet date back to research commissioned by the United States government in the 1960s to build robust, fault-tolerant communication via computer networks. While this work, together with work in the United Kingdom and France, led to important precursor networks, they were not the Internet. There is no consensus on the exact date when the modern Internet came into being, but sometime in the early to mid-1980s is reasonable. From that point, the network experienced decades of sustained exponential growth as generations of institutional, personal, and mobile computers connected to it.

The funding of a new U.S. backbone by the National Science Foundation in the 1980s, as well as private funding for other commercial backbones, led to worldwide participation in the development of new networking technologies, and the merger of many networks. Though the Internet has been widely used by academia since the 1980s, the commercialization of what was by the 1990s an international network resulted in its popularization and incorporation into virtually every aspect of modern human life. As of June 2012, more than 2.4 billion people–over a third of the world's human population–have used the services of the Internet; approximately 100 times more people than were using it in 1995. Internet use grew rapidly in the West from the mid-1990s to early 2000s and from the late 1990s to present in the developing world. In 1994, only 3% of American classrooms had access to the Internet while by 2002 92% did.

The Internet has no centralized governance in either technological implementation or policies for access and usage; each constituent network sets its own policies. Only the overreaching definitions of the two principal name spaces in the Internet, the Internet Protocol address space and the Domain Name System, directed by a maintainer organization, the Internet Corporation for Assigned Names and Numbers (ICANN). The technical underpinning and standardization of the core protocols (IPv4 and IPv6) is an activity of the Internet Engineering Task Force (IETF), a non-profit organization of loosely affiliated international participants that anyone may associate with by contributing technical expertise.

## Terminology

The Internet, referring to the specific global system of interconnected IP networks, is a proper noun and written with an initial capital letter. In the media and common use, it is often not capitalized, viz. the internet. Some guides specify the word, when used as a noun is capitalized, but when used as a verb or an adjective not capitalized. The Internet is also often referred to as the Net or Web.

Historically the word internet was used, not capitalized, as early as 1883 as a verb and adjective to refer to interconnected motions. Starting in the early 1970s, the term internet, as a shorthand form of the technical term internetwork, the result of interconnecting computer networks with special gateways or routers. It is used as a verb meaning to connect together, especially for networks.

The terms Internet and World Wide Web are often used interchangeably in everyday speech; it is common to speak of "going on the Internet" when invoking a web browser to view web pages. However, the Internet is a particular global computer network connecting millions of computing devices; the World Wide Web is just one of many services running on the Internet. The Web is a collection of interconnected documents (web pages) and other web resources, linked by hyperlinks and URLs.

As another point of comparison, Hypertext Transfer Protocol, or HTTP, is the language used on the Web for information transfer, yet it is just one of many languages or protocols available for communication on the Internet. In addition to the Web, a multitude of other services are implemented over the Internet, including e-mail, file transfer, remote computer control, newsgroups, and online games. All of these services are often implemented on any intranet, accessible to network users.

# DEDICATIONS

For my Loving Mother

For my Loving Father

For my Loving Sister Sharon

Tom, Marty & Staff from CCR

Kathy McNeil and Dick Baldwyn from the Chubb Institute for Information Sciences and Dunn & Bradstreet

Joanne Kuleba – First Mentor & a Beautiful Woman from Dunn & Bradstreet

# YEAR 1991

# PART I

# EQUITY

# CHAPTER ONE

Getting older feels great until Luke discovers Martha reruns on Lifetime television. At a chance pause while channeling up to Fox News, he catches Martha holding up in her right hand, a beautiful Red Delicious apple, looking directly into the camera with a warm, Connecticut working-farm-girl smirk. He has heard of Martha before – Who has not. – But he has never seen her. He pictures her nude, and right away becomes quite aroused.

A classically antonymous version of Morticia Adams is she, with her strong and perfect lines, talent, and spirit live. Luke sees her all heritage and pride, the broken heart from Jersey. He is a sucker for her face and that wispy hair. Martha stands light rider poised; frosted, rooted, golden all around, and goes on to describe the fruit to him smartly and precisely as, "…so tight, sweet and (oohmmm), drippy."

Annie chuckles at that. Luke involuntarily squirms in his seat as he cautiously eyes his way over to her. His erection that night is more than his wife is and he had shared in months. Matter of fact, the next day at work - the transmitted scene of Martha, with that drippy Red Delicious apple glued to the walls inside his head - Luke masturbates right there in the executive commode just to relieve the tension.

Later that same night Luke guiltily crouches in the corner of the basement, haunted still by the celluloid posters of his Compost Queen. His own careful, filthy graffiti and dark edition does not quite manage to mar Martha's glow of charm and sexy garden attire. Perfect. There, at three in the morning he kneels, sitting on his feet like a naughty altar boy. In his mind's eye, Martha holds the apple, modifiers rolling off her tongue, expressions knowing and loose. He wonders, for only a moment, if each line is canned, written for her. Perhaps she simply delivers on demand, like the true professional she is - just for him. Nevertheless, he is alone; never to share what comes after.

The notion that it is not participation, exactly, yet it is super-mutual activity, even if it is involuntary; everybody is getting older, all at the same time, saddens Luke to a degree. Then he embraces the mere thought that if nothing else, everyone on the planet is doing that one thing all together. Luke once again holds in his right hand a record breaker, which bleeds out all anxiety in pearly off-white, down into the palm of his left. Moreover, it was there, in that forced pool of what might have been, under different circumstances, the future, a whole world cast down in his fucking hand. Yes, it is then he realizes he has not really grown that much older at all.

*Still lonely. Still playing around.*

As we decay with age, Luke believes, hope may not always accommodate. Abridging hope in a material world, with hope for a better world, diminishment and expansion may unitedly deliver. Otherwise, Luke sums it up in his own head that hope decomposes with us…as we do. Luke does not hide or try further to defend the unorthodox, sexual or spiritual aspects of his life from his wife. Like dangerous truths, however, these topics are typically unspoken or downplayed. Truths they dutifully ignore, or tip toe over. Most of the nonsense serves as a buffer for his wife, Annie, who, after treading through a few too many of what Luke coined as "Cathological" (rhymes with pathological) punishments in her early life, cannot consistently deal with any color outside black and white. Luke dare not think that chances are she may never.

Openness, just yet, whether slight, radical or perverse, remains uncharted.

"Those kinds of trips can make holes," she comments, speaking in general terms about altered states of mind, and Luke's view of awareness and constant practice to reach such highs.

"They can also open doors," is what Luke replies.

Moreover, that is okay. Luke travels better lighter. His reach for the sky continues, recycled many times over.

*I have reinvented myself more times than Burt effing Reynolds!*

From that corner, on his knees he spies and spaces at a rack of unused, rusting guns on the wall; his guitar stringed with cobwebs dumped in the corner behind him. He turns his head and saddening makes out a couple curling photographs of himself astride his beloved Harley, one mounted, the other trodden underfoot on the floor. Coming of age during the sophomore and junior generations of rock and roll music he treasures and cherishes and his spirit. He only hopes the Information Age and Technical Revolution will deliver a new outlook and living unto him. He digs the money a software consultant makes, but he remains rather bored and unchallenged.

A persistent sexual tension keeps Luke vital with stamina. The energy eases for a short span when Annie and Luke first connected. She divorced her first husband after five years of marriage; the man to whom she delivered her virginity, yet through and with whom she had never experienced an orgasm; not one. Luke reasons that he has a twenty-six year old virgin (!), and that is what keeps the line raised for a short span of time.

Luke has no qualms with his belief that virginity is lost upon first orgasm, not first penetration. He tells Annie that anyone, anything can penetrate, but it takes a little artful finesse from either or both partners to bring on climax of release. So, the novelty of the Annie's newfound orgasms keep Luke's tension low for a year, or so, but soon the woman's leftover hang-ups and lack of assertion, not to mention reciprocation, begin to take a toll on him. Annie, Cathological shield ever poised, never even masturbates herself to climax, nor has she ever, shattering Luke's sense of the essence of being a woman…being human! "Not once?" Luke marvels. "Not ever?"

"Not even alone in the dark, Luke."

This is pure Annie. Luke used to wish she would learn, but eventually decides he is thankful she did not. He knows he would not enjoy knowing it, after all. Would a cheap rubber dildo steal away his cock-thunder? Would his split-lickety-lightening seem less exciting once she started digitally exploring herself? Would she share with him if it did?

"No one could replace you, Annie." Luke may ever to her repeat in cliché (because no one, beside his lost loves of the past, truly place at all). Annie is not a fun smoker, and dull in bed, but her intentions are good, and clear. Luke fulfills the gaps in desire the only way he knows how. He will sheepishly deny the truths of condition, just for her, favoring her smile to her tears of naivety. Why would *he* ever need to masturbate if *she* did not, after all?

*If she only knew…*

Some of this foolishness is, admittedly, for Luke's own sake. He is not yet completely comfortable with the idea of sharing all that make-up his personal universe: even within the sacred and respected co-individual confines of marriage. Somehow, he rationalizes, the magic would be lost with the introduction of another, who comes along with the high and dire need for constant attention and repeated explanation. With that in mind, Luke keeps and entertains Annie.

*Hell, I am already there.*

The realities that live spirits and parties serve Luke's social rewards, but then not like they once did, and he rarely does anything exciting with friends at all anymore, cumulate to his diagnosed depression and other behavioral disorders. Most of the books in his library are deep in dust. Food has no taste anymore. His base feelings are that he thinks Annie's breasts are ugly. So is her face. He thinks back on the day they met. Nothing special sparked the direction they took together nonetheless.

"Hi," Luke smiles. "My name's Luke… new in town. What's yours?"

"Annie," Annie thinks he is cute. "So, where ya from?"

"Eagle Lake, Maine, originally: I'm living here now. I came down from Massachusetts."

"Like, what do you do? You know like, where do you work?"

"Merck, right now. I'm an Information Science consultant."

"No way! I work there, too. Fulfillment."

"Oh yeah? I am in a bullpen over at the Headquarters with a bunch of other consultants. Programmers…Analysts…"

"Wow," Annie knows programmers make a good living nowadays. "Nice job."

"It is," Luke agrees. "I like it. It's a decent living… clean"

"Another coffee?"

"No, thanks," Luke declines the offer. "I'm going home to play with some new toys." Luke chuckles.

"Oh yeah… Don't tell me. Computer stuff, right?"

"Yep."

*

They make the motions through a quick courtship, and then Luke buys their house in Washington borough when they marry. It is a Primitive-Colonial in Western Jersey that the previous owner – an ex-Amish carpenter – remodeled and rebuilt to such perfection and attention to detail, it is quite beautiful, if not just a bit small. During the gutting, the Amish fellow salvages and reuses as much as he possibly can. New fixtures and treatments reflect the timeline of the original home to the point of irresistibility. When he calls it complete and puts it out on the market, the home reflects that age in time one-hundred-fifty years prior impeccably. Both Luke and Annie are quite happy and satisfied with their find, and ultimately with their existence in the model-home.

Seems long ago, yet never out of reach, those years of life on the road in a traveling rock-show, which is far away from mainstream society. Prior to his landing in Washington Borough with Annie, Luke never experiences neighbors and community. Conceptualism, based on family life growing-up, throughout his childhood, leads the way toward his current assimilation. He reflects on his two decades on the road – how they fostered personable patience, multisided perspective and other traits – that help him get along on this old-style, Victorian, rural avenue.

Luke knows the importance and impact of a decent next-door neighbor. With this thought in mind, he tells Annie: "It is easy to make friends as a youngster, but most adults aren't capable of *making* friends. Children have the flexibility, resilience and innocent openness in their favor. Tolerance, if not acceptance are practiced by default. Adults, however, will have been hardened and learned by the truth behind error, and fearful of risk and loss. Adults tend to *find* friends, not make them, because adults cannot make other adults into anything, period; therefore, we must look for like individuals." He believes he makes his point clear, although it sparks nary a comment from his wife.

Through all he learns, the pain he has felt (and that he dealt)... Luke is thoughtful, selective and cautious about letting others into his world. The low point comes as those in that selective group invariably begin to loom and hover. Luke likens all of them now to a suspiciously dark, inhibiting ring around his own intuitive nature. He recognizes, believes and counts on God as his conscience, and Holy Spirit his witness. In addition, Luke holds court daily inside his head: his Church of Conscience, Temple of Soul, Jesus.

Regardless, Luke continues. "All of life is a personal thing, Annie. Everyone is the center of his or her own universe. Shame..." Although Luke is certainly not anti-social, he is devoted to living his life, day-to-day, happily and peacefully, on his own terms.

"Is that how you measure your own success? You know; in that way?" Annie finally contributes something to the one sided conversation.

"Not entirely, Annie, but certainly in part."

This, he shares with those close to him, is his simply complex mission in life. He soon becomes masterful at leaving work at the office, and leaving personal issues at home.

Thankfully, he does very well, even during the worse, periodic bouts with his disorder. At best, he currently *feels* great, and that, says Luke, is ninety percent of it.

*worst case better left unthought-of…*

Nonetheless, Luke knows the blessings a good neighbor brings. Therefore, he and Annie try to get along with most of those families on the block. They are particularly hopeful about Kat and Stone, the couple in the Victorian right next door. The neighbors on the other side are not worth messing with, as the house is a duplex apartment conversion, one upstairs, and one down. Tenants come and go with the wind, it seems and never worth the trouble: Most all of them turn out to be dysfunctional and low-life.

Kat and Stone are a little younger than Luke and Annie, but seem likable and amicable. They have two children, polite and good kids. Luke and Annie make efforts to befriend the family. "Kat and her kids seem okay, now that we are getting to know each other deeper and deeper," Luke says to Annie, hope in his voice. She offers no reply, which troubles Luke a bit – for he merely mentions another woman's name.

*

"But I think that Stone is just a big prick," Luke continues. "I'm sorry, but I think he has a definite problem." Why Stone on this night came to be the subject of their bedtime conversation, Luke does not even know. Annie and he are only talking light and easy about their prospects of the friendships they seek week by week in their new neighborhood.

"And, you know what? There is something funny going on with him, too." Luke looks to Annie for effect, lifts an eyebrow, and whispers gruffly, rolling his R's like a horny pirate, "Marrrk me worrrds, young Lassie; heheheheheh. 'E'll tear yer bloody eye balls out and skull-fuck ya!"

"That's gross, Luke." Annie says.

For better or worse, they typically share something too wordy for Luke before bed. Luke is always thankful when they discuss someone else's problems or imperfections rather than his own. If he had his way, there would be no deep conversation just before bed, or just after waking. Other than the dinner table, however, these are the only times Annie has lately to talk to her husband.

"Like most of us, he was traumatized as a child," Annie shares. "Kat confided in me that Stone's father left him when he was quite young."

"Shit. Too many fathers are flying, dying or going to jail," Luke begins. "None of the living should be running!" He was merely thinking aloud, but hearing his own words make his balls extra-large and snotty, so he continues. "Now he is just a frustrated actor, doing stage production with the local troupes; How sad." With that, Luke hears himself again, and suddenly empathizes.

"Fuck, Annie that would be like me going back to playing bars again. You know… at my age…in my circumstances, for money."

Annie thinks Stone is one of the most unfriendly people she ever met, and she means it when she says it.

"What do you think of him, really, Luke?" She asks facetiously, then follows, "Is he the ass hole, or is it me?"

"Cheeziz' Annie, do I… I mean, *he* is," Luke knows he had better be careful. He knows Stone is an ass hole, but he thinks Annie could also use an attitudinal and disposition adjustment. Nothing like the issues Luke has with Stone, but specific and various attributes that make up her persona.

"Ever since that time I asked him for help taking that fucking lawnmower out of the trunk of the car," spit Luke, recalling too vividly the petty incident.

"I should have asked *her,* ferchryssake! Kat would've been glad to help… always is!" With that, he knowingly and carefully quiets. Annie, adding to the issues list with a recollection, asks rhetorically, "What about using their swing set?"

"I still can't believe Stone reprimanded us for using his kids' backyard swing set without his permission! On the very day we hold Mal's Baptism party!"

"Yet, Kat already told us we could," Luke, prompts.

"I know and I would guess," Annie resolves, "that Kat and Stone don't talk much." She then laughs a little.

"His cocky attitude bugs me the most, I think," Luke says. Luke has a very low tolerance for people who think they are superior, for whatever reason, to anyone else, period.

"The greasy hair and Pinocchio face reminds me of Chad." Annie always goes with looks, Luke gut feeling, but this time Luke has to agree. Chad is Luke's sister's ex-live-in, a moocher, that no one liked.

"Stone does have an overall look that is very much like Chad's and a skewed, if not any sense of goodness whatsoever."

"I don't like Chad any more than I do Stone, either." Annie admits for the first time. So there it is…more garbage for the fire.

"He constantly references the kids back by the creek… partying, and *smoking their POT!*" This is a sore spot on Luke, once for the sake of childlike affinity, and twice as a proponent of marijuana.

"…like that's such a crime… like he never had any fun, or got into any mischief when *he* was a kid," Ann adds. This beckons a rambling, thoughtful narrative from Luke, but thankfully, Annie interrupts.

"Well, maybe he didn't," she offers. "You know… have any fun."

"Sure… that's an issue," Luke deadpans.

"I don't know what his problem is," chortled Annie, "…what their problem is!" Annie does not really care for either one of them.

"Oh…here I am thinking that you are okay with Kat, but I guess I am wrong, after all, admittedly." Luke responds to Annie's declaration.

*

Kat is quite attractive, so she is used

to being ogled, after having to walk up and down Manhattan's 66th Street every day and night, but never desensitized. Even though, she does not notice that the looks from Luke over conversation, over the fence as she moves about the yard, gaze far too long, up and down – all over. She does notice that he keeps her eye when conversing closely, instead of undressing her all over, as other men do. She likes that, and Luke knows it. She manages to keep her ballet dancer figure; tall and very thin. She has longish blonde hair, white even, a sexy flat chest, and beautiful form downward. Her eyes are a hypnotizing bright blue.

Luke is readily adept at remaining below feminist radar. Luke develops the stealth personality into second nature almost subconsciously, by virtue, simply, of his many relationships, particularly with females, back in the days of great sex, decent drugs and all-out rock and roll. He recalls the day he moves-in and sees her the very first time… his attraction.

*Now,* Kat *is a good neighbor…*

*

Beside the anger over his deadbeat dad, Kat also shared with Annie, Stone's vow long ago that he never would leave his family in the mess that his father did his own. On the inside, however, Stone, reaching for Synchronicity, recognizes that his father left him with something positive: the strength to know a child can survive without. However, Luke's father died; he did not fly. Sadly enough, all the strength left is just enough to give in. "What a sin to turn synchronicity inside-out." Stone obviously keeps unwittingly in the back of his head, itching nervous and tense more often than not.

The thought of his own kids growing up without a full-time dad continues to eat Stone up with regret. It makes the path he is on appear skewed, and the internal nagging is so loud it drives him nasty. Consequently, Stone barely tolerates his two boys, and downright degrades and belittles his own wife… when he is home. His only source for warmth is a secret he cannot divulge. He is a sad man with secrets: Especially from Kat.

*

"Mmmm… I don't know," Luke says almost in the form of a question. "She seems okay to me. Moody," he adds quickly, almost too loudly. "Sometimes cold… I don't know…" His voice trails off into his pillow, frightened. Luke, around Annie, very carefully words what he says about any other woman. He knows he will have to answer to the slightest inflection, someway, if not immediately, someday. His wife, bless her heart, is so very insecure.

"Is it us?" she asks.

"Well, is it us?" he returns.

The memory of last December, when they plan a big Christmas Gala, still slightly bothers them. Luke and Annie invite most of their friends, and stock-up on gourmet food and spirit. Then, no one shows-up. Not one guest attends. That hurt. All that food... all that booze… the bummer that it is. They continue to reach…

"Did she find that joint you've been saving forever in the coffee table drawer?" Thankfully, Annie changed the subject, but Luke can almost feel the blame coming on. She lightens up, sparing him.

"You know, baby-sitting the other afternoon? She could have, you know."

Then, just like that, Annie turns back, to peg Stone once again.

"In a word, I guess I'd say he's arrogant."

"Yes, that too," Luke agrees. "But, sociopath also comes to mind, Annie."

Annie loves to hear Luke giggle like that.

"Good night Luke." He does not feel assured.

"Night, Annie." She does.

Then, as always, they say their "I love you" to each other, like singing in near perfect unison, roll tidily over together, and fall slowly to sleep, buttocks to buttocks.

# CHAPTER TWO

Ever since attending the Problem Solving Leadership workshop, Luke is fond of declaring that he no longer rides the guilt donkey. He adds that he has learned to be accountable, and to take ownership, however, it is a prayer, and a hopeful blessing that guide Luke through, like a Hopi man in a maze.

*God let me continue to evolve spiritually, grow intellectually and develop personally, individually and professionally. Now that I am a father, make my most sincere intentions and deepest desires to parent and husband successfully, forever. Amen.*

No one who knows him realize that he lifted that straight out of Kekich's Credo. That is surface Luke at the shallow end, but the deep end is darker. He does not try to fool himself into believing that he is not unlike everybody else. Like every other man on the block, Luke works to escape the insanity of home life, and he rejoices time away from work at home. The new and improved Luke finally becomes comfortable once again, but comfort comes only now that one fierce year has passed since nearly killing himself over Kat's shellacking at work.

At the time, Luke is the premier architect in the Information Sciences department at Merck and Kat is a data Security Analyst. Her hidden interest in Luke has her monitoring his every move; particularly the web sites he visits. It is a widely known policy for Security to perform random monitoring of phone calls, emails and web sites visited for all, but Kat keeps a much keener eye on Luke.

Luke, however, as technically perceptive as he is, picks-up on Kat's nosey habits. He tries to nail her on something – anything – but cannot. She is squeaky clean. He is her neighbor, but nonetheless, she feels she must report his questionable choices for time spent at work, which leads to a lay-off. The report writer accusing him remains anonymous, banner headed only by "I.S. Security" so she feels safe and secure, but little does she know that Luke knows all about her crucifixion.

Hello, what is this? Luke and all of I.S., experience a power outage and surge. The Facilities Department's generators are buzzing now to keep throughput humming along. Luke can see in his Task Manager a network thread coming from an anonymous source. This makes him, by nature, a tad suspicious, so he decides to investigate. He cannot immediately tell what is running through it on his machine, but he intends to find out.

It is merely a semaphore at this point – a leftover piece of whatever it once was in memory, yet it remains in Luke's computer memory after the outage. Very strange, indeed, Luke dwells in his quandary, stroking his chin. "Someone is hacking me" he deduces, as he remains regularly aware of any middleware or system changes and happenings of any kind, anytime as part of his position in the I.S. department.

He decides to restart his machine. He then installs a CPU and network monitor to see if he can pick-up the intruder if there is a next time around. He hasn't much to worry about, as he is caught-up with all his work – he by virtue remains two to three weeks ahead of the game; always. Lately he has been perusing the Allman Brothers web site taking virtual tours, viewing the thousands of available images, reading posts in the forums, checking out the front page news, and even found the published a story he wrote about Gregg and him meeting and jamming together from years gone by: it was titled 'Gregg and Jam.'

Luke is hooked on the tour of the Macon house, the diner where they ate, the cemetery where Betts wrote 'In Memory of Elizabeth Reed' and of course the tragic pictorial and narrative accounts of the motorcycle accidents that killed Berry Oakley and Duane Allman. He was so enthralled, that he decided to continue until his next assignment came along, instead of going to management and seeking it out as he usually does.

Lucas is so far ahead with his work that he has close to a month to spare. He spends time at 'The Dead' site, as well, reading the biographies, history of the band, looking up tour dates, reviewing set-lists and other activities he could not resist. Hey – there it is again! He can see CPU and network activity additional to what was there before. He carefully traces the thread and finds it… a small daemon running from just outside the kernel, all but undetectable. He runs an application extraction module to view the source code of the little spyware program.

A CPU Stats daemon tracks everything from keystrokes to Internet activity! Son-of-a-bitch, Luke curses to himself: Someone is spying on me! In stealth, he backtracks the thread, very delicately, and finally, after an hour, discovers its origin. It is the I.T. Security firewall. It is going to take some serious hacking, but Luke is determined to see who is spying on him. Not that it matters, because the deed originates with some security analyst for some reason.

"Knock-knock..." It's Luke's boss Margie at his office door.

"Hi Margie."

"May I have a word with you, Luke?"

"Of course," Luke replies as he makes visible only his desktop, keeping hidden his exploratory mission. With a slap and a bang, she drops on his desk a stack of computer paper almost three inches thick.

"Luke," Margie begins. "This report reflects the fact that you have been visiting and spending multitudes of time on the Internet instead of performing your assigned job duties. You have been neglecting your responsibilities for close to an entire month at this point. The report contains every site you have visited within the past month. Although you have not visited any forbidden sites, most are clearly not business-related in any way. Do you care to explain?"

"Well," Luke begins. "Having finished all the projects I've been assigned ahead of schedule, I've been out of work. I think I deserve a little breather, so I have been surfing the net a little bit. I'm so sorry if this upsets you…"

"This is more than 'a little bit' Luke."

"Haven't I always exceeded your expectations and come-in on-time and under budget, Margie?"

"Yes, you have, however that does not justify the way you've been squandering company time and resources over the past four weeks."

"Okay, so I promise to stop immediately – just get me some more work," Luke finishes.

"I'm afraid it's not that simple or cut and dry Luke," Margie adds.

"What's the matter?"

"I am compelled to open a probation report on you, and share it with upper-management and Human Resources."

"Oh, come on… please."

"I'm sorry, but that's the way it has to be, whether you are the star of the show, or not." With that, she tersely pivots and heads away from his office.

*Shit! I have to get back to the task at hand…*

His utility finally drills through the

firewall and to the I.T. Security Supervisor's workstation. He accesses the full machine credentials and discovers the spy is none other than fucking KAT!

*God damn her!*

Lucas swears to himself that he will – he will – bring her down someday, somehow. He does not know yet how, but he is already beginning to scheme. Luke goes home and remains downstairs in his office room for the night contemplating what occurred earlier that day at work. Margie is up his ass, no telling where she is heading with her allegations… he discovers Kat is using spyware to investigate him for some unknown reason… and Luke is eaten-up inside by both matters.

# CHAPTER THREE

Luke is in his easy chair just in time to see Martha feed her audience a taste of master woodworking, on a field trip to Boston. She is there to visit local Master turner Longfellow Goodmount, the owner of a woodshop renowned for custom spindles, balusters, railings and finials. Mr. Goodmount, on cue, offers a stock explanation of the features, differences between and virtues of each. Martha, in her follow-up, drills the noble New Englander for more. In a mere two moments, she covers in totality every necessary process and part, and labor. She then summarizes.

*She is so good.*

It is obvious to Luke that the penetrating follow-up questions intend to benefit her audience. Even so, sweet as must be, she sometimes sounds as if she underestimates the mentality of her target. Luke does not care for that much. He is tempted to change the channel, but decides not to when he sees old Longfellow bring on a strange looking tool of some sort. As Martha and the older fellow delve into the topic of lamination, he gives her a brief demonstration of his Moisture Meter.

"It's an antiquated and utilitarian looking piece," Martha comments, "with a look of another time."

"I invented it myself," Goodmount explains. Martha bubbles over at the sight of it, coming into stance with a face of pride that even outshines Longfellow's own. She knows what it is, and she cannot hide it!

"Well Maahtha," the man remarks in a perfect Bean pot accent. "Ya just have ta place the prods onta the subject and look at the readin' right heeah," pointing to a clouded, little, yellowed window.

"I wonder what it would say if you pointed that meter at *me*," queries Martha, coyly smirking. She was clear enough in her lead-in to prompt the man to hold the device out to her. Grabbing the instrument and pointing it inward, toward her midsection, the old man nods when Martha asks with a giggle, "Okay now… do *I* seem to be moist enough for you, Mr. Goodmount?"

"Oh, yes, deeah," the straight man responds. "You do seem plenty moist, ayah."

"Good then," Martha says, smiling, satisfied. "…On to turning!"

Luke complains in thought, as the reading on his own meter – his Peter Meter – draws down from his brain the precious thought's blood. Some of the dialog cooked up for Martha could drive a stew bum blind. With all the innocent suggestiveness arching forth, B-caliber porn sometimes comes to mind.

*On the other hand, is it I?*

Visually, Martha has a way of camouflaging all the warm references with a perfect recipe of cool, collective sweetness. Her timing is professional, absolutely to a fault. As an ex-drummer, Luke relates to timing, and he loves that flawlessness about her. There is no chance she is not for real! No chance, he thinks; she is just too good… delivery and timing, like a well-versed comedian… so, so fine. Blood enriched endowment fills Luke's hand, any thought flying with fuel of fantasy instead.

*

For all the contempt Luke harbors for Stone, he holds multitudes more in affection for Kat. Her betrayal of him at work makes her even more attractive to him. He does hold deep-down resentment and carries some anger and notions of vengeance; revenge, but his attraction to her tends to outweigh all that. Every wrong altercation with Stone delivers to Luke long, soothing excuses, singsong dismissals and smiles in response from Kat. Even she is beginning to see, at times, what a jerk her husband can be. Luke feels guilty that he ever derogatorily calls her *Alice*, referring to the lilting way Kat seems to float in her home from room to room – Luke peering through the blinds – she light blonde-haired woman of hair, and fair of face. He is on track in mind and fronted by eminence. As he watches Kat, she innocently plays each day out as a banausic adventure in domesticity.

Luke imagines her sunken frustration harbors a longing, but he cannot have known. Kat often wonders secretly if others suspect the dolor, she carries inside. The next thought is always the sad reality that she feels it as strong as it felt to her seven years before. After a lifetime of dedicated practice, Kat had turned the dream real, and she, in the classic sense of the phrase, had "made it."

After a lifetime of foot swelling and bunions, not to mention the daily, dietary madness and exercise, her dream becomes her reality. Her professional dancing career is the payoff. Her gig with the New York Ballet Company is a major milestone and priceless achievement. With immigrant parents behind her, Kat truly lives The American Dream. Having a flat chest, she discovers, has even finally paid off!

Meeting Stone in the early, melancholy beauty of that moment in time, still bright and shiny with her own arrival, is the abrupt awakening she wishes would never come. In a few short months, he manages, archetypically, to snare his wife-to-be into a lifestyle far from what she knows and what she truly wants. Once the finest dancer in the troupe – The New York Ballet Company - Kat tip toes and twirls through a life that's now merely leftover… …With kids.

Stone mistakes her malleability for contentment now, just as he did back then. Her dream ends exactly the moment she meets him. She adores the Bohemian-slash-Socialist wardrobe. He does not even call it that! He is in theater, too! He could become a famous Production Designer someday, you know…

*She is in love…*

*She does want a family…*

*Just not now…*

*Later.*

*Sure.*

Her success in finality nullified, the issue inevitably resurfaces every time she and Stone argue. She cannot keep it down. Sadly, she cannot talk about it, either. Therefore, the regurgitated feelings roll about the throat until the next family crises calls them up again, or, until her own self-administered mental flossing blows them all away, albeit temporarily.

Along with Kat's sanctity, Stone stole her cherry. The wide-open, educated, and splendidly liberal life and spirit, fostered by her parents, ended the day she married him. Her Swedish mother and father, world-renowned scientists each in their own right, struggle ever since the inception of the relationship. Even the proud Grandparents now recognize, as Kat the happy young Mother does, that bearing Stone's first child snuffed cold completely her dream and the would-be life of a star. Then, there was another… and there went her ambition and virtually all chances.

On the good days, that is how Kat feels and what she thinks. It is worse on the bad days. Explaining it away as PMS comes too easy, for too long: She knows that, too. Until the computer guy and his wife moved in next door, she held it all inside, all the time. What little pride Kat has left over, she guards with passion. However, she opens up gracefully to Annie, and sometimes even to Luke. At first, Kat felt oddly less self-assured around Luke. Toward him, she feels conditional, prejudicial and skeptical, but does not know why. Yet, at the same time, Kat feels somehow attracted to Luke's cool disposition and simply decent attitude. His manners are impeccable, and he treats her with respect and understanding. He listens to Kat, and now appears to her a gentle and caring Earthy peacemaker.

How Kat manages to keep herself in such great physical shape, Luke cannot begin to fathom, especially after having given birth – twice. He never witnesses her working-out regularly, keeking from behind the mullion. She runs on a constant wave of kid delivery and crises, Luke witnesses, rushing in and out of her house, and jumping in and out of the car, like a woman run mad. Watching her now, Luke tires of this daytime.

Kat is as slim as she appears in the graduation picture on her wall. She knows it, but does not act as if she does. Dancing instruction for the local ballet troupe in Hackettstown keep her toned and fit, too. She easily recognizes, especially now, the only blessing left applicable, yet first realized long ago, would be the obvious ease small ones naturally afford her dancing.

"You are the only mother in town whose tits aren't down to your knees," Annie so vividly points out to Kat. Sunning together on the deck, Annie can see also, with some amount of disgust, that Kat's breasts are actually concave. Annie's comment is an attempt to be nice. If not for Annie's raucous, yet keen observation, Kat may never have thought about that additional neighborhood pay-off. Kat knows deep inside she is the only mother on the block - probably in the entire Borough – whose breasts ride still… way up firm and high… just like the old song sings. A woman raised to be proper, however, Kat cannot even allow herself to think it, let alone say it, or barely believe it.

Kat always wears a bra, Luke notices, although in the classic sense, be believes, she would arguably need one. One might presume she wears them for the extra padding the small-cupped versions offer, but that would be wrong. She wears them merely to keep her nipples – the most ample part of her bosom - from pointing provocatively through the fabric of her blouse. Even sweatshirt weight garments do little to keep them contained. Annie notices that, too. Luke often wonders what they really look like...

In seven short years, Kat turns from being a promising young ballet star living on Manhattan Island, to being a young mother, stranded with children in Western Jersey. That lately feels to Kat so apparent, and truer than ever. Why can't she simply admit it?

"Oh yes," Kat begins. "Stone has been working so much lately."

"Really…" Annie is not much of a conversationalist, but loves to prod others along for the scoop.

"He's in demand, you know, doing a lot of out-of-town shows," Kat adds, almost in defense.

"That's good," Annie tries again. "I guess…" but then blows it.

Kat stops before including Stone has also been sleeping at the school lately - when working over. Annie, who lacks the communicative wherewithal to resist the inclination to voice her own thoughts on the subject, tells Kat straight away that she "could *never* handle that kind of existence, ever."

"A husband working nights is bad enough," Annie declares. "I could never tolerate the travel, too…and the sleeping away? No!"

Annie's first husband legitimately worked

the night shift, but that made it convenient enough for him to have the affair that would eventually break them up. She believes that his spending so much time away from home solely contributes to his having that affair. She fails to recognize that at the foundation of it all lay her own catholic-illogical behavior.

Lack of living does not help, either. Neither Annie, nor her first husband ever does much living, together or apart, outside of the work life they share. Apart through their teen years, together as young adults working to get ahead at Dunn & Bradstreet, working life is all they ever know together. They are both Italian. They are both Catholic. He takes her virginity. The parents do all the driving from there. That is all the couple need know.

"Oh my god, Stone would never do such a thing," Kat laughs. "He always says that he did not ever, *ever* intend to do what his own father did to him…" Stone's father essentially abandoned his wife and kids. Stone constantly smatters talk about his colleagues, known cheaters on their spouses, blatantly, disgustingly, having affairs with students, let alone with each other!

"How disgusting it all is!" Stone reiterates to Kat.

"Hmmm," she involuntarily hums in reply. If he is not having an affair, or fooling around, why isn't he making love with me anymore? She wonders.

Annie cringed with a sympathy that should have been saved for the coming truth, as Kat relays all that to her. For, Annie trusts no one. She and Luke share that one temperament. However, emotionally, they share little else. Therefore, they already know what is really going on, even if Kat does not.

*Kat did not know the ugly, patroclinous inheritance. After his shielding fronts, implying his own bluesy, fatherless childhood, Stone finds himself facing the dilemma he's always feared. He has no idea how to deal with it, except to live with it, keep it at bay, lying to all along the way. He is biding time, as fate waits to step in from the wing. Luke frowns.*

✳

Enter Luke – from stage left. His disdain for Stone turns over the years almost to vengeance. Luke keeps close his own motherwit, but the contempt for Stone grows nonetheless. No one really knows what Luke's current life is all about. No one… Not even Annie. The evanescent identity of Luke is indeed alive and well in one Luke L'Italian, however, even if he has to practice life as though he is in his own self-imposed, virtual witness protection program.

Luke subconsciously envies Stone, because Stone has managed to stay in the business, in the game. It is not Broadway production, but at least Stone is still in it for the money. That thought once led Luke to think his own life had become too viatical.

*My own ex-sound technician still tours with premier artists, and makes good money. Nevertheless, in the end, they are still, both, just roadies. That is all they will ever be.*

*At least my star still shines high and bright over those who remember...Luke rests.*

At the core, it comforts Luke to know how Stone must suffer daily from under that rotten manqué. <u>There is nothing worse than being a frustrated artist, except having to answer to one</u>!

Luke's new life – different from his old one – remains peregrine in nature. Where Luke spends the better part of two decades roving the highways in a midcult, saluting the rock and roll way of life, he ramps up and onto the Information Super Highway during a third, eventually becoming the well-paid geek-hip tech-wallah he is today. Like a cat, he always lands on his feet.

# CHAPTER FOUR

Under the greenish effulgence of his basement room, Luke masters a domain of networked servers that keep thousands of web users up and online – and he keeps it all up close to ninety-nine percent of the time. For the better part of nine months, on those nights Luke is not teaching at The Institute, and after the day gig was done, Luke slaves assiduously over the racks, black boxes, machines and software. Parting ways with Merck offers Luke an open door to ownership of his own consultancy.

He names the Internet Service and his S-corporation 'Equity' and it is the least expensive and most reliable ISP server in all the surrounding counties out in rural Western Jersey, and lately even the Metro area! Annie views it all as some kind of nimiety, either superfluity or excess. She pegs him on negligence, and he accuses her of perpetual niggling.

"If you made any effort to remain more aucourant," he reasons, "you'd realize that I could be on to something big."

It is already something big, truth be told, but she is none the wiser and he is glad of it. She will someday no doubt, thank him for his devotion, he adds in thought. Annie backs-down if for no other reason than to escape the potential, if not impending, harangue. Luke learns to curb the Southern twanged invective he picked-up during his travels through the South, but not the verbosity. Indeed, both their respective admissions and accusations would be wrong. Luke enjoys the money and power over others being master of the domain afford him. He also craves the seductions that come with his insider information. Annie is simply a woman who can and will find a way to either dismiss or deny Luke any endeavor that does not interest her, or that does not include her.

Within nine months, Luke secures a multitude of lines for Warren County, the surrounding counties, and the tri-state area, providing local dial-up, and broadband services for those willing to pay a small premium. He keeps his rates a whopping seventy-five percent less expensive than the leading service providers do. He urges his customers and clients to take advantage of those savings by connecting to their favorite Web portals, and facilitating their e-mail and back office systems through his host servers. He gives personalized guarantees of support, and, he delivers on them.

Luke already recoups the initial investment of thirty-five thousand dollars, and he is turning a monthly net profit of almost fifteen thousand dollars. His monthly gross revenue had grown to forty-eight thousand dollars, over and above his new day job - personal contracting - salary as a technical consultant that pays fife-hundred-fifty dollars a day and his night gig at The Institute that pays forty-two dollars per hour.

Luke's work becomes his escapement. The thought that he is but a mote specimen in a glimpse of life reaves his otherwise felicific disposition, replacing it with machination. The malaise feels equal to mistaking raillery for the derogatory. Where Luke was once as peaceful as an old curandero, he, in strange atrophy, is surely growing into a nervous computer doctor on the verge of electronic malpractice. He feels the seduction, but does not recognize it, entirely. It holds his interest like nothing else does.

Annie knows nothing, still. She does not know anything about the business, little about the money, and nothing of Luke's basement office escapades. Annie is blind to it all, admittedly so. Her upbringing underneath an extended arm of the Celentano Family taught the potential and eventual importance of self-imposed ignorance.

*

"Luke!"

Annie yells often, so this one is futile.

"Luke!" This time, she yells down into the kitchen floorboards, as if that may offer a different response.

"Come up here…" She adds thoughtlessly, "Now! …And hurry!"

Luke hears her, but selectively ignores her. Finally, Annie's stomping, full force on the pumpkin-pine floor gets Luke's attention. That move gets his attention every time, and it is enough to get him out of his seat this time. It also gets his gander going: Repeatedly so.

"Fucking bitch," he mutters under his breath. He has been doing that a lot lately.

When Luke bought the old home, there was no way to get to the basement without going out the back door, down the deck steps, and back in through the old, rickety cellar door beneath. Remedially, while remodeling the basement for his network, he cut a hinged trap door in an upstairs closet floor. To completely allow passage down to and up from his new office space, Luke mounted a hard wood ladder-type stairway to a joist.

The hatch, canal and ladder-stair he finishes in an attractive, dark oak stain. It is a fun idea for a transition, but does not change Luke's hatred having to respond to her bothersome outbursts. The built-in convenience of his cool trap door did not make him want to jump up to deal with her any more than it made the laborious ascent seem attractive to him.

The floor door slowly opens, wider with each step up, inch by inch of Luke's head appearing through it. It swings back on the hinge over the crest of the arc, hitting the wall behind it with a bang, as Luke's shoulders appear through the hatch in the floor. Every trip up was like a birth – the cellar hatch-door delivering the soul of the man Annie can recognize.

Between Annie's cries, despite the severity of his hearing loss, Luke can vaguely hear strange voices coming from within the kitchen. They remain unrecognizable as he treads apprehensively across the small living room. He passes by the fireplace, through the arch into the dining room, and can see that Annie is alone in the kitchen. Yet, he hears the voices getting louder with each light step. He cannot make out the conversation, but it sounds to him as though he is hearing only one side of it.

Annie stands crouched at the counter below the microwave hutch. Her index finger to pursed lips signals for quiet. With her knees slightly bent, Annie looks like the field hockey star she never was. She has her right ear to the baby monitor with a facial expression so intense, she looks like she is listening to a wise man tell her his ultimate secret. To Luke, Annie appears impatiently mesmerized. His stance, right next to hers, Luke can finally hear the cause of her fussing.

The voice on the monitor is not immediately recognizable, but after hacking the situational theme, Luke is able to identify it. He knows that the spoken voice was a man in his kid's room. The new Dad was babying his infant with talk about the crap found in the little one's diaper. Luke, hearing nothing but goo-goo and gaga from both adult and child, looks down at Annie and gives her a nudge.

"That's the new Christian guy down the street, Annie," he points out, whispering.

"Shush!" Annie has no patience or interest beyond what she hears coming from behind closed doors. That quality sickens Luke, but he just as smartly justifies his own instinctual probing. This conversation is pure innocence, but overheard nonetheless, which, by virtue, Luke believes, ultimately removes harmlessness.

"Annie, most everyone knows their cordless phones can put out signals that police scanners can pick-up. But they have all but ignored that baby monitors can share electronic signals, as well." Luke explains. That first impromptu eavesdropping compels Luke to discover his seeming in-house formula, and he does. He wires two transmitters and receivers: each in a different room. Both transmitters and one receiver were off, but the other receiver is on, and Luke switches the small unit to the alternate frequency. That configuration invariably delivers Luke's wife an abundance of ash, which darkens warmly the white of her soul. Luke, only half-jokingly and to only he, equates her heady addiction to emotional heroin.

*

"You know Luke," Annie begins another goodnight conversation. "That new guy we first heard on the monitor that night?"

"Yeah…" Luke wants to sleep.

"He sings songs and reads stories to his

kids every night." Annie sounds like a proud comrade, adding, "Mostly Christian stuff."

Luke grows accustomed to hearing the day's latest every weeknight. Upon returning home from work, or just before they fall asleep, he can depend on an update. Annie could barely get a greeting out before spilling over with the gossip. She is used to having to hold it in some evenings, when Luke blows by her at day's end without much more than a word. To her credit, she learns to see and to notice when her husband is accessible, or not.

"Cheeziz Annie," Luke is tired, "If we were to just gather Mal around the monitor every night about 8:00 PM, we may never have to read another fucking bedtime story again!" He is not really pissed, but his impatient sarcasm sounds like contempt, making Annie feel small. He is just cracking a joke, of course.

"He yawns between every sentence," Annie says, "just like we do."

"Of course…"

*Relief.*

*

By the time he celebrates his first anniversary online with "Equity," Luke regularly eases his way into the virtual lives of almost every woman on his local neighborhood network. He basks enchanted by the joy chatting with all of them, but thrives on conversation with the ones from *his* block in Washington Borough. Luke masterfully maintains dozens of disparate, online personas. His technical prowess, and the shrewd humility, carries-over from teen-hood, keeps him busier than a character in a Dylan song.

No matter the conversant, every one invariably relay to Luke the same, exact themes: The pleasure over the ease with which they seem able to relate to him, and the dissatisfaction with their spouses. Luke chats up women usually, but knows the men on the block quite well by now, too. Unlike with their spouses, he (or she, as Luke plays anonymous women as well as men online), "is so easy to talk to…" Luke loves that.

*Heh heh heh…*

Luke's online characters are sincere, but neglect the innermost emotional fragility most of his friends carry. He is aware, but much too indulgent to care. Luke serves up psychological, even physiological and philosophical slices of liberation. He is masterful in the art of non-threatening condescension. He is peacefully invasive. Night after night Luke effortlessly hosts, as people spill their guts to him entirely. Trust appears built into the abandon cyber space and lends to the ego. Writing alone, behind the curtain of anonymity, as opposed to speaking, helps many to open up, let alone that anonymity they obviously believe exists there. Luke hates to admit that it is self-serving circumlocution, nothing more, but must.

*Maybe I should be writing a book...*

*

Blatant eavesdropping keeps Annie wonderfully entertained. She rearranged nap schedules, to set the monitors up at peak times. In the living room, most afternoons, she listens through the baby monitor to half conversations. Annie nonetheless comes to know and recognize who is who from the neighborhood, and when.

The voice she hears now, however, does not sound familiar. The voices in the conversation she is listening to now are unlike any she heard thus far. It is a woman and a man – that much, she could tell – but the sound was not near as clear as other conversations she had thus far heard. Listening carefully, Annie can clearly make out the woman repeatedly calling the man "Daddy." She listens on;

noting the man repeatedly addresses the woman at the other end, "Baby."

The conversation continues, but unpredictably so. The scratchy distortion frustrates Annie. She thinks she recognizes the voice belonging to the male, but there is a definite discrepancy. Therefore, Annie tries to think of any man in the neighborhood with a daughter having a voice that matches the one she hears. The female voice is soft and lilting, as a child's might be, but the chuckling laugh she coughs out after every "Daddy" give the woman away. It is driving Annie crazy that she cannot, for the life of her, figure-out who belongs to that fucking voice!

*I need to have a cup of tea.*

Annie turns the volume up higher on the monitor before walking into the kitchen. As she paces back and forth, waiting for her water to boil, Annie sees Stone sitting on the picnic table behind his house.

*I am* not *watching the kettle – why won't it boil already?!*

Passing by the window, still pacing, Annie gazes right through all that is out back. Past the direct scene peripherally, she looks beyond to the mucky creek, wrapped-up in the frustration she feels. She knows she has heard that voice before. She walks by quick, and pretends not to look out, as her guard is most always up. Why, neither can she have any neighbor thinking the good Mrs. L'Italian spies out her windows! Oh, no, that would not do!

Hurrying by the back door window again, the impact of what she thinks she sees brings Annie's defenses urgently down. She, this time, stops directly in front of the windowpane. She hastily turns to her left, switches on the kitchen monitor, and then rushes back ducking to the window. Stone stands up, which makes Annie jump back behind the curtain's hem. The teakettle whistles. It instantly gets louder.

*Shit!*

The only louder noise is the abrupt crackle and pop coming through the monitor, as Stone looks down at the phone in his right hand, and pushes the off button with his left.

*Oh...*

*My...*

*God!*

Annie shakes with tension, as she absorbs and processes what she believes she just witnessed. Luke is aware of the possibility all along, but not until this does Annie discover the monitors can pick-up cordless phone bleed, too. Validating the male, whose voice she thinks she heard, however, makes her tremble more.

*…but Kat and Stone do not have a daughter…*

*…And that voice did <u>not</u> belong to Kat…*

*

The monitors innocently set in the other neighborhood homes continue to send syllabic messages of stimulation to the bored and nosey homemaker. Annie finds comfort on those nights Luke taught at The Institute, usually honing in on pillow talk. She adores the phone calls of women endlessly complaining with girlfriends over their matrimonial and sexual frustrations. They tend to validate for Annie the notion that Kat was not alone.

Luke typically pretends to detach himself from all that, but found it difficult to brush-off the debriefing on the conversation between Stone and the mysterious "Baby." Secretly, Luke enjoys the occasional, useful tidbit Annie inadvertently throws out. He can always use some hot information online, although most of what Annie had thus far was old news to him. This time, Luke does not even hear the end of Annie's news broadcast, finding it difficult to concentrate at all after the debriefing on Stone.

*Baby.*

It is a logical continuum of growth; Luke points out to himself. He can imagine the weight, sometimes the horrible stress and humiliation behind the forced facades. The coded elements of the language and abbreviated actions impose on the sincerity factor, Luke knows well. He sees Stone in this light merely as one closer to Kat. Luke's own approach toward the infatuation with Stone's slender dancer build uncomfortably, but make Luke feel invigorated, excited and challenged.

*

Stone's focus on being unlike his father could not keep the knowledge that he was, from resurfacing. Stone's familial devotion and success drew the young woman to him in the first place. Ironically, the success his mistress enjoys, having found her father figure, turns all righteousness bogus. Dawna was only narrowly confused when Stone's flirtations finally tickled hunger and self-centeredness, despite the innocence in her heart. The lunches out together, far enough away from the eye of his naïve wife, the couple act on their attractions. Subtlety gave way to comfort, which eventually lent itself to uninhibited fantasy.

Administrative assistants do not usually travel with the production crew, and this will have been their first road trip together. Thoughts cross her mind throughout the day, every day leading up to their planned departure. The vividness makes her wanting, but Dawna knows she can never let it happen. She does not plan to give herself to him on the road trip to Pittsburgh. Stone behaves the passive-aggressive he is, as though the thought had never crossed his mind either. Gentlemanly-like indeed, yet riding a never-ending wave of flirtation, Stone knows she will give in the end.

# CHAPTER FIVE

Somewhere between the back of his head and the front of his pants, Luke has it hard for Kat. Everywhere within the South walls of his home, there are vantage points of view into her house next door. Like a fronted schemer, passive in demeanor, Luke looks - gazing, and dreams. Images of Kat hang all through his head, like celluloid pin-ups of a skinny calendar girl. Ooh! Martha is on!

"I like them in all shapes and sizes, and choose them according to mood and occasion," Martha shares. "Sometimes, for instance, when I'm after The Big Chill, I use a big one. Its length, wider girth and tendency to drip unpredictably mad, lend a mood reminiscent of the good old days."

*Man... She is so good.*

"Other times, machine-perfected, non-descript and near "dripless" tapers lend the prefect essence of reservation when entertaining thoughts of prouder shirts, ties and jackets."

Martha is the expert, Luke surmises, yawning from the couch. As with all other aspects of pleasing one's self, Martha explains it in a way Luke can understand. Each episode he happens to catch adds some nugget of fuel to his next dark, cornered fantasia. He opens his eyes to see the tabletop crowded with candles behind which the expert stands, speaking, instructing.

*

Now that 'Equity' is mature, babysitting the system is not near the requirement it once was. 'Equity' thrives on all the latest gear, due to Luke turbo charging his monetary success back into the resources. Like a lucubrating author, however, he spends as much time in his basement office as he ever did. Yes, Annie continues in her blindness by second nature, not that she even cares. Ignorance is a lesson that Luke knows all too well, and he's satisfied that she usually manages to leave him alone when he is down there, and that she resists asking questions that may provide answers, that perhaps she does not want to hear. He understands completely, and that keeps tension for the most part, at bay.

Luke frequently downloads and saves multitudes of nude female images, and has over the years, but never did much with them beyond storing them in categorically named folders. Until the coming of Martha, and now Kat, he masturbated regularly to the slideshow of his choice. Identified by some all-encompassing bodily attribute, thousands of downloaded images reside organized within the folder most appropriate. However, they are strangers. Martha is distant, but Kat is for real, and right next-door.

He admires in his My Pictures folder a private, hidden, encrypted and protected directory called 'Samples.' The subdirectories therein span every type and characteristic of pornographic feminism one can imagine. Looking over the folder names: Dark, Light, Celebs, Hair, Lips, Toys, Young, Old, Red, Assorted, BJ, Y&C (Young and Cute), CU (Close-Ups), merely several of many, many more, Luke decides with each "File>Save As" exactly where to place his latest subjects. The sheer quantity of pictures is impressive, but Luke is stimulated more by the fine quality of each, and the ease with which he can navigate to his immediate preference. Like Martha and her candles, Luke can always find the appropriate album to match the affected degree of arousal.

*

Stone enjoys the road trips with the theater troupe, but each one leaves Kat colder and lonelier at home. The communication, camaraderie, participation and companionship that Kat thinks should constitute marriage are all but gone. She eventually learns that she must try to enjoy her life, with a personal agenda by now well outside of Stone's, with or without him.

Stone plays the part of the martyr magnificently on holidays and birthdays, when it matters most. Posing as the sacrificial traveling breadwinner is a byproduct of his mercurial control drama. Forced to face his children at those key times is the emotional hardship he faces, not necessarily mourning over, or patronizing the marriage, all but abandoned Kat.

Kat takes her kids on weekend trips to see their grandparents in Ohio whenever Stone takes a long weekend away. It helps keep her mind on family, yet free from the marriage and sometimes freer of suspicion. The relationship Kat shares with her parents never waned, but even they were curious over the influx of weekend gatherings.

Kat conveniently arranges for Annie and Luke to watch her house whenever she went away.

Kat and Annie speak with each other often, but aside from their city-girl existentialism, they have little else in common. Underneath it all, Annie does not trust Kat – for Annie trusts no one – and Kat cannot particularly relate to Annie's raw delivery and juvenile timing. Flawless mannerisms and Luke's shear duende are what get Annie and him the key to Kat's home. To Annie, this means she has Kat's trust and validation. To Luke, it means the dark chance at entry into her house.

Luke can hardly wait for the time he would find himself left alone in his house, with Kat gone away from hers. He typically flourishes in solitude, always taking time to masturbate, and, over the past year or so, legitimately spends a lot of time building upon 'Equity,' extending and up scaling his underground, neighborhood network. Nevertheless, bustling and laboring less turn his thoughts and actions seamier. He is an unsuspected, innocent narcissist. Moreover, he is free of maleficence, too, yet as premeditated as a thief is.

Annie leaves for the afternoon to visit her mother and father down in Warren. Luke stays home to work on 'Equity.' Two years ago, Annie would have objected, complaining of Luke's social inadequacies, but now that Luke regularly, and somewhat mysteriously, showers her with all the little gifts - delivered for no special reason whatsoever - she looks the other way. She feels good about herself for being able to do so. She suspects that Luke's little cottage industry might be bringing in a little money after all. She would have balked if Kat had been home, but since she knew Kat was away for the weekend, she left Luke alone easily.

Annie's departure with the kids and Kat's home vacant for a time stages the scene. Certain Annie is sufficiently away, gone not to return for anything forgotten; Luke takes a short walk to the far end of the back yard. He scopes-out the situation; he looks down the streambed, glancing discreetly up the meadow toward the yards adjacent to his. Wanting to obtund his presence, trying to appear as though he is down there for nothing more than a stretch of his legs, or perhaps a passing of gas, he breaks his own rule and whistles. Luke could just larrup men who whistled, or hummed, especially outside the home! He regards it is cornball goofy and sounds insane. He does not admit that he is nervous. He will not. He cannot.

He has to make sure the old woman that neighbors Kat on the other side is not in her yard. She is forever in the garden Kat shares with her, squawking at her dog, chasing her cats. He sees that none of the Mahoney girls are out, which seems a bit queer - they spend as much time out of the house as possible - unless the whole clan goes out somewhere. Daughters of a ruddy Irish guy who drinks himself mean on a daily basis, taking it all out on his wife but good, nightly, all three girls are stunning in each their own ways. Intermittent cycles of fair-to-middling times, with a steady dose of bad, make it seem like they are stuck in a loop of time within which they cannot escape.

*Mama – she know how to wear a nice shiner, chile.*

*"The StuckInRutters."*

Luke decides that the houses further down do not matter, but he is compelled to look to his left, past the hedge that separates his property from the old person on his other side. She rarely sees the light of day, except to drag her terriers – Toto and Benjie – in and out of their smoke-filled existence.

*"Dorothy."*

Neighbor Connie, however, has her head out her kitchen window yelling at the group of children, grandchildren and teens assembled in her backyard. Connie is always pregnant, and she already has a house full of kids. Some of her kids have kids already. Luke thinks it sad, as her face reflects more cigarette lines, booze-hounding and toothless cave-in than the middle-aged woman she actually is. Men were always a welcome problem.

*"The WhoMyDaddies."*

Therefore, self-involved and convoluted the scene, Luke dismisses them harmless and saunters back up the yard toward the basement door underneath the deck. He enters, proactively leaving the door unlocked after closing it behind him. The stats check out on the network, but he double checks the scripted utility, running to simulate his own system presence and activity, before going up the hatch. He wrote that homegrown utility especially for times like this.

*…Stealth mode…*

Luke always follows his instinct, flowing intuitively with life as it presents itself, as best felt fit. It occurs to him often how fluently he makes the journey to each disparate destination in life. Even the painful trips are bearable, and invariably more educational than the easy ones. Experiences alone make Luke an expert chameleon-like being.

Up the hatch and to the kitchen, Luke is primed and ready. He has an adrenaline high, but is otherwise finally quite calm… considering his intention. He stops short, reaches into the fridge, and grabs a bottle of Newcastle. He pries off the top and guzzles the entire 12 ounces in one tilt. The loud belch that follows sends him briskly out the back door out onto the deck. Confidently bounding down the stairs and stepping into the back yard, his long strides carry him swiftly through to Kat's yard. He ascends the back stairs to her mudroom. Taking a slow, deep breath - by now, Luke is past any possible point of detection - he reaches into his pants pocket for the key. Working it into the keyhole, Luke feels a tug of guilt in his gut, but then, a stir in his jeans.

Luke has been inside Kat's place a few times with Annie, and he concentrates particularly on the layout more with each visit. He put extra effort into memorizing her personal effects over the old Victorian floor plan. He is here to borrow photos that he can use for his project, and he knows where to go to get them. Quickly out of the small room Kat uses to can her garbage, Luke sails through the kitchen, then into the dining room. There, just beyond the doorway, he squats. Then, taking another deep breath, relaxes on his knees. Looking around, he sees that all the drapes are drawn. He wants a picture in this room, two from the hallway, and two from the sitting room.

Walking toward the dining room portrait of Kat, Luke feels another odd mix of erotic pleasure and dark guilt. Smartly, he shifts gears before either distraction can overcome him. He plugs in his portable scanner and scans the image. Luke feels overheated and frustrated after capturing the two photos of young Kat in the hall. He wants to continue. He is fighting the urge to masturbate right there, and he will not run home, mission unaccomplished. He walks into the sitting room.

Gazing into a picture of Kat sitting at her piano, Luke imagines she is looking back over her shoulder at him. It arouses him to stand there at the very piano bench upon which she sat for the shot. It is like a picture in a picture, he thinks briefly, but she is not actually here, and he, of course, is encroaching. His eyes fix on her fine and lambent hair. Luke is now uncomfortably and visibly aroused, as he thinks of the fine hair of hers that he cannot see. Forcing his hand from the grip on his crotch, Luke grabs the framed photo, strips it, scans it and replaces it. Working like a professional, he destroys all traces of action. All the pictures are back in the frames, back in place and dusted within the half hour.

The scanner tucked back under his arm, Luke hustles back home. Mission accomplished, he sits back in his basement, editing photos, as he sips this time his favorite brown ale. Luke continues Project Kat over the next few weeks. Under the dim light misting from within his case mods, Luke meticulously cropped, sized, stretched and rotated hundreds of images of Kat. He found himself hard in hand sometimes three times a day as he layered her polished headshots onto the anonymous bodies of various nudes.

Initially, the thought is to merge Kat with bodies that were distinctively different from the shape of hers, but after weeks of internal struggle, he decides to change his scope. As much as Luke adores Kat's face, the mystery of that dancer's body, what is within, drive him bat-blind. She is right next door almost every day. That body is real, but Luke cannot have it. Merging Kat with only those images of bodies that look like her own, as far as he can tell, Luke sets out on another digital quest for visual perfection. Selectivity was difficult because it was subjective to a man whose only hope is fantasy.

*

"Luke!" Annie hollers from the front door: "Tickets to 'The Nut Cracker!'"

"Wow! Nice… from Kat?" Luke asks.

"Yeah, she had extra… there's only three, though."

"Hmm, that's okay. Take the kids. They'll love it!"

"Yes, they would. Are you sure?"

Kat plans at least two trips a year with her kids to Manhattan. The Nutcracker musical ballet show at Christmastime is an annual event, but throughout the year, they spend the occasional casual weekend there, as well. Kat is genuinely pleased with the house-watching arrangements, and feels confident asking Luke to watch the house again before booking the ballet. Luke is always happy to oblige.

Knowing the ballet is coming along with Christmas causes a childlike excitement around the holiday Luke has not felt in decades. He wastes no time organizing a plan in preparation for the opportunity to pay another visit next door. Even though he will continue to serve himself well by the custom pictures within his Kat folders, his lonely world echoes with cries for more. Thinking more than anything else about having something to have and hold of Kat's, makes the second trip into Kat's back door much easier than the first.

He walks briskly through the Rossinski yard. Kat's kitchen leads to the doorway leading into the dining room. There, he squat thrusts into a position that allows him to scoot quickly through the dining room and up the hallway. The front door is always shaded with a shear, opaque curtain, but Luke, looking AWOL and out-of-uniform, scoots anyway. He is deep in his thoughts as he circles left and bounds three treads at a time up the wide, curved stairway.

Entering her bedroom, Luke feels the emptiness he imagines she feels at night. He is there to sniff her panties; perhaps he will steal a pair, too. However, an old temptation hits him. He once found his cousin Gini's dildo under the sink in her master bathroom. It is a reproduction of the Virgin Mary, dressed in a light blue robe with white undergarments. It was phallus shaped, with a battery-powered vibrator built-in.

*Oh, Mother…*

Luke finds nothing like that in Kat's bathroom, but he is happy to hold the panties he pulls out from the hamper up to his nose and inhale. He stokes as if he were sucking a hookah, deeply as possible. Savoring the odiferous sensation, a medley of every secretion and misjudgment of her day before, Luke suddenly starts when a throaty groan involuntarily escapes him. He folds the soiled panties and stuffs them into his left hip pocket, and then shuffles back down the hall returning to Kat's bedroom.

As he carefully rummages through her drawers and cabinets, Luke admits to himself a hope he will not find any toys. On one hand, knowing such truths could be a turn-on, he thinks, but on the other, flaccidity in self-doubt. He hates the possibility of finding anything even remotely similar to the huge motherfucker he found in a stranger's house as a young teen. He remembers sneaking into the home only because he heard from a friend that the woman living there had one, and he wanted to see it!

Penile envy was not an issue for Luke at that young an age, but now, the thought of Kat inserting one of those into her vagina drove him green. Uncomfortable, sweaty and depressed, he takes a pair of clean, light blue panties from her top drawer and wipes his forehead. The cotton feels good and cool. He shoves them into his pocket along with the other.

There is one bedside table in the bedroom, giving Luke an intimately thoughtful vantage point: The side of the bed she sleeps on. The edge of the bed she sits on in the morning, and at night. Where she keeps her bedside needs. The place she holds her comforts and luxuries. If there is anything in here, Luke thinks it will be in the bottom drawer, but with living sustenance, first pulls open the top. A book on dreams, a physics periodical, and a tube of 'Blistex' do not impress him. Reading glasses and a corkscrew are a mere dite more attractive to him, but the promise of that bottom drawer beckons.

He opens the bottom drawer slowly, and with one eye carefully spies into the space. In it, he sees a small white workout towel. It is neatly folded, so that the grommet stapling the tri-folded length shows right on top, along with the black embroidered 'Halston' logo. The inert excitement keeps the curious bulge in the middle unobvious at first. Smiling, like a slow-motion magician with a scarf, Luke lifts the clean towel to expose the prize. There, in the open case it came in lay Kat's diaphragm. Entranced, Luke stares at the object, but does not know exactly what he thinks he wants to do with it.

Thankful for the procrastinator in Kat, Luke savors the scent and touch. Kat had apparently neglected to rinse or wash the device since, at best by looks, last use. Once again hypnotized, Luke stands mesmerized by the curl of the pubic hair and the fingerprints amidst the dried mucus. The erotic feel of the latex begs his fingers in both hands. The sheer sabulosity of the object might have turned another man off, but it charges-up the sexy source inside of Luke.

Back from the kitchen, baggy in hand, Luke sits on the edge of Kat's bed. Gingerly, he picks up the rubber disc, and lifts it to his face to take another deep sniff. Glancing down thoughtfully, he gives it long, loving look, as though he were holding a masterpiece of progressive art, instead of the filthy, rubber contraceptive that it is. It was one last look before stripping the contraceptive of all the hairs and residue, storing it all in his makeshift specimen glad bag along with the rubber disc itself.

# CHAPTER SIX

Martha is working her compost today. She has gardening-gloves on, but the earth and rich mixtures in her hands and slathering through her fingers is, Luke knows, reflective of exactly who she is: Earth Woman. She looks to the camera and stops what she is doing with an eclectic grin on her face. She has a wooden rake-like tool she typically uses to stir-up the heap of waste-turned-nutrient, but for the sake of her audience gets her hands dirty in it all instead.

"Ooh! Look up there," she says to all watching. "Oh, it's a male turkey! I hear him gobbling. He is a huge specimen that appears even larger as he preens puffs and fluffs his feathers. Look at him dancing along the dead limb of that Fir tree!" Rarely has Luke seen Martha so excited. "Point the camera over there to the end of the branch, please. There's the hen he's trying to impress!"

"Males are polygamous; they mate with as many hens as they can. Male Wild Turkeys display for females by puffing out their feathers, spreading out their tails and dragging their wings. This behavior is most commonly referred to as strutting. Their heads and necks are colored brilliantly with red, blue and white. The color can change with the turkey's mood, with a solid white head and neck being the most excited. They use gobbling, drumming or booming, and spitting as signifies social dominance, and to attract females. The phallus becomes more and more prominent."

*Who knew Martha knows so effin much about effin turkeys?!*

"Oh my goodness be!" Martha chuckles. "He certainly appears confident she likes what she sees, though to you and I, the female looks bored with it all, simply pecking and waddling around. The giveaway is how she shifted her tail feathers to the side and eyes the male, even if merely quick, little glances. You see, though most male birds do not, many waterfowl and some other birds, such as the ostrich and turkey, possess a phallus. When not copulating, it is hidden within the proctodeum compartment within the cloaca, simply stated, just inside the vent. The male does have two testes, which, by the way, become hundreds of times larger during the breeding season to produce sperm. It is stored in the semenal glomera within the cloacal protuberance prior to copulation."

"That's enough of the technical jargon. Suffice it to say that, by goodness and by the looks of… things… this male is ready to mate!"

*

Fat Sharon from across the street is online. She is very unhappily married to a fellow just as fat as she is. He lies on the couch every night after work and drinks beer until passing out. Luke decides to vent a little and give to her what he knows she always wants from him. His handle for her is "BigDude1." He transposed her cryptic handle to 'FS.'

*Here goes…*

FS> Oh, BigDude1 – it's so good to see you

FS> Give it to me – please

BigDude1> in our bedroom

FS> Oh, keep going BigDude1 - please

BigDude1> you're just finishing your shower after a swim

BigDude1> you're in the master bath

BigDude1> I'm already clean and dry, but my hair is damp - towel around my waist

FS> Oh, keep going - please

BigDude1> I am lying in bed... waiting...

BigDude1> shshsh

FS> Yes

BigDude1> The thought of you returning from the bath with just your towel has me aroused to no end

BigDude1> I lay there touching my own nipples with the tips of my fingers and when they harden I squeeze them gently too

BigDude1> My penis is getting bigger and harder, it longs to be free of the towel

FS> Yes! Yes!

BigDude1> I hear you roll the TP dispenser and flush the toilet and know that you will be coming out shortly

BigDude1> I get up without making a sound and go to the door - standing behind the hinged side so you won't see me when you come out

BigDude1> You open the door and stroll through it and just as you call my name all whimsical, quizzical and breathy...

BigDude1> I grab you from behind, gently, and hug your waist

FS> Do it

BigDude1> You have the towel wrapped as women do around the chest - under the arms - tucked in the front to the side a little

BigDude1> The length of the towel just barely covers your genital area -- that is a huge turn on

BigDude1> I can just make out barely your sweet ass and privates from below

BigDude1> I continue to hug you and you hum a little appreciation for me

FS> mmmmmmmmm mmmmmmmmm

BigDude1> and begin to sway a little bit as if dancing - my face is in the back of your neck... I am tugging and tickling the little hairs at the neck line and kissing your neck all over licking it too

BigDude1> My hands roam upward to your head and begin to massage your head, temples, all around messing your hair all around.

BigDude1> you can feel my erection from behind though my towel and yours

FS> mmmmmmmmmm

BigDude1> poking your rear end a little… You are already wet

BigDude1> You were wet with anticipation fresh out of the shower but now even more – my hands are at your breasts now

BigDude1> I want to wait to undo your towel but I can wait no longer

BigDude1> you can't wait either because you go ahead and pull it off of yourself just as I begin to do it

BigDude1> this time we both let out a mmmmmmmmmm and I gently yet firmly ravish your breasts with my hands

FS> mmmmmmmmmmmmmmmmm

BigDude1> they make their way down your torso lightly tracing your stomach and belly, your tummy, your pubis and finally to your sweet and gorgeous vagina

BigDude1> I wiggle my fingers – the tips like doing a trill on a piano, around either side of it, gently flickering the lips back and forth, in and out.

BigDude1> I do this for a moment then run a finger up your slit and it feels so fucking good to me I have to do it again and again…

BigDude1> then I let the finger travel

up to your clitoris and I massage it for a moment

BigDude1> you groan oh, and turn yourself around immediately, placing a long, sexy, wet, and yes, sloppy kiss on my mouth

BigDude1> you are intensely turned on, moaning and groaning as you kiss me with more passion than I have ever known - I know that your lips are almost swollen, and they are eating mine!

BigDude1> And your tongue is darting in and out of my mouth finding my own tongue twirling with it and then you begin to suck on my tongue as if you were performing oral sex with it - and you ARE

BigDude1> I do the same to you, as I always love to do.

My tongue slides in and out of your mouth as you suck and release suck and release.

BigDude1> It is so intense now; my erection is poking at you in the front.

BigDude1> one of your hands reaches down and touches it - you groan again and grasp it

BigDude1> you give it a couple pumps then stroke it nice and gently

BigDude1> my face is at your breasts

BigDude1> I alternate sucking each nipple

flicking them with my tongue as well - doing both

BigDude1> your nipples are erect

BigDude1> your clitoris is engorged and your special place is sopping wet. I am incredibly turned on by it all and you know it

BigDude1> you feel the pre-lube at the end of my organ

I feel the warm ooze of your own secretions

BigDude1> we both settle into a standing position

BigDude1> you crouch slightly spreading yourself to offer her up to me and I ease between your lovely, lovely legs and slip him into you

FS> OMG, I am going to let go soon!

BigDude1> you feel so fine to me, oh god, I tell you so.

Sweetness, you feel so fine. You ARE so fine.

FS> ILY

BigDude1> and we sway, we rock a bit, and we sway, ILY, as if in a ball room dance marathon in the twelfth hour, slowly, methodically, so I do not fall out we must be sensible, controlled, to continue to enjoy, and we are, we do.

BigDude1> My hands are so busy at your breasts, my manhood is engulfed by your womanhood, and our lips are now locked into forever

BigDude1> I want to come, but I want to also wait until you come at least once before I do…

BigDude1> I ease both of us to the bed — it's like doing a sack race, still in you, we collapse onto the bed

BigDude1> I am once again between your legs in a second and still inside you too

BigDude1> your arms are up over your head, my face is in your underarm, kissing, sucking, licking, and you are going crazy as I thrust strongly, smoothly into you

BigDude1> deep

BigDude1> deeper deepest

FS> OMG

BigDude1> every one

BigDude1> my belly rubbing against your clitoris with each long stroke, the making love to your underarm, which no one has ever done to you, the penis so smoothly lunging, so deep into you, and the belly hair over your button send you into a massive orgasm

BigDude1> you are moaning from deep within and whimpering my name -- BigDude1 -- and I keep going -- you arch

FS> OMG I am coming!

BigDude1> it breaks the rhythm but I stop and give it to you once more, deeply, and hold it there with your meeting arch as you come so big and grand

FS> OMG

BigDude1> I am so huge or at least I feel like I am, and harder than the average.

BigDude1> you roll me over so I am on my back. I am almost there,

BigDude1> this time when you come, I'm coming with you,

BigDude1> I'm thinking, and you straddle me, knees to either side of my waist

BigDude1> you guide me into you and it's as though it was the first time I had ever felt such warmth

BigDude1> I'm so nasty, I'm so horny, my mind can't help it

BigDude1> I would never say it out loud, but I can think it without hurting my baby, and you begin — you are gliding up and down, pressing yourself against me and rubbing up and down, riding my shaft, taking long strides, but being careful not to go so far as to let him come out

BigDude1> With each thrust, your breasts come just close enough so I can lick and kiss them.

BigDude1> I also play with them with my hands every so often, and we lick each other's tongues

BigDude1> You pick up the pace and you are breathing heavy.

BigDude1> you are going for it now. I think I can tell

BigDude1> I want to go for it too - I grab your sides and push and pull with every thrust you offer - it's frenetic, it's crazy, it's fast, deep, you are coming

BigDude1> you are coming, it's intense, NOW and I come and come and come with you

FS> OMG I am going again!

BigDude1> I'm so vocal that your hand covers my mouth, so I lick the palm and you jump with joy… you lay atop me

FS> Oh GOD - I am there! I am there! Oh God!

BigDude1> and you feel so good against my skin your breasts on mine your belly on mine your pubis on mine and we kiss

BigDude1> you rest your head at my shoulder and rest dearly all over me, and that is where I wish to stay for the rest of my life.

BigDude1> Hi!  :-)

FS> whew!

BigDude1> Was that good for you babe?

And so it went with fat Sharon. It feels good for Luke, and he knows it feels good to Sharon. He gives all the girls on the block the same treatment – different names, story lines and scenarios, themes; same games. Luke admittedly believes he is quite creative in how he makes up these stories right off the top of his head. Each one is unique, yet just as sexy. He never seems to disappoint.

# CHAPTER SEVEN

Lifetime Television is promoting an upcoming special on doublets using an image of the subjects, perfect Siamese twins – two arms, two legs, one torso, and two heads. Plugging the news magazine event live, Martha begins each narration with, "Still ahead…" and "This, just ahead…" has Luke laughing aloud. He is not sure exactly why, except that it is not 'just a head,' it is two! He decides, laughing again, that the writer of an intro for a story about an essential two-headed person might avoid using the 'head' word at all. Of course, as long as it is Martha's spoken word, so be it – it is okay – no worries – it has to be good.

*

Slowly, yet surely, all the townspeople, those in all the surrounding counties, as well as virtually all the folks from all over the Metro Area, switch to Luke's new 'Equity' ISP. On this early evening, Luke considers, reasons and thinks about, generally, over-all, his success, work, and his play. The services are less expensive and superior to any comparable internet service provider available in and around Northern Jersey. Equity's chat engines are much more open and adult-themed than those of the (heavily censored) big name ISPs. However, for most of these folks, 'Equity' remaining much less expensive is the big selling point. The sexually charged chat and innuendo typically propels an evening justified for most men, according to the popular "buying 'Playboy' for the stories…" mentality. As for the women, well, let us just say it is all about sex, clothes, make-up and shopping – in that order.

Luke maintains multiple personas, handles, which he uses at will, depend on the respective subject at the other end of the thread, or the room in which he spies or moderates. No one in town, including Annie, know that their own Luke L'Italian is the sole proprietor of 'Equity,' though he feels he knows most do assume he simply must be online right along with everyone else. If they find he is an active chat room participant, let alone his ownership and administration of their piece of cyber space, Luke's world would be a much different place.

He picks-up volumes of neighborhood homemaker trash, but he patiently awaits nightly the inevitable arrival of Kat. This, he knows, admittedly so, everyone suspects Stone, except her. The shame is that everyone is chatting about it, too. Unexpectedly, under no premeditation, Luke's entire dissertation pays off: Kat finally registers. It is another work night for Stone, she has heard enough about this new online community, and now she wants to login too, by gawd! Luke is sure Kat will learn soon enough about the chatter going over her and Stone.

*K1tty.*

How cute is that? She thinks. K1tty… Like a Cat, but cuter: Luke gets a kick out of her transposing the letter 'I' with a number '1'. He, knowing about Stone's escapades, spawns also an understanding of Kat's understated vulnerability. Luke has IP addresses that map to every personal computer and woman on the block, let alone the entire membership. He can just barely keep-up with the neighborhood Borough, never mind those from elsewhere. It is a fringe benefit to be able to go outside the day after a particularly hot night and look his cyber lovers in the eye. Luke reluctantly lets Kat surf a while. He stays his course, yet knows it is just a matter of time before he is ready to pounce.

*

Kat is at first leery of chatting with anyone, in general, which has her starting rather cold online. Other women in the neighborhood, frequenting or hosting favorite chat rooms, come off very differently while online. Like any online community, they may wonder, but do not know, with whom they chat. A few, however, behave as though they do. Sharon, across the street is a gadfly, but she reads like a sexpot online. To speak with her in person is a pathetic gabbling. She chooses to remain anonymous online, but Luke knows her when he sees her out there in 'Equity.' She sees a line in a room stating, "Sharon's pussy must be entirely hircine ordure." That did it. Luke multifariously develops his personable craft, and he behaves with the precision of a gimbal. He is not exactly laconic, though he natters upon first meeting. He presents himself with pastiche without appearing tasteless or unctuous.

Kat's first impression of 'Equity' is ontological, as if she enters dark penetralia, however, the more time she spends there she also recognizes a comfortable lucency of it all. She is the most educated woman on the street, which makes obliquity naturally impossible. Her initial findings brought yawp and moue in the sexually charged chat rooms, but in time, delivers as well a strange new effectiveness like a charge and a talent. Fun in fact! She smiles.

Luke figures she will warm significantly once Stone leaves her. Actually, when she is not around him, she is fine nom, in the L'Italians' opinion, but when Stone and she are together, they are both cold. Luke understands the chill she carries around self-infects the otherwise wholesome, likable Kat. Meanwhile, the once lonely nights become welcome mini-vacations for her. Online almost every night since her first, she becomes somewhat of a doyenne in several of 'Equity's subspaces.

*

The July 4th holiday vacation to Ohio is a tradition in Kat's household. It is a well deserved, if not token visit with her parents, and, a chance for them to see the kids. Weekend trips in Stone's absence slow since her discovery of 'Equity.' Kat cries when Stone announces over dinner that he has to work out of town this coming fourth, as their two boys, used to the absence of Dad already, look on with consensus.

*

Annie is on the deck sitting at the patio table sipping tea while Kat is in her yard playing with the kids. Kat finally works up the muster to ask Annie for the favor.

"Annie," Kat calls out. "Stone is working out of town again this coming weekend."

"Isn't that your Ohio family time?"

"It is. He will not be coming with us."

"Well," Annie consoles, "we'll keep an eye on your place while you're both away."

"Thanks, Annie."

As Kat turns to go, she sputters out the departure and arrival dates to her neighbor.

"You can count on us for your ride to the airport, too, Kat," Annie adds.

"Thanks, Annie." Kat is not happy with Stone's self-exclusion, but she would not miss her annual, extended trip to Ohio, or the kids seeing grandpa and grandma, for any reason. She fears for the first time ever that all the chatter over an affair going on in the neighborhood may in fact describe her Stone. He travels excessively often and supposedly far. Online in the chat rooms, he is secretly known and referred-to as "Dunce."

Annie is in the living room with her baby monitor on. It is so ironic that the only woman not online misbehaving these days is married to the person responsible for it all. Luke chuckles. She is perfectly content listening-in on the noise bleeding through her monitors. Suddenly enough to make her jump-start, she hears a loud dial tone transmitting. "Stone is on the phone, coming through the monitor again!" she says aloud, even though she is the only one in the room.

Annie must have missed him pulling into the drive on the other side of his house. It makes her crane her neck in a whiplash, as she pulls aside a blue-checkered, handspun curtain. His car is out front! Annie smells something funny.

"Luke!"

Luke is in his lab. His first reaction is to take no action.

"Luke!" Annie bellows, louder this time.

"What?" Luke sounds upset by the urgency, though he is used to the interruptions.

"Come up!"

"Fuck…" Luke knows his ascension is inevitable. "Coming…" He yells to her.

"Hurry!" Luke thinks Annie sounds overly excited or over reacting, one.

"Cheeziz." He makes his way up the hatch, sighing, and sees Annie in her chair spying out a living room curtain.

"What." He deadpans.

"Stone is here." Annie whispers just loud enough for the nearly deaf ex-rock and roller to be able to hear. Her excitement is contagious this time, however, and Luke quickens his pace. He runs to the kitchen and looks out the kitchen window. Stone is out back at his picnic table again, and he is on his cordless phone. Annie and Luke can hear only Stone's side of the conversation this time, which adds to the wonderment, but disappoints as well. Annie appears to be freaking out over hearing the conversation unfold.

"Calm the fuck down, Annie, will ya? I can't fuckin' hear him."

After hearing Stone give directions from elsewhere to his place, Luke and Annie are confident he is planning a rendezvous with someone. They know also that whoever it is will be showing up at Stone's house at six tonight. Luke and Annie, eager to nail Stone's balls to the wall, assume he has planned a date with his mistress. They establish battle stations, and arm themselves with a 35mm camera for Annie and a Cannon video camera for Luke.

"This reminds me of Mike's affair," the memory of her first husband upsets Annie. "I couldn't believe it, or the pain it caused me. I feel kind of sorry for Kat."

There is lots of tension, but it fortunately winds down in just a few minutes. Hearing Stone out back on a sunny summer day on the cordless helps:

"I couldn't sleep at all last night."

"I miss you, too, Dee."

For once in their lives, Luke and Annie share the same wish, at the same time. The wish to be able to hear the person Stone is talking to pulls strongly. This thought spins for a moment in Luke's head.

"Who the hell is Dee?" Luke wonders aloud.

"I don't know! I don't know."

"Shhh!"

"I love you, too." Stone reciprocates, after dictating detailed directions to get his invitee, Luke knows, now, from Edison to Washington. It currently sounds to Luke like Stone is anxious, as he attempts to warm some cold feet.

"No, no… it's ok… I promise…," Stone continues. "Everyone is gone! I can come get you, if you want." Stone paces back and forth between his picnic table and the swing set. He looks about, at nothing in particular. Luke, still listening, returns to the back door. It is obvious the man next door is struggling.

Luke goes to their upstairs bedroom window with the video camera. He will take the vantage point toward the front. Annie sets up a stool between the kitchen island and the back door with the 35m camera and a cup of tea. She has the back yard, door and drive. They wait impatiently for five-thirty to come, and then, as the time approaches, retake their battle stations.

A man in a pickup truck parks, and then walks toward the house. Luke awakes from languor and smiles at the thought of Stone being a closeted bi/gay guy. His smile widens when an extremely young girl parks in front of Stone's house, but then walks right by his walk way and Luke's, up the street. …Another false alarm…

Both Luke and Annie have a monitor in their assigned hideouts. Stone calls out again at about five-forty, and asks for Dawna. She is not there: He begins to pace. Annie, looks out back, and realizes that area must offer the finest reception on Stone's cordless. Could mistress call him back - he looks panicked. Annie's focus went from phone reception to adultery as she both hears and sees it roll out before her.

Ten minutes later, Dawna pulls up in her car. She has a spot directly in front of Stone's house, and in front of his vehicle. It happens so fast that it hit Luke like a coup d'état. Even though he has been waiting for this very moment all day, it still comes as a surprise. Luke's seconds, however, pass more like minutes at this point; he has the camera up and focused within a short three seconds.

*So, it's not a man, not a youngster, but clearly a young female at least fifteen years his junior...The Motherfucker...*

Stone reclines on the padded white bamboo chair, calm and debonair on the porch of the old Victorian house, waving and smiling nonchalantly. After all, he is an ex-actor. Luke and Annie, in another moment of uncharacteristic commingling, softly yell that she is here. Dawna sheepishly approaches, smiles nervously, blows a kiss and waves to Stone. Luke notices the pink short shorts.

*She looks too good for him - but certainly no beauty.*

After a quick smooch, they sit together on the porch and share a beer Stone has open. They are both out of Luke's sight, so he runs downstairs and peers through the living room curtain.

After coaching Annie, Luke counts to four and they burst out the front door, on the silent five-go!

*I just want to video tape my wife… No big deal.*

Luke poses Annie in front of the short, picket fence right where she also put the two adults behind her in the frame, the direct line of focus. Luke shoots, and keeps shooting as Annie performs. She giggles happily, and asks Luke to interview her. She loves doing that – acting like someone famous, important and glamorous. Stone is visibly spooked when Annie's laughter breaks him away from his mistress's spell. They both look suspiciously over at the L'Italians and without knowing it inside each other, scare, and then quickly jump up and stride to the front door.

*Got it!*

"Let's go in and get cozy," Stone suggests to Dawna, then continues with another bum line just to get them into his house.

"Yeah, let's do. I'm getting chilly." She quickly agrees with a white lie.

*

"What did you get?" Annie asks Luke. "…Anything good?"

"About three or four minutes of her on his lap," Luke replies. "That includes half the walk from her car to the porch before, and the smooch when she got there."

"Oh my God," Annie cries. "This is awful. This is terrible!"

"Haven't we been suspicious?" asks Luke. "Come on… We got the fucker!"

"I guess…"

*

Dawna feels a nervous chill, odd in July, coming out the front door. She grabs a bag from the car, feeling quite rigid, this being her first sleepover and all. Nevertheless, she put a lot of effort into this night, bringing with her, sparkling wine, negligee (nightclothes), and gourmet food. If that does not make its way to his heart, nothing will!

Luke and Annie are apprehensive the next morning. That feeling makes the day seem to pass by slowly. The two illicit lovers dash out together at two-thirty in the afternoon, only to return fifteen minutes later, pizza and soda in hand.

*…One night of glamour, and the next of grease…*

At four-twenty, Dawna retrieves books from her car, leaving it parked, and joins him in his car. They drive away and do not return until eight-thirty the following night. Annie remains upset by all that has thus far transpired - trembling and crying with hurt for Kat, as well as herself.

She, uncharacteristically boldly, wants to get a hold of Kat to let her know what is going on, and Luke does not object. Luke, tapping into his mischievously minded internally, devises a plan. Annie searches around frantically for Kat's number in Ohio. She finds the number scribbled on a sticky note in the coffee table drawer. Annie punches it into the living room receiver.

"Kat," Annie begins, "I'm afraid I have bad news for you."

"My house didn't burn down, did it?"

"No Kat, I'm sorry, Stone is there…" Annie chokes, and starts to cry, so Luke grabs the telephone.

"Kat, Luke… Listen, Stone has another woman in your home, and we thought you might want to know. We know you've been wondering…"

Kat wants to know, all right. Annie and

Luke tell her the whole story, from the baby monitors to present, including the video tape.

"But," Kat interjects. "How can I catch him?"

Kat's mother weaves her way into the conversation, and wants the neighbors to butt-out, and for Kat to do nothing.

"Why stir things up, Kat?"

Kat's father has a different take, and hands her the airfare in cash. Annie agrees to pick her up in Newark, and Luke invites Kat to stay — you know, stake-out - with them, and catch him red-handed, red-faced.

"I have a plan, Kat. Don't worry." Luke's voice sounds comforting to Kat.

Luke volunteers to make Annie's promise good, drives her to the airport, and pick Kat up. They know Stone and his girlfriend will be back because her car is still there. Nevertheless, they want to — must — get back before Stone does. They are on Route 80 heading west, toward home. Kat, on her cell phone talks with her parents, and plan her trip back to Ohio. She plans to execute swiftly and smartly. Then, live happier ever after.

Luke's plan seemingly thwarted - the lovely couple next door do not return home tonight – and it is getting late on this, the night after. Kat is crying, knowing her children are waiting for her to return to their grandparent's by July 4th. Kat is dictating to her mother a confirmed flight number and time when the stars of the show finally, suddenly show-up. She hangs-up on her mother while both L'Italians try to tell her what she already knows. The guilty couple is home. Her neighbors pep and prep her, while Kat rehearses repeatedly in her head what she plans to say, to whom, and what she will do. She shakes and shivers as she gears up for the confrontation, as she knows it could turn to conflict.

Stone and Dawna carry several bags of gourmet food, like oysters, escargot, clams, steak and lobster, fresh fruit, and champagne. The three spies could see food protruding from each sack. Kat collects to calm and rational, giving them a few minutes to settle-in before she barges quietly in for a visit. Stone is in the downstairs bath - peeing - with the door open. Dawna is at Kat's sink rinsing the fruit, fancy food sitting on the table, most yet unpacked. Kat stands quietly across the hall from the half bath.

"Look at yourself, Stone," Kat spits looking slightly to the right. She turns left toward Dawna, down the hall. When Stone zips up and turns, his chin hits the ground and his eyes go wide.

"I lost my invitation," says Kat, and referring to Dawna, continues "and I do not believe we have been properly introduced." She sounded snide, facetious, sarcastic, hurt and mean. Right now, she is.

Dawna immediately wets her pants. Stone tries to act cool and offers a bogus introduction, "Kat, this is Dawna. Dawna, Kat."

"I am so, so sorry," Dawna is dumbfounded, crying. "He told me you knew, and that… I am so sorry."

"Stop groveling!" Kat uncharacteristically yells. "I want you to hell out of my home, now! You get the fuck out of here now, and if you EVER show-up here again I will summon the police!" She has not used the "F" word since High School. Oh, but Kat is not done.

"And Stone, you stay right here, husband of mine." Then, sounding just as sweet as could be, "We have a lot to talk about."

Dawna runs out through the front door leaving her belongings and lots of choice food behind. Stone is not far behind, but she waits not and drives away as fast as she dares. After a short chase on foot, Stone slithers back into the house to face his distraught but taught wife of eleven years.

The Mahoney girls watch almost knowingly from their front porch.

Kat demands he drive her to the airport. On the way, she lays out the new rules. He shall see her in court! Meanwhile, all that great food sits on their kitchen table rotting, turning spoiled and rancid. Stone will be cleaning up that mess shortly, he knows, along with a nasty mess Dawna and he made upstairs two nights before.

*

Stone stays out of the way, save his visitation pick-up and drop-off times. Kat not only continues to live lively without skipping a beat, she expands her life. She takes a college credit course in physics, dance classes – given and taken – but it is the Project Manager position at Merck that make her the superior breadwinner, post-divorce. Stone and Dawna move a mile across town, but still stay away from the house as much as possible. That is not bad for Kat, but she worries about the kids.

Luke monitors the chat rooms he thinks he is more likely to find Kat. He directs messages to her: Mostly several occurrences of mild flirtation. He alone has an Instant Message engine that will display the end-user real name, if he chooses. Luke knows them all. Holy shit…He has Kat on a thread!

DrJMrJ: here, k1tty, k1tty

K1TTY: a/s/l

DrJMrJ: nice k1tty

K1TTY: what kind of doctor are you?

One night, when Kat feels especially lonely, Luke gently prods her into a private room. She accepts. Kat asks all the questions people want to know.

K1TTY: a/s/l

DrJMrJ: 39/m/NJ – U?

K1TTY: 33/f/NJ

DrJMrJ: Hmm

K1TTY: What kind of doctor are you?

K1TTY: It's you.

K1TTY: I remember you.

DrJMrJ: I cannot tell a lie

DrJMrJ: it IS I

K1TTY: The Laughing Doctor.

DrJMrJ: That sounds like the title of a gore movie.

They converse idly for almost an hour, ad

nauseam, until Luke has agita and is too tired to play nice anymore.

Kat believes DrjMrj is a Socio-Psychiatrist within moments. Kat shares her innermost feelings with him, including, but not limited to love, dispositions, and her difficulties with other peoples' difficulties. He listens with the patience of a professional psychotherapist and likewise responds. There are no judgment calls, no bias, no come-ons and no sexual innuendo. Kat likes that, but does not share the fact with her special new friend. However, she does add him to her Friends List. Luke's souvenirs keep him hungry. The potential for fantasia keep him enticed.

# CHAPTER EIGHT

"It's one of the most pleasurable things with which we indulge ourselves that is measured by the inch," Martha smiles. "I bet it's not what you're thinking," she continues, smiling wider. "It's not an Inch Worm. I am talking threads per square inch, of course!"

"At a minimum a two-hundred-sixty thread count, and for the most luxurious go with four-hundred-twenty-five minimum." She goes on to explain why, and where cost comes in to play when selecting quality bed sheets.

Luke is still way back on measuring by the inch. He wishes to know what Martha's dildo looks like. He speculates that she has one at all; billionaire she is, why, any man or woman would have her. Luke knows better. She simply must. He thinks about it, and it does the trick for the night.

*

Luke's chat community thrives, now with a membership of thousands. Most members reside nearby, in western Jersey. Besides Washington County, 'Equity' reaches out to Hackettstown, Phillipsburg, beyond to some in Easton and Allenton, Pennsylvania, and, the New York City Metro area. The city members are almost too freaky for him, but Luke prefers to hang locally regardless. He works persistently and slowly, almost exclusively, unfurling a seductive rug toward Kat.

On the portal home page, Luke decides, on a lark, to advertise a free service, more an underground group, and even more precisely, a growing band or ARMY of new confederate missionaries: "The DayAfters." He begins recruitment targeting his own neighborhood, where, for every six-figure family, there are six substandard – some bordering poverty. Word of "The New Confederate Missionary" page, and "The DayAfters" spread quickly. "The DayAfters" spawn from the Grand Mother on Annie's side, over her habit of holding out for the sales. Luke sees it as militant, in that the ultimate objective is to spend the least amount of money as possible earmarked for retail sales. Beside the week-to-week and holiday-to-holiday savings, the objective is to get the group large enough to stop buying everything – completely – and anything for one week or two at a time. It causes the monopolies and capitalistic to listen to the message – to hurt them, Luke believes. Implicit boycotts followed by explicit buycotts.

The group celebrates Christmas the week after the actual holiday to take advantage of the after Christmas sales. The group modus operandi is to do the same for every holiday. Luke continuously tries to embed a frugality mindset as second nature for every aspect of consumerism. The members take their vacations off time and off-location. The primary intension is to cut commercialism down to size, although he presents the idea first simply as a money saver.

Luke's previous online enterprise was non-surgical penis enlargement, which graduates in price by product choice to market and quality. The low-end solution – twenty-dollars – is a pair of premium pubic hair-styling shears wrapped in a bonded linen bag with a comfortable font instructing the user to trim back the pubic hair. This does the trick; exposing the penis in its full length, thus looking considerably larger to the on-looker. The use of a tie line is the mid-tier solution, and tying a pair of sneakers beneath the glans and throwing them over the side of the bed when ready to sleep is the next tier up.

Sub-portal – portlet – pages feature both

enterprises as third party ads, but it is all Luke's profit. People are so self-conscious, trusting, satisfied and believing. He earns his first million when a little over fifty thousand men in the network respond to the initial ads by sending "Natural Goodness Enterprises" twenty dollars each to learn how to optimize their minimal assets. "Natural Goodness Enterprises" is an otherwise unknown affiliate of 'Equity,' but no one had reason to know, let alone complain. Once he reaps reward from the penis nonsense, he drops it and destroys all traces of it. The "DayAfters" remain in full bloom.

Luke approaches his enterprise as simply as possible. He forms an S-Corp with outsourced payroll, and Tax Preparation. Affiliate money goes to a PO Box in Hoboken. He knows a gumshoe agency online that will screen applicants registered, but he knows he must keep a low profile. It is peculiar to him that no matter how depressed he may be his focus at work does not waver. Outside of having some – any - focus, he suffers. He has grown weary of network chat, unless it is with Kat.

Her chat sessions with him have grown beyond flirting to the point of sexual in nature. Kat is a naive, lonely woman who turns to on-line chitchat to fill a void: THE void. What starts with sharing recipes and dress patterns, graduates to sharing fantasies, desire and feeling. She plays with herself. They all play with themselves...Especially when they have Luke's respective character on the wire.

Luke persistently keeps his eye on her. He makes a decision, even within the foggy symptoms of his disease. The intention to become her all out, online, mate, match and lover does not seem as lofty a goal to him as it once did. After recording and studying her behavior online, he is ready to make his move. He scripts several scenarios speculating on how she is likely to respond. He has hundreds recorded from all the pleasure he has spread around the neighborhood the past couple years.

She is online now, in the Romance queue, no less.

K1TTY: Hi – you again

She sends him a red message, to which he promptly replies.

DrJMrJ: oh hi

K1TTY: Feeling good?

DrJMrJ: okay – a little lonely tonight

*Tonight is the night apparently...*

K1TTY: Aww – Anything I can do?

DrJMrJ: Wanna cyber?

K1TTY: What is that?

DrJMrJ: sexy talk online – fantasies, and what naught

K1TTY: Hmmm

DrJMrJ: never done it before - have you?

K1TTY: No.

DrJMrJ: would you like to try it?

K1TTY: No. I don't think so.

DrJMrJ: why not?

K1TTY: Seems perverted.

DrJMrJ: really…

K1TTY: Well, I have thought about it.

K1TTY: My husband recently left me, and I have been lonely…

DrJMrJ: I am so sorry…

K1TTY: I think I would feel funny doing what you suggested.

DrJMrJ: funny isn't bad

K1TTY: No, it's not. Go ahead. How do we begin?

DrJMrJ: I will start, I guess, and you can respond only if you feel like it.

K1TTY: okay

DrJMrJ: fair enough?

DrJMrJ: okay

DrJMrJ: all right… here we go:

DrJMrJ: in our bedroom

DrJMrJ: you are just finishing your shower after a swim

DrJMrJ: you are in the master bath

DrJMrJ: I am already clean and dry, but my hair is damp

DrJMrJ: towel around my waist

DrJMrJ: I am lying in bed... waiting...

DrJMrJ: The thought of you returning from the bath with just your towel has me aroused to no end

K1TTY: mmm

Luke goes on to describe an exquisite sexual fantasy worded with appreciation for the female form as well as animal bravado. Kat cannot help but issue a virtual moan every ten or twenty lines, or so. Every response of hers equates to fuel for Luke to build up again. He cannot know it, and Kat only assumes it is the very point, when she climaxes in her computer chair.

DrJMrJ: you rest your head on my shoulder

and rest dearly all over me, and that is where I wish to stay for the rest of my life.

    DrJMrJ: Hi!

    DrJMrJ: :-)

    K1TTY: wow!

    DrJMrJ: Was that good for you sweetness?

With that, K1TTY signs-off in a hurry, to go clean herself off. Luke does the same.

# CHAPTER NINE

Martha spends her airtime today at the Portland Public Market, in the coastal Maine city. She is featuring fresh vegetables – of the phallic variety, such as cucumbers, zucchini, et al. She features a few of the exotic variety. Martha talks with ease about the virtues of all.

*Of course she does.*

"Given its phallic shape, asparagus is frequently enjoyed as an aphrodisiac food," she explains, poker faced.

"Feed your lover boiled or steamed spears for a sensuous experience. Be careful of overcooking – the spears should not be limp or soft. The Vegetarian Society suggests 'eating asparagus for three days for the most powerful affect.'"

She holds up in her right hand something

that looks familiar, but Luke does not know what it is.

"The banana flower has a marvelous phallic shape and is partially responsible for popularity of the banana as an aphrodisiac food," she begins.

*No wonder she has the ratings...*

"An Islamic myth tells the tale that after Adam and Eve succumbed to the Apple they start covering their nudity with banana leaves rather than fig. From a more practical standpoint, bananas are rich in potassium and B vitamins, necessities for sex hormone production."

Finally, banana in hand, she says what Luke wants to hear:

"It is a darn, Nice Thing."

*

Luke's anonymously submitted story lines continue to deliver online seduction at its best. The excitement flowing through the neighborhood lines, women sharing their experiences with someone they believe is their very own online lover, has Dawna curious to the point of making it a habit to login right after work. She starts her 'Equity' chat messenger secretly hoping that a mysterious man will someday login and give her what makes so happy, she hears, the others in town.

Luke sees Dawna signs-in from five-thirty until six-thirty every weekday evening. He figures that must be the difference in time between her arrival home and Stone's. She sometimes spends hours at a time online on weekends, mostly idle, when Luke guesses Stone is out of town. Luke is almost solely interested in Kat and Kat only, but to date he has cybered most of the neighborhood women into climax, including fat Sharon, Deloris Mahoney, and young Laura Carnes… others… repeatedly. Now he badly wants Dawna. For one thing, she is somewhat cute, but moreover, she belongs to Stone. Call it seduction for spite, if nothing else.

Dawna walks in and hangs her jacket in the hall closet. She is feeling tired but decides to login, as usual, lay down on the couch, and do absolutely nothing. She hopes the dull ache in her head will be gone by the time Stone gets home. Luke is monitoring Dawna's online activity, but sees she has been idle for almost twenty minutes. He decides to try to chat-her-up. He would adore a little taste.

anoMan: Hi ☺

anoMan: anyone home?

Dawna jumps at the whirly-chirp sound her Instant Messenger client makes.

DawnaBeeBoop: who r u?

Replacement of words by letters suggests she is an experienced I.M. chatter. Luke wants her, but does not want to lose her. He must groom first.

She has been, she knows, started and startled into excitement and interest, yet not without apprehension.

anoMan: Like the name says, anonymous man.

DawnaBeeBoop: k

DawnaBeeBoop: haha

DawnaBeeBoop: hi to you ☺

DawnaBeeBoop: a/s/l

anoMan: 35/m/NJ

DawnaBeeBoop: 27/f/NJ

DawnaBeeBoop: ? in NJ

anoMan: Anonymous, NJ.

DawnaBeeBoop: lol

anoMan: ☺

anoMan: Are you married?

Dawna wants to say she's spoken-for, but

simply answers, "No," instead. She answers his question truthfully, which is important to her. Luke easily lies, replying that he is single, too. Well, his character is, anyway. He is okay. They continue to chitchat for another ten minutes about topicality, mostly esoteric. Luke breaks the ice with an innocently posed question.

anoMan: ←{Hmmm… she mentioned being lonely}

anoMan: ←{wonders if she might want to cyber}

Dawna does not know how to answer. If she says yes, in order keep his attention, she might come-off whore-ish, yet if she said no, she might come-off as a prude. Finally, she answers with the truth. She truly enjoys the company of this man.

DawnaBeeBoop: IDK…you?

anoMan: maybe

anoMan: any interest?

Just then, Dawna hears Stone pull-up. He is surprisingly early. Flustered and frustrated at having to stop her conversation short, she reluctantly tells anoMan she has to run. She parts with a final acronym:

DawnaBeeBoop: ttyt

*poof*

Luke gets the invitation for the next day, and feels positive about the experience today. He feels he made significant progress with her. He is glad because he knows Kat should be online soon. He goes upstairs for supper, watches Martha, and then some news on television. Ever since 'Equity' came to be, these are some of the few times Annie ever sees Luke anymore. Rarely does he remain in the living room with her, though they will occasionally take in a movie, or a night of throwaway sitcoms. Nine o'clock rolls around, and Luke gets up and goes back downstairs.

"What do you do down there all the time, anyway?" Annie uncharacteristically asks.

"Software upgrades, hardware upgrades, debugging, troubleshooting…"

"Never mind," Annie hears the words <u>debug</u> and <u>trouble</u>, which confirm she wants no part in any of it. "All right, see you around eleven."

"Okay…Sounds good."

*

K1TTY: hi – is the doctor in?

DrJMrJ: why, yes madam, he is

DrJMrJ: and how may I help you this evening?

K1TTY: oh, I have this ache inside

Lucas knows what Kat is hinting at. She wants more.

DrJMrJ: oh, how wet thy gully – how sweet thy lips…

DrJMrJ: May I please, please, please…

DrJMrJ: lick-start your motor?

K1TTY: mmm

Luke kicks-off another string of sexy occurrences that weave into a full-fledged and full-bodied sexual experience for Kat. She admits to him afterward that he took her to orgasm twice. He waits until they finish, then navigates to his "Kat" folder, runs a slideshow, and relieves him-self. These nightly activities keep him disinterested in making love with Annie. He feels tired of her lackadaisical, needy, yet selfish approach. She is not exactly passionate, or giving. She takes well, but is completely unsure of herself when it comes to letting go and giving, uninhibitedly.

Luke also spends a lot of time in the basement monitoring. He works on 'Equity' or perhaps picks a female to cyber with, Luke eavesdrops in the neighborhood chat rooms and private IM conversations. He knows who says what to whom. He records during the infrequent times he cannot watch live his neighborhood goings-on. He does indeed perform all of those tasks he told his wife he does, however more seldom than he implied. Luke spends the majority of his time watching and diddling around.

It is ten-thirty, and Luke is contemplating an early night when he sees Stone login and call-out to someone in the city with the handle Sweetlilgreek. He cues them up and watches. Stone dangerously calls his presence "Stoner" online. His last name is Rossinski, and he is far from being a stoner.

Stoner: So we are lying there...

Stoner: It is bedtime, but we are not exactly sleepy, but a little worn from the day. I am sprawled on my back, hands clasped behind my head; you are on my right, on your side, facing me. You love the way I am just lying there, nude – as a king, and you love that you are naked too, under your tee and panties.

Stoner: Your right arm reaches over and caresses my chest and belly for a while, and you know how I love you to loosen me up down there a little, so you do it to me, playing gently with my hydraulics – I nicely grow a tad…

Sweetlilgreek: OMG

Sweetlilgreek: Mmm

Stone Rossinski lit into a scene that literally captivates Luke: He is dumbfounded. Not bad, he thinks, not bad at all. More arousing than watching the session is the knowledge that Stone is cheating on his mistress-partner. This, Luke can use.

Sweetlilgreek: Nice for you?

Stoner: Yeah – you?

Sweetlilgreek: oh yeah

Stoner: Good night sweetie

Sweetlilgreek: nighty night

# CHAPTER TEN

Martha celebrates a Thanksgiving second to none. It is a fact; Luke knows, judging by the ad for it that features a trailer from the year before. Martha offers blessings and honor to her invitees. Around her table, sit family, as well as a few stars to round-up the ratings. Of course, unlike conversation between Martha's rehearsed relatives, which she can rely on remaining G-Rated, it is not so with the often outspoken costars. It makes Martha regret fulfilling the wine rider. Live show business is always an understood risk.

Yappy guests, asking boring questions, sometimes risky, get through a grimacing smile responses like "Oh… Dare I say coining 'It's a nice thing' probably before you were born?" She chuckles to soften the under-the-table blow. Not unlike a nun, who would dare not appear scolding, she is just one to scold mercifully (also not unlike sometimes-said nun).

One star asks how she survived her divorce, with a child, and all… Martha replies, "Am I the same girl? Yes, I am. Personal life events either change or offer opportunities somehow. I believe that is to some degree true for all people."

Martha describes herself as a 'girl' and the mere mention by her of the word "girl" to describe herself turns Luke on. He gets-up and goes down to the basement.

*

Opportunities on weekends were few, and the last evening chat Dawna is a narrow escape. Nevertheless, Luke wants Dawna. He wants her to know about Stone's online activities. Luke wants to have her without having to have her. It's Saturday, Kat has taken her kids to the city for the weekend, and Luke is lonely.

*Tonight would be perfect for Dawna*

The chat between Luke and Dawna aside, even suggestively three or four times, Luke, until now, does not feel the time right to go for it, but if she logs-in tonight, he shall. He looks through a few folders of Kat while waiting. He makes a few pictures of Dawna using converted video cells edited into nudes from the Web, much like his initial takes on the 'Kat project.'

*She is not Kat, but she is a damn cute redhead.*

Moreover, here she is, ding-dong, it is the big hour of seven past seven, and it is mind over matter. If she does not mind, it does not matter to him.

anoMan: after a long hike through Acadia, we return to our cottage.

Luke is not in a hurry, does not want it to hurt, but he does want to cut right to it if she can handle it. What is the worst that could happen?

DawnaBeeBoop: uh, Hi {?}

anoMan: You are a bit sore from the walk (so am I, but I do not admit it).

DawnaBeeBoop: ok – I will do it

*Oh Jesus, yes*

anoMan: I slowly peel your clothes off…

anoMan: like this...

anoMan: Your outer layer, top button, up, comes off, over your shoulders.

anoMan: I loosen your belt and unbuckle your pants just enough to let your tee shirt out and I pull it up over your head.

anoMan: Your arms are in the air and I peel it off and toss it on the divan.

Leave it to Luke to bring it on within moments as the cyber-story of love making in a cabin that sets the place ablaze! Finally, at the finish:

anoMan: We fall in for a nap...

anoMan: Do you feel good sweet ONE?

*

Luke signs on anonymously and sends DawnaBeeBoop an email message. As the administrator, only he has the ammo to do such a thing, so he uses that power.

Dear DawnaBeeBoop –

You do not know who I am, but I have evidence of your fiancé having an illicit online affair. I do not care about him, nor do I wish to meddle, but I have a soft spot for unknowing and wronged women, and you. Attached, please find a recent, intercepted IM session of theirs, as an example. I have more.

Signed,

No One

Dawna does not know how to react. In her reply to that email, she begs for more information, but it comes back undeliverable. She thinks about how Stone is doing what she is doing with AnoMan. She reasons that if they are both out there essentially having sex with another, they must not mean much to each other anymore, let alone belong together (forever).

Her heart bleeds over it, but it more pounds now with charged emotion. When he pulls the care in to the driveway, she feels almost as nervous as she was the night his wife caught them playing house together. Once he is through the doorway, she confronts him with it. She simply hands him the email and attachment. She says nothing, and goes to sit in the living room.

"I left my wife and kids for you!" Stone bellows, shaking the papers in his hand.

"You've been fucking another woman, STONE," she spits. "And DON'T BLAME ME. I have been a catalyst. Pack and go."

Stone acts as if he is mad with regret as he packs and departs. Therefore, he leaves begrudgingly, regrettably: over a mistake? Now, he drives straight for a certain New York City girl. He is going to find and meet the girl he met online a couple months ago. This time, it is going to work. Stone leaves

Dawna for a NYC girl who said more than once that she could get him professional work, so this is a good move. Regardless of his promises, and regardless of his follies, he self-serves.

# CHAPTER ELEVEN

Martha's hands are in the dough today; she kneads the mixture carefully, according to the instructions from a special mid-century, stone-ground flour bread recipe. She moans and groans, as if she were the dough instead, yet between the unintelligible, she explains in detail the entire process for her audience, "Because it does matter. Feeling and knowing the full course, from source, in-ground, tree or bush, the ocean or terrain, matters much to every good chef."

*I am listening…*

"You want to work this dough, knead it, as though you might your partner on those times you really need his attention, if you know what I mean," Martha winks.

*Wink.*

The writers at "Saturday Night Live" immediately write a script for Ana Gasteyer where she plays a topless Martha in the kitchen, playing in the flour. The show airs this very night! Oh my God, between Martha's kneading and commentary, and SNL's fulfilling moment, Luke needs help getting himself to sleep.

*

Headley smiles as K1TTY leads a group of Youmans Avenue women through a dialog fit for print. Almost every night their conversations are enough to make him play with himself. He fears it, the embarrassment, but it feels so needful. He loves her. Online, Headley is a young woman from New York City typically, who is all but silent, yet friendly. He occasionally red messages with men or women under his guise, but men unusually.

They all appear to be talking about different, yet equally sensational men, all of them. It makes him wonder. He lets his thoughts take over. When there is an unknown, it is all one has. Imagination… it is boundless. Headley tries to get out of this nasty habit and vows he will someday approach Kat for real. She needs more time after her divorce.

He mows lawns and does odd jobs all over town. Headley works part-time at Merck, East on Route 78, but spends his spare time working the neighborhood, and town. Face to face, conversations with the townspeople reveal a common thread…sex. Even he sometimes feels like the Pepsi guy in the wife-beater as he walks through town.

Instead of watching tonight, Headley plans to take the big step: he is going to hack. He once swore he would never, but now the action seems vital. There is a man or woman encroaching upon the marriages of virtually every woman on his block, and now he simply must know who is behind it all. He goes to Circuit City and buys a second computer, which, unlike the other machine, dedicated to work, he will use as a worm can and a sandbox. Once he wires and sets-up his utilities, system, and his search and destroy software, it does not take him long to narrow the source down to the county. So now, finally, the three days of work reap the harvest. Night two brings him right into the Borough, the third, to this side of town. Headley has a hunch, but it soon turns into potential deduction. What is going on is by one man or party of low down and close men.

Headley watches some of the chat, like a kid in the bushes spying on his big sister and boyfriend. It sickens him to see that Kat is involved. It is so unlike her. She must be so lonely. Certainly, she would prefer the real thing. He does not want to hurt her,

but he does want to bring the chat master
down for a fall.

*

DrJMrJ: You are wearing...

Short shorts unbuttoned at the top, zipped
most of the way up, with a loose, .sleeveless
halter-top, no bra, no panties

DrJMrJ: I come home to you… you look in
my eyes, and scurry away from me

DrJMrJ: I chase. You run. I threaten to
spank. I catch you.

K1TTY: We agree it is so much more fun to
catch than it is to chase.

DrJMrJ: You slide quickly my belt from
the loops, slip my sweater over my head and
attack my trousers like the craved sexpot
that you are.

DrJMrJ: You grab my shirt and rather than
unbutton it you simply pull it apart and the
let the buttons fly about the room.

K1TTY: I get "mad" and wrestle you to the
floor -- we rock --

We roll -- you are on top of me.

K1TTY: (I let you "win")

DrJMrJ: We embrace and share the longest kiss we had ever...

You then slide downward…

Luke is satisfied he pleases Kat. He knows he does, as he reads her intermittent moans, groans and declarations of her climaxes to him.

DrJMrJ: You collapse straight downward, and I too fall and rest on your perfect ass and back. I never want to leave. We roll and turn toward each other. We exchange a loving glance, we hug, you cry, and then we nap.

K1TTY: Good night sweetheart

DrJMrJ: night

DrJMrJ: *poof*

As Headley wipes the semen with a wad of tissues from his right hand, panting, he notices a post-activity hit on the IP tracer program.

*

Luke spends so much time with his online harem; he neglects 'Equity' some. When once he would have updated operating system, firewall, and virus protection related software daily, he hastily automated it all. That gives him time to spend bringing it on with the neighborhood women than with any systems related efforts.

The worm enters the network at 3:00 AM, and by five o'clock Headley has firm inquiry control over most of 'Equity.' He cannot change anything, but he can hijack, redirect and watch. Moreover, ever did he watch! 'Equity' snooping became his secret passion. Luke L'Italian is getting it on with virtually every woman on the block, and others, too, but Kat believes he is all hers. Headley makes a promise to himself that he will bring Mr. L'Italian up front and center, then down, and down hard, flat. He is a scientist and engineer, for Christ's sake! Surely, he can manage a project to ruin a man, and win a woman! Even the renowned Information Sciences Architect he ran into once in while at Merck.

Within a month, Headley knows almost as much as Luke does about the neighborhood folks. Stone's affair, Dawna's escapades, Sharon's secrets, and those fantasies of every other woman on the block – he works them all during Luke's downtime. He nails all their online partners down to one man: Luke. However, Luke seldom ventures out or seen outside his house, it nauseates Headley to see him in his yard or driveway whenever Luke does for something – a walk to the diner, corner store or the occasional yard sale.

*

Luke wants a face-to-face meet and greet with Kat. He wants her to know how he feels about her. He wants to stop the nonsense involving all the others, but he is having trouble doing it. It is comparable to addiction. The subtleties, heterogeneities and nuances of each woman satisfy him, as Annie never does, even though, in reality, he faces loneliness at night's end, with only Rosie Palmer, her four daughters, and sister Thumbelina.

Kat worries about her secretive behavior around her kids, an uncomfortable façade that, come bedtime, discomforts her. Why can't she just meet this wonderful man? He comforts her. He satisfies her. He seems to adore her, whether they are engaged in online follies or intellectual conversation. Why?

*

Hed: Hey Kat – it's me Headley

K1TTY: Headley the yard guy?

Hed: Well, I work part time at Merck

Hed: Engineer/Scientist

K1TTY: OMG

K1TTY: I had no idea

K1TTY: I work there too

Hed: I know

K1TTY: You know? How do you know it is Kat?

Hed: It is a long, long story

K1TTY: Well?

Hed: A story perhaps better told in person

# CHAPTER TWELVE

Luke cannot believe his ears. He cannot believe his eyes. There is Martha on Fox News: under arrest for insider trading, or wire fraud, or something: Both! He is immediately alert, unlike the very moment before, drowsing to the drone of the day's headlines. She may be going to jail…, which, in an eerie way, breaks Luke's heart. He is clearly in love with Kat, but his celebrity fantasy with Martha, even after all this time; still feels equally near as fulfilling. He tries to curb his concern and loss. She has finally lost him.

*

"Have you heard the jokes about what Luke has going on in his basement?" Headley asks Kat.

"Yeah," Kat said. "I understand you said he was growing cannabis… or mushrooms."

"Under those creepy looking lights… all night… all the time. But listen to this, Kat."

"Well, come-on! I've been waiting."

With that, Headley dives right in with what is actually going-on in Luke's basement. He spills as much as he knows, including all the chat sessions going on.

"That's, that's…inscrutable!" Kat feels utterly betrayed, hurt, embarrassed and nothing less.

"Unscrupulous indeed… I'm sorry, Kat"

"Kat," Headley continues. "We've got to get Luke over here."

"But why here…How can we do that?"

"Look… You know he knows who you are. He does not know you know who he really is. Next time online, invite him over. Tell him you think it's time you met."

Headley and Kat devise a plan should Luke decide to make some kind of move. She is horrified to know what is going on under the covers – more so behind the cellar windows right next door. It maddens her to think she is just one of his many: She is his alone.

"So, Headley, you want to and think we can set Luke up for a fall?"

"Logon, Kat," Headley impatiently suggests. "You can ask him to meet you."

"You're kidding, right?"

"No. Even if he freaks out initially first, he'll show." Headley is confident.

"I know he will." She is sure.

*

K1TTY: anybody home?

Luke hears the prompt and scurries to his workstation.

DrJMrJ: I am here, sweetie

K1TTY: I think I am ready.

DrJMrJ: for what?

K1TTY: to meet you

K1TTY: I want to meet you.

Why, won't he answer? She wonders. Okay… nothing to worry about, she reasons. I will give him time.

DrJMrJ: WOW - OK

DrJMrJ: where

K1TTY: My house. My kids are with their father, so it will be okay for a first meeting.

We will feel free and have the house to ourselves.

Luke is sweating buckets and shaking like a hound dog shittin' razor blades...Nervous as a four-balled tomcat.

DrJ&MrJ: Wgen?

DrJ&MrJ: When*

K1TTY: I don't care. How about now?

DrJ&MrJ: All right. Give me the directions.

*

Luke takes six 10 mg Valium and chugs a New Castle. He is so keyed-up; he is compelled to have a rare, off-schedule movement. Luke, through plenty in his life, cannot help but think this move could easily take him once again from one life to another with another huge change.

Luckily, Luke reasons, Kat thinks he is a New Yorker, so he gets some extra "travel time" in order to get his head together. Kat and Headley think the same thing, as they plan again the event as they hope it will occur.

"Luke is busy at home planning for the same thing. He will divulge all to me in time, Headley...right?" Kat remains anxious to the point of tummy aching over it – rightfully so, Headley acknowledges.

Meanwhile, the women on 'Equity' buzz amongst themselves, oblivious to the reality of drama that, as they chat, surrounds their cyber community. They all agree that they miss their dates tonight. They all reiterate their disgust with their own husbands. These women are gratified, satisfied and happy just to masturbate. It is better than no one at all, and much, much better than hairy backed apes, drunks, fat men, abusive spouses, and playboys that mean nothing at all.

"So, you'll open the door, Kat," Headley instructs. "You will have to act your way through the surprise of identity, but he will to. Just try to keep calm, Kat."

"Uh-huh…"

"Then, lead him into the dining room, through the hallway, and insist he sit with you over an adult beverage."

"Okay…"

"I'll take it from there." Headley deadpans.

*

Kat answers the door in jeans and a sweatshirt.

"Oh my God; it's YOU!" Luke smiles widely.

"…And YOU!" Kat hugs him, giggles, and leads Luke down the hall.

"I can't believe this," Luke carries on. "I mean I couldn't believe it when you gave me your address!"

Headley steps out from the living room and around the corner.

"Neither could I when I discovered what you've been up-to." Headley says. "You are fucking despicable!"

Luke goes white. Kat comes from the kitchen, around the table, and slaps Luke across the face. She then steps back and puts her arm around Headley. He hugs her close.

"So… What's 'Equity' worth to you, Mr. L'Italian?" Headley facetiously, yet curiously asks.

"That is your name, isn't it?" Kat spits.

"Keep in mind," Headley adds. "I know everything, and I mean everything you've been doing with your computers systems and network."

They could not have planned for what was to happen next. No sooner than Tom Headley begins to speak his rehearsed piece, Luke, quite nonchalantly, reaches into his jacket and pulls a three-eighty semi-automatic and shoots four, silenced rounds, two for him and two for her – fucking Lovebirds!.

*Of course, they had no idea who they were fucking with.*

"God damn it!" Luke is pissed at himself… He is angry at everything. "Fuck!"

They each have a clean hole in their foreheads, barely bleeding, and a hole in the chest, bleeding into their clothes. Kat and Headley lay lifeless folded together on the floor, eyes open. Almost makes Luke throw-up a grotesque scene. Thank gawd Kat's kids are with Stone, after all.

*Holy shit, are THEIR lives about to change…*

*Holy shit is MY life about to change…Again.*

Luke forms the bodies into fetal position and wraps each of them with plastic tarpaulin and duct tape. Thank God, she had both, and more in the cellar. Kat is light as a feather, but Headley is heavy, so Luke kicks him down the stairs. Luke laboriously rolls both of them in a large throw rug, and seals it with more tarpaulin and tape. Luke drags each to Kat's basement freezer. He empties it of everything in it. They both fit nicely together, sixty-nine, in the bottom of the cold rectangular box. He refills the freezer of all he previously took out of it to nicely and deeply cover-up the bodies.

Luke is home within ninety minutes. He kicks-off the Erasure software, swiping the discs of 'Equity' for good, performing a cascade of deletes and swipes. If he hurries, he can make the bank and disappear in the city before anyone knows anything. He has to go back to either Florida or to Portsmouth. Shit! He needs someone he knows right now, but there is no one left.

A day and a half later, Luke is still swiping the servers and customer clients, and hacking into Headley and Kat's machines. Luke contemplates this as he does all he can do: Wait. If he runs, they will chase for good reason, so, he remains there in his basement room, his sanctuary – waiting. Ann and the kids should be home shortly.

# PART II

## JUSTICE

# CHAPTER THIRTEEN

Luke knows there is plenty of planning and acting to do. Will he stay or will he run and go? He leans toward staying then lets his mind wander the paths of possibility. There are fundamental measures that he must put into place, and they have to be complete fast. He decides first, he will indeed stay, and second, he will make sure that Stone takes the hit for the crime. Third, he must put this basic plan into play tonight, and augment as necessary. He knows he can do it. He is a professional problem solver, after all, very fast on his feet and keen in mind.

Sweating profusely, Luke sits in his office and outlines the steps he must take in order to stay below the radar, and make certain that any evidence he can, tie to Stone. Luke is nervous, but he is determined to push his super-logical mind to the limit to overcome this sticky situation. He resigns to the decision he makes to leave the bodies where he put them. Discovery of the frozen corpses is inevitable upon the initial search of the home. Even the Washington Borough Police Department cannot be that incompetent! He starts with the obvious: The gun.

Complete darkness finally comes, so Luke prepares to take his first step. He is going for a short walk, Luke tells Annie, to help release a little stress. That, of course, is not far from the truth whatsoever. He puts on his winter jacket. Then he reaches into his top left drawer, and grabs the firearm. He buries the .380 deep into the right-side jacket pocket and walks out of the basement thru the back door leading to the back yard.

Luke walks around the house and continues up the avenue before he crosses the street to cut through the pathway to the local, Public Park and playground. From there, he takes another pathway that leads, almost directly, to the back yard of the house Stone and Dawna rent. He walks the path thinking about where exactly he will dump the gun. His first thought, was to put it into the flowerbed in the front yard, but he second-guesses and changes his mind. The front yard does not make sense…too obvious…too simple-minded, even for Stone. Luke decides to give the .380 a shallow burial along the tree line just to the side of the path but in the back of Stone's yard. Luke is satisfied this is much more feasible than his first idea for a spot to leave the smoking evidence.

Almost there, his stride slows a bit. He must remain quiet and careful upon approach. The trees and brush remain thick right up to the back yard, but Luke remains keenly aware and sharp, and makes sure there is no one, a neighbor, perhaps, by chance, out in their back yard. Now that he reaches the tree line, he sees that neither Stone nor Dawna is outside; no one is, as far as he spies. He takes a few steps to his right and mindfully creeps along the back yard border toward the corner. He is comfortable with the location, and crouches down. Knees bent, his rear end resting on his heels, he begins to brush away the layer of leaves left there from autumn.

Reaching ground, Luke, with gloved hand, digs a shallow crevice into it. He pulls the pistol from his jacket pocket, then, in the small grave, he lays it to rest. He hastily covers the gun with the dirt brushed away moments before, and then replaces the ground cover of leaves. He meticulously places the leaves to make sure anyone investigating will notice a small disruption there. While he is deliberate as he knows he must act, he is eager, if not anxious, to get back to his office to take-on his next task.

There. He is done in Stone's yard, and

with that gets up not without a bit of pain in his knees and back. He briskly takes his walk back home, intermittently looking back for footsteps he might have left. There were none; just the leafy ground cover there just as he encountered it while on the way. The path is wide enough so he does not have to worry about broken twigs hanging off the brush into it. He stops for a brief moment, puts his hands on his hips, elbows bent, and takes a nice big breath of clean, cool winter air. Thankful there is no snow on the ground, he trudges back home, and goes in through the same door he exited thirty-five minutes before.

Luke goes to the hatch, opens it a crack and yells to Annie that he is home and will be working in the office for a little while. He gets the "Okay!" then hurries over to his desk. Once into the systems he needs to access, he sets out to recover all the chat threads he deleted yesterday. The recovery process takes about an hour. This pleases Luke: He thought it would take much longer. He can delete only the threads between his IP address and everyone else on the Network, including any threads the end-users saved in the interim. This task requires him to write a few scripts, but he is good and quick, as always with this stuff, and has them written within the hour. He smiles as the scripts complete. He validates the results.

*"Finis! Voila…Success!"*

He logs back out of the system.

*Now, for a cold and well-deserved New Castle!*

"So, what are you doing down there this time of night?" asks Annie. She is only trying to make up a conversation. She does not actually care.

"Oh, just typical systems maintenance that I put-off for too long."

"What does that mean, exactly, Luke?"

"Well, you know how on your computer I run the Clean Disc and Defrag utilities? It's kind of like the equivalent on 'Equity'."

"Oh." Anne deadpans.

"Yeah, that's all, really…" His voice trails off.

"What do you want to watch, Luke?"

"Is Martha on?"

# CHAPTER FOURTEEN

Waking slowly, Dawna is feeling lazy and well, warm and Sunday morning sexy. She hopes Stone will hear the stirring as she ruffles the covers and issues several sweet-sounding whimpers, yawns, moans and groans of morning. She thinks about what she wants while lying there, rolling back and forth on the bed, and thinks of Stone coming in with a touch and some words of love for her. As her mind wanders, she begins to think more about touch than the spoken word, and soon finds her own hands wandering. Please Stone, please. He never shows up. She waits no longer. One hand goes to her breast and one to her crotch. Oh how she wants him to come in. She feels this excessively often lately, satisfying, and relieving herself...relief and release.

Stone knows Dawna is awake. He can hear her in the bedroom. She sounds wanton of attention, but he does not care. He does not feel like going through those motions again right now period. He sits in his recliner, sipping on coffee and dreads going to his Ex-wife's house today, but he must return the kids after his weekend visitation. It is indeed *her* house ever since the divorce… and the tightly scheduled visitations with his kids. They are an award from the fucking court, fercrysake!

The short ride over won't come until a little later on this evening, just after dinner, at about six-thirty, but here he is worrying about it at nine-thirty in the morning. Stone has the bad habit of chewing on his fingernails and he engages in taking those nails right down to the quick. Why must he be so nervous about doing this? Enough time has passed, months, and he should be over it. Why is he unable to live it down? Why can't he merely be…comfortable? He knows the answer; it is simple. He let everyone down... his wife, his kids, but most of all, himself.

Dawna reaches another in what has become a long string of self-provided orgasms, and then eases out of bed, going into the bathroom for a nice morning shower. Under the streaming hot water, she thinks about why and how it has come to this. 'Why doesn't Stone want me anymore? Ever since I nailed him for carrying-on with that online 'friend' from New York City, he remains distant, and aloof. She is quite aware of his persona, troubles and guilt over the incident that led to his divorce, but after all, he now has her…his Dawna! Surely, at some point, he has to reconcile with God or himself, both, and enjoy a life in love again. Maybe he does not really love Dawna as he says he does. Maybe he is seeing someone else. You know what they say: If he did it to someone else, he will do it to you, and, inattentiveness is the first sign of a cheat. She cannot think about this anymore. She wants to have a good day today.

She has, in the meantime, shampooed her hair, lathered her entire body with soap and rinsed without even being aware that she did so. Dawna grabs her towel from the rack to the left of the tub, and methodically dries herself off. She is mindful of drying completely every crevice, every curve and every part of her body, between the toes and all. She takes the towel and makes a head wrap that looks like a turban, then puts on deodorant. She reaches for the body lotion. After she covers all those parts susceptible of dryness, finally, after putting on undies and a bra, Dawna goes to the door, takes her robe off the hook, puts it on, ties the front, and walks out of the bathroom. She treads through the bedroom, down the hall and into the living room to see that

Stone is indeed there, sitting quietly in his chair, staring out the window. There is no television, no music, no nothing, except an empty coffee mug on the end table next to him.

Dawna stands behind Stone seemingly unnoticed for the longest time, looking down at him and wondering. 'what is going through his mind <u>right now</u>?' She nearly screams as her heart starts when Stone abruptly and suddenly says, in a rather loud voice, "Good morning, Dawna."

"Good Morning Stone. How did you sleep last night, honey?"

"Oh…I slept alright, but I was up and asleep again all night long and couldn't sleep-in this morning."

"Apparently not…" Dawna does not intend to air disgust, but Stone picks-up on her tone of voice and sighs loudly. She ignores it and walks to the kitchen to pour a well-deserved cup of coffee. Sitting in the living room airs a silence between them that is deafening. He has nothing to say to her, and she has only negative thoughts lingering from the questions raised in the shower, so she says nothing.

They both hear the two boys awakening and talking in their room. To them, it is a bit like camping at Dad's house, because they have to take turns sleeping on the floor in a sleeping bag. The other one gets the single bed. Stone put a Television in their room to keep them happy and occupied. They use it for their games most of the time, however on the weekend mornings they watch cartoons. Stone listens to the sounds, the funny cat-chasing-the-mouse music, the odd voice-overs, and of course, the loud five-minute commercials every eight minutes of the show.

Dawna gets up to fix a hearty, Sunday-morning breakfast for everybody. She knows she has some leftover ham and baked potatoes, and with them, she makes ham and eggs, home fries, and toast. Without realizing it, she begins to sing while preparing the meal. Even though she has to handle it on her own this morning, she feels quite satisfied and at ease. This beats thinking about the possibilities revolving around Stone, thoughts that, for now, totally escape her mind.

The smell of the food cooking raises Stone from his seat and he goes into the kitchen. He walks up behind Dawna, who is at the stove stirring the potatoes, puts his hands on her hips and says, "It smells good, Dawna. I can't wait to eat."

"It does, doesn't it?" Dawna says cheerfully.

"Sure does… Listen, I'm sorry I've been so quiet this morning."

"That's okay. Is there something bothering you?"

"I just have a lot on my mind. That is all. The new show next week, mostly."

"Oh. Well Stone, don't worry so much. How many shows have you pulled off successfully at the university? Huh?"

"Yeah, you are right," but Stone is worried more about why the girl from New York has not been online in the past several days. Dawna, on the other hand, has not given much thought to her online acquaintance. It was intriguing, given Stone's absences and inattentiveness, but she is not a cheater. She only hopes that he is not either. 'Stop it!' She tells herself.

"How do you want your eggs this time, Stone," she asks. "Scrambled or fried?"

"Let's have scrambled…with cheese." Stone replies and takes a seat at the dining table.

Dawna walks to the children's room and knocks on the door, then opens it, and says in singsong, "Boys? Breakfast is almost ready. Wash up and come to the table." She is not a yeller. Stone would have hollered from table at them if she had let it go much longer before summoning them. She goes back to the kitchen and stirs the eggs. Everything else is done and keeping warm in the oven.

Everyone gobbles the food down, as though they are ravenous, even Dawna is eating fast, which is something she is not in the habit of doing. She takes notice, slows down, and wishes everyone else would too, but does not say anything. She does not want to start trouble. It pleases her to hear the expressions of approval – the sounds the boys and Stone make between bites, and, as always, she is impressed that they all chew with their mouths closed. Kat, she believes, trained them well.

"So, boys, want to go to the park today?" Stone says more than asks.

"Yeah," Brian and Timmy answer excitedly, in unison.

"Okay, good. We'll leave here at around noon."

Stone gets up, refills his mug with the last of the coffee, and returns to his chair in the living room. He kicks his feet up, breathes deep, and tries to relax and remain calm. Dawna is no longer surprised that he skips doing the dishes together, with her, as he used to. Again, she refrains from saying anything to him, for fear of stirring up the nest. The boys, back in their room, stay there until it is time to go out. Dawna clears the table, wipes it down, and finishes the dishes.

She decides she could use another cup of coffee, so she asks Stone if he wants more. He does not, so she brews a two-cup pot. She fills her cup with fresh coffee, adds cream and sugar, then goes into the living room: She wants to relax. She has no difficulty as she gently sinks into the corner seat on the couch – her favorite spot. She has an end table there, a reading light, two throw pillows and of course, a couple books and magazines. As tension emanates from Stone, she leans on one pillow, hugs the other, and occasionally sips her coffee.

"Stone, do you mind if I put the TV on?" she politely asks.

"Um, no, I don't." Stone says. "Go ahead."

Dawna watches The Food Network to see if she can pick-up a new recipe or two. Besides, she cannot seem to break through the 'Stone wall,' referring to his indifference and absentmindedness. 'So, I might as well do something at least half-way productive and fun for me.' Truth be told, she really does want to go online just to check and see if her special friend is there. If nothing else, he has a good ear.

"Are you coming to the park with us?" Stone finally breaks his silence.

"Ah…no, I don't think so – not today, thanks." Dawna tells him she wants to stay home and relax this Sunday.

"Oh, okay." Stone does not really care one way or another.

"It's noon Stone. What time are you leaving?"

"Oh, I'm going to get the boys ready now." Stone gets up and heads toward the kids' room.

"Okay kids," Stone yells through the door. "It's time to go now."

"Okay Dad," Brian yells back. "We'll be right out."

"Remember to dress warm. It is December and chilly!"

The three males go out the back door and cut through the back yard to the path that leads straight to the park. Eager to get to the park, the boys walk fast. Not eager to do anything, Stone walks slowly and falls behind. "Not too far ahead of me, now," he hollers up to the boys. They slow down slightly, but not much. Stone does not walk any faster to catch-up with them either.

Dawna wastes no time logging into 'Equity' and waiting for anoMan. She waits patiently, yet knee jerking nervous. 'Where is he? Come on, anoMan! Come on!' she says aloud. Dawna finally gives up and logs out, but she becomes so turned-on by the thought of AnoMan, his seductive stories, while waiting for him, she cannot help to masturbate a third time for the day. She is hasty with her actions because she does not know exactly when Stone and the boys will be home again. She feels no guilt about what she does more and more of late, because, she reasons, Stone is not fulfilling his manly duties: He is not satisfying her innermost needs. Surely, he must know what he is not doing.

The boys start with the swings: Who can go the highest? Both of them let go a loud 'woo-hoo' with every swing up. They swing so high that it makes Stone nervous, on top of his already feeling tense. He silently says 'Thank you God' when the kids move-on to the tilt horses, which are mounted on big springs cemented in the ground. The kids bounce back and forth with all their might.

"The horse's nose almost touched the ground," Screams Timmy.

"The tail, too," Brian echoes.

'Well, at least if they fall now, they are

close to the ground…' Stone is tired and unnerved. 'Why must I obsess over her?'

Stone, through all the nervous tension, sees danger in everything around him, especially his kids' rough playing out there in the park. He cannot make his gut shut-up. He cannot slow his mind down, no matter how hard he tries. He feels like he can easily jump right out of his shoes right now, damn it! It all turns in his stomach – it all blasts in his head. It is a sick, guilty feeling: The kind that triggers when you do something wrong and it is relentless inside.

The merry-go-round brings no reassurance to Stone. He can just see one or the other boy, or both, centrifugally forced into sliding-off. They would hit the ground rolling, hopefully, and not get hurt. They push the round ride fast and jump on it only to hang half-off the thing, using one leg for turbo boost. That extra kick of speed is worth the effort and their hearts pound as they burst out laughing, all while clutching with their lives the bolted-down railings to keep from wiping out.

*

Luke is a busy man. It does not matter that it is a Sunday: He must finish this. Thus, today's Sunday is not typical at all:

The only time he usually allows himself to just…well…be. He would rather sit in his upstairs office, or the living room; and vegetate. There is no chance this Sunday. He sits at the edge of his chair while typing at one of several keyboards; this one is standard input for his UNIX boxes. Luke uses this UNIX cluster to interface with his store of the databases, but he now works natively from the command line – no pretty interface. This is the only way he is able to do. He must erase, not delete, but erase the hard discs of every trace of every chat that involves his IP or that contain references to any given chat handle of his to date. He leaves be those sent by Administrator and those originating from his personal space as Moderators. Then, he erases the performance footprints of the Erasure utility. Erasure makes thirty-seven swipes at the segment in its run parameters. One of Luke's favorite mottos: Anything is possible. In this case, anything can be un-done.

Luke has no intention of logging into the chat regions for any shenanigans. He plays it very cool during the whole debacle. Will it ever come to a resolve, an end, and blow-over? He knows, of course, that it will become legend in this small town of Washington Borough. It will never blow over. It will, he knows, come to resolve, and if it is up to him, Stone will take the heat for it. Luke feels no guilt.

He is at the point where he can walk away for an hour at a time for four hours. Therefore, Luke makes the journey up through the hatch and enters the living room. Annie is there in her recliner with baby Mal. Luke says "Hi," sits down and leans back in his recliner. His mind is a fury of color and noise. He remains, fighting the urge to want to shake, and tries to take a couple deep breaths. He does not want Annie to see he is upset in any way.

*

Stone watches his boys on the jungle gym now. It is actually one of the new-world wooden, nylon and rubber contraptions set on top of wood chips enclosed in a large, landscaped oval. Stone takes in the surreal vista floating in front of his eyes. He holds a keen view of the lower block of the avenue; the treetops, the rooftops, as well as a close up awareness of his kids on the gigantic magic ship they call a gym. Stone holds that gaze – it is mesmerizing – for too long, and it dissolves into tiny multi-colored, non-parallels, bubbles of partials, before his eyes. Life, as he knows it, at the atomic level he can afford to see.

With his head in his hands, Stone stares down into the grass. It is beginning to freeze in the thirty-eight degree sunshine. Each blade shines in its own peculiar way, and makes room for a range of shimmering green and bluish colors. He no longer hears the intermittent sounds of the children's voices. He hears only pink noise coming from within his head. 'Why can't I hear the kids?' Stone knows his anxiety is causing the deep thoughts and gazing. 'Okay, it is time to snap into the now… Damn it!' Stone feels guilt. That is it! His discomfort, however, stems from every wrong thing he has ever done… all at once. It takes considerable concentration and thought to maintain from moment to moment.

Stone looks down at his watch and it surprises him to see that three and a half hours passed by already. He gives the kids a ten-minute warning, which also prompts him to prepare himself for the walk back home. He must calm-down, but he's not sure how to make it happen. Deep breathing helped him this morning, so he tries it again. It has a relaxing effect, which pleases Stone. Ah… finally, some peace…without the visuals.

"Okay kids," Stone raises his voice. "Alright, let's go. Let's go now."

"Aww," Timmy is not ready to go home.

"K, Dad!" Brian is ready.

"Good boys – come on, let's go"

Stone leads on the way home, as his boys wearily chatter and follow behind.

"Tired you out," Dad begins. "Huh…didn't it?"

"Yeah," Brian says.

"Sure did," replies little Timmy.

Stone cannot help but smile. He feels more grounded now that he is up and walking, and talking to his children. He is relieved all of a sudden, and he does not want to do or think anything that will change it. Therefore, he keeps talking:

"So, are you all ready for Christmas?"

"Oh yeah," Timmy yells.

"Oh yeah," Brian chimes loudly.

"Great, now each of you tell me what you want the most of all," Stone wants to engage them. It is keeping him sane right now. "Brian, you go first."

*

Dawna sits in the living room, curled-up in the corner of the couch, book in hand and iced-coffee on the end table. She jumps at the sound of the boys bursting into the house through the back door, but pays no attention to them as they come-in. She ignores Stone, as well. She feels no guilt. The two young boys kick off their shoes and run to their room. Stone leaves his shoes on and ambles into the living room. He sits down on his chair, and tries to think what subject he can raise to converse with Dawna…Anything to keep his mind shutdown.

"Do you want something to drink?" Dawna asks, as she gets up with her empty glass and walks toward the kitchen.

"Yeah, please," says Stone. "Whatever you're having is fine."

She made another full pot of coffee and used only a third of it in the pitcher. She pours two tall glasses full, so there was just enough left for one more glass each.

"Ice-coffee," Dawna tells him.

"Sounds good," says Stone back. "Ah…" Stone sinks into his recliner, legs up, and within moments, is asleep. Dawna sees and watches him sleep for a moment, then places his beverage next to him at his table. She returns to her spot and continues to read. She sips the coffee and wonders about his dreams. He never says. She never asks.

There is something wrong going on with him, and she vows to find out what it is. He never talks about his feelings. He does not share in that way. He is going to, however, even if it takes a confrontation, because Dawna believes that it is a key in a successful relationship… communication and honesty.

In addition, what she believes matters, you know. AnoMan taught her that. She cannot stop thinking about him. Why, in the middle of thoughts about Stone would she switch to thoughts about anoMan? She wishes she would have saved some of those chats, and could have sworn she did. There are no transcripts in her Message Box. Weird, but oh well, she must have deleted them. She would not want Stone stumbling on to them.

Stone dreams of nothing, actually, his mind lately total mush. The experiences in the park, stirred in through the mush, emotionally wore him out. His mind is as empty as a closeted suitcase. Dawna cannot help but believe he is dreaming of another girl. That is indeed a part of his apprehensiveness and preoccupation, but it is just a portion… nothing more. She will have to wake him for dinner at five. The rule is that they return the children with a full belly, and he has to have them back to Kat's by six-fifteen – six-thirty. He has an hour to sleep. She has a half-hour to read. Time goes by too fast.

"Come on out for supper, boys!" Dawna will wake Stone at the last minute.

She places the bowl of spaghetti and sauce with meatballs on the table. Everyone has water. Everything is okay.

"Stone," she calls out softly beside him. "Wake up for supper – it's on the table."

"What?"

"Dinner is ready."

"Be right there."

"Okay. Want me to make you a plate?" she asks him.

"That would be nice." He feels good after his short nap. It's routine from here on out.

"Okay, we have plenty of time," Dawna says. "Please eat slowly."

She smiles and gets smiles around the table. All around her, they are eating slowly.

"And please don't forget your salads when you're done with your pasta." Dawna happily chirps. "I happen to know that a following salad is healthier for you than a before-salad." She winks.

"Did you boys have fun this weekend?" Stone asks his sons.

"Yeah!" comes in unison, the enthusiastic boys' answer.

"Have all your stuff packed for six…Okay?"

"Yup"

"You have twenty-five minutes."

Moreover, Stone has twenty-five to unwind on the chair. He offers no word at all about dishwashing with Dawna. She sure does not like it, but lets it slide – again. Stone does not give it a thought. Whatever his issue is; she has no idea, but she still intends to find out, one way or another. This man must talk. Her new quest: Get him to talk. She almost giggles aloud. She imagines administering an inquest over him.

Visibly smiling now, Dawna catches on with some composure just in time. Stone stands in the doorway to the kitchen, and simply says, "I should be back by six-thirty." He turns to leave. As an after-thought, he comes back to Dawna and gives her a little kiss on the cheek, and says, "Love you."

"Love you, too. Now you have to go."

Stone's frustration shows with each series of knocks on the door. Each rap was five long – like a cop's – but each time he repeats the code, it is louder and louder. He feels rejected at first, because he sees Kat's car at the curb. He then reasons that she could be out with someone, albeit a little late, according to the settlement, the agreement. What is he going to do… take her to court? This is stupid. He accepts that he has to get off this porch and go back home with kids in-tow. He calls and leaves a message…a good message.

Stone's nerves shot, he grabs a cold beer from the fridge. It sure seems like every day-life moments challenge him in a way they challenge an infant. He has to snap out of this immersion, this depression. This is it, he resounds loudly from within, no more worries, an attempt to shock his brain into a new disposition. He will live day-by-day, one day at a time, no expectations, no assumptions, and no disappointments. Forget that New York chick! He lives with Dawna! She is young and beautiful: A prize of a girl.

"Yeah… She isn't home," Stone says to Dawna. "I don't know where the hell she is."

"Well, after the message you left her, I'm sure you'll hear from her soon – as soon as she gets back."

"I hope it's soon, otherwise, it's up to us to get the boys to school tomorrow."

"Oh yeah, that's right!" Dawna continues.

"You know, that's not a big deal, Stone. I can do it."

"Okay," Stone responds. "That would be great."

"Okay."

They wait and wait, but the call never comes. Stone calls Kat once more, but he does not leave another message. How can she be so selfish? You stay out late on Saturday night, not Sunday night. This presents a milestone test for Stone's newfound world of no worry. He reminds the boys to finish any homework that might be leftover, incomplete. That is necessary, and checks the task off his list. Some deep breathing is in order, so Stone kicks back in his stuffed recliner and proceeds with it. Dawna sees he is doing it again; something he has been practicing for the past couple weeks. It is some kind of meditation, or something, but he is taking deep belly breaths though his nose, and exhaling slowly between pursed lips, like a runner.

Brian finishes his homework while Timmy quietly watches a nearly mute television. Dawna remains quiet and watches Stone apparently trying to relax. All the while, he is deep breathing, and his feet are twitching. That is not a sign of relaxation, Dawna thinks as she looks on, and then away. Poor man...

So troubled: She must ask him if he wants or needs to talk when he appears awake enough for it. Even if he seems uncaring toward her lately, she still cares about him. Sexual neglect hurts her, but not as much as this. The scene plays-out every night, and it bothers her. No, it scares her.

Dawna puts out a sad expectation. Be ready for another night of deafening silence out here in the living room, restless sleep in the bedroom, and, no sex. She is not impressed with the new routine, yet she is willing to try to understand it in hopes to break it. Questions continue to reiterate in her mind. What is he thinking? What is troubling him? She wonders, but cannot let it drive her mad, because it is up to him to open up; she cannot help with a solution if she does not know the problem. Dawna knows, of course, as much as she needs to know about the chick from New York, but she does not know that the situation causes Stone to contract a depression over it. All Dawna knows, in addition, is that there must be something else, too. She hopes it is not her.

Stone makes another call to Kat. This time he tells her in a message that he will keep the kids overnight and bring them to school in the morning. She is responsible for being home when they get out. He is not pleased that she has not called. It is past bedtime already. The decision made, he checks that one off his list of worries for the night. There is nothing to wait for anymore, just sleep, blessed sleep.

# CHAPTER FIFTEEN

Stone is not the only nervous man in the borough. Luke rests easier Saturday night, the gun taken care-of, 'Equity' all cleaned-up. Now for the third and hardest step: witnesses. Is there any chance anyone saw him, without Annie, enter Kat's house? No. He thinks not. However, how can he be sure? He cannot be. It is as simple as that. He tries to accept that, but it is stressful to the point of naked worry. It was dark out and he was wearing black; that is two in his favor. He went from the back door to the front door, not front to front. That is another plus, as it kept him out from under any lights, beside Kat's dim porch lamp. How quick did she answer the door? How long was he standing there under the light?

*Think!*

It is all going to come down to the time line of that particular night, the night in question, and since, so Luke does his best to dig deeper into every detail and trace of his movements. Everything remotely evidentiary comes to mind and ties it, and his stomach, in tight-knotted cornrows. He has two additional firearms he must get rid-of. Put that one on the list, and move-on. It does not escape him that he may become, at some point, a person of interest. That alone, regardless of involvement, drives him mad. He can barely sit still, or off the toilet, but must fight the feelings down, especially in front of Annie.

It is widely known by the forces in town – police, fire and emergency paramedics – that Annie and Luke hold Kat's spare house key, in case it is, for some reason needed. Therefore, it stays. It is a straight face test anchor for Luke. If he were trying to hide anything relating him to Kat, certainly he would not leave unhidden, a key to her place! What else is there?

*Come-on.*

They will be at his door day one. Annie will be in on it. He will provide the key, no questions asked.

*

"Thank you, Mr. L'Italian," says Earnest.

The local Deputy Sheriff takes, like clockwork unfolding before Luke, the key.

"Anytime," replies Luke easily.

"Who was that?" Annie walks from the kitchen to the living room and asks.

"Deputy wanted the key to Kat's house…"

"Why?" Annie's gasp-reaction is entirely what Luke expects.

"I didn't ask," Luke says. "It's none of my business."

"Well, we have to find out."

"I'm sure we will, along with everyone else in town, once word gets out why he is there."

"Luke," Annie pleads. "Go over there! Ask if you can help, or something."

"No! I am not going to get in anyone's way; period."

After he knocks, Earnest slowly turns the key in the lock and opens Kat's front door. He yells, "Hello" and gets no reply. Walking slowly down the hall, and then circling around through the dining and living rooms, he sees that nothing seems out of place. There is no sign of a struggle here. He goes into the kitchen. There is no meal set-up and left. Nothing is there that should not be, if she is away: No phone, no keys, or pocket book.

That is it Earnest, she met someone and stayed out late. She has that right. She is an adult.

He knows he is there because of the calls, inquiring why Kat is not meeting her daily responsibilities. This is not an emergency. He should check the basement just in case. His hand massages the stairwell wall to find the light switch. A string runs the length from there at the top of the stairs to the fixture below through small eyelets screwed into the joists. He gives it a yank and the light goes on. Out of nervous habit, he yells "Hello" again, "Anybody home?" He gets no response. Earnest carefully descends the wobbly staircase and steps into the basement. It is mud-floored. There is an area for lawn tools at one end, and there is a laundry area in the other. There is a freezer between them. He walks over and takes a quick peek in the freezer. He does not know why he bothers. He sees only frozen food and shuts the freezer lid.

"Thanks again, Luke." Earnest says, handing the key back to Kat's neighbor.

"What's going on?" boldly asks Luke.

"Oh nothing, I don't think: Just a single Mom taking some time off."

"Gotcha," Luke says, as Earnest gives him a wink and a smile.

"Be good, Luke!" Earnest says loudly on his way out the front gate.

"You too!" answers Luke.

"Was that the cop again?" Annie's interest did not fade.

"Yes — He gave the key back."

"What's going on?"

"He said Kat was out unexpectedly. He said it is probably just a single mom taking some time off."

"Well, she didn't tell me!" as though she knows it all between them.

Well, that was over with quickly. Luke wonders how long it will be until he receives the Sherriff's next visit. He figures it is only a matter of time before the squad conducts another, secondary investigation. Luke makes an effort to stay ahead the curve. Kat is not magically going to begin showing up places. Day three, her place of business calls her home phone and her cell only to reach voice mail. They make another call to the Borough's local authorities.

Annie calls Kat's parents in Ohio and asks them if they know where she went over the weekend. They do not know…they last talked with her on Saturday morning. She was at home, they said. Luke stays put in his office for the day. He knows Annie is making calls, but he does not care. He cannot believe he killed Kat and Headley. If he does not believe, does that make it untrue? He will conduct his life as though it does.

# CHAPTER SIXTEEN

Dawna gets up on Monday morning, ready to get the kids off to school. Everyone is pleasant, but rush to make it on time…Stone to work and the kids to school. Stone leaves for work at seven-o'clock, but Dawna does not have to be there until nine. She walks the kids to school just two blocks to town then one more after crossing the busiest street in the Borough. Dawna reminds them that they are to walk home after school, as usual, to their house. She has their suitcases in her car, and plans to drop them off at Kat's house on her way to work. Once there, she sees Kat's car out front, which makes her scared to approach.

Dawna takes the suitcases out of the trunk of her car and carries them up the porch steps to the front door. Her thought is to put them down, ring the doorbell, and run back to her car. She decides to just drop the bags off at the door and leave it at that. Mission accomplished, she goes to work without another thought about Kat, or the kids. Her mind remains on Stone and anoMan. She is almost too preoccupied with her personal issues. Her work comes with difficulty.

Stone seems fine at work, probably so involved with what he is doing he has no chance to dwell on his demons. She does not see much of him when he is working on a show, but she sees him four or five times throughout the day, otherwise. They keep talk on the work at hand or pleasantries, holding off on anything personal until they get home. She can tell, however, that in this element at the university, he seems much less stressed and more into his job. Dawna plans to confront him tonight to get to the real subjects in mind.

Even though Dawna's hours are nine to five and Stone's are eight to four-thirty, she beats him home every night. Upon pulling into the driveway, she sees something that causes her stomach to get instantly queasy. Brian and Timmy are sitting on the front steps. They get out of school at three o'clock, so they have been there for well over an hour waiting. Dawna parks the car and circles the house to the front yard, and asks, "Boys… What are you doing here?"

"Mom never came home at four-thirty, Dawna," Brian replies.

"So we came here!" Timmy is somewhat excited because of the break in normal routine.

"Hmmm," Dawna thinks. "Okay, well, let's go in."

"Do you know where my mom is?" asks Brian.

"No, Brian," Dawna answers. "I don't. Neither does your father, but relax. You will be fine here. Your mom will show-up soon, I'm sure."

"Okay."

"Are you guys hungry, or do you want to wait for dinner time to eat something?"

"Can we have a snack now and dinner later?" Brian asks.

Stone is livid upon discovering his kids are back at his place. Dawna explains to him everything she did that morning and afternoon for the kids, and how she came to find them at the front door steps. He immediately gets on the telephone and calls Kat. He leaves another message saying that she had better come get the kids ASAP, and that he does not appreciate the run-around. He then does something that surprises Dawna. He calls the police and reports Kat missing. He does not really think anything is awry, except that she is ducking her responsibilities, and he does not like it. Therefore, typically Stone, he opens the assortment of issues, and has no problem with that!

"Are you sure you don't know where your mother is?" Stone asks the kids.

"I'm sure we don't." Brian answers. Timmy shies away when he sees his father upset.

"She doesn't tell us all the time," Brian adds.

"Okay. She will be home soon. Everything will be okay, Timmy."

*

Kat's mother and father are worried to death. Kat has only once done anything so irresponsible, getting pregnant by, and marrying Stone. Granted, those remain significant to them, it simply boils-down to a life event. This is no life event. This is a strange and uncharacteristic event. She has been out since Saturday night or early Sunday for going on two days now. They decide to call the Washington Borough police one more time.

"That's another call about Mrs. Rossinski," announces the desk Sargent to the Chief. "… her parents, from Ohio"

"Okay," Chief Deckham's disinterest diminishes. "How many calls is that so far, Sargent, and how long has she been missing? What's the latest?"

"In total, seven calls from four callers. We got two from the dance school; two from Merck; two from her parents and one from her ex-husband."

"And it's been how long?"

"According to her parents, she's been gone since Saturday, sir, possibly Sunday morning."

"Well, she is an adult and has a right to come and go as she pleases," the Chief says. "Let's wait another two days before putting out word. Ernie reported that everything looked fine inside and outside the house."

"Okay, Chief," the Sargent says. "We may receive call-backs in the meantime. I'll just log them."

"Good," the Chief looks back down at his desktop, signaling the end of the conversation.

The Sheriff receives directly, six additional telephone calls within two days, and he now begins to feel the pressure. He works on a case all night and presents it to his force in the morning. It is quick and dirty, if not immediate and filthy. That will have to suffice; however, it is all he has…at least for now.

"Okay here it is for the day Officers, Deputies," the Chief sounds nonchalant. "We have a possible missing person case open, okay a missing person case open for Kat Rossinski; Missing since last Saturday night to Sunday morning. Not seen or heard from since – today is day four. We searched the property once already, but I want it done again. Walsh, get a team together and take it deeper this time. Everyone else be on the lookout until further notice. This could escalate at any time. That's it."

Walsh jumps to action, gathers a team of Investigators and grabs a conference room. He lines the situation room with magnetic white boards, corner flip charts and a large corkboard. Markers lay around the tabletop. The men take seats around the makeshift bullpen table in the room.

"Okay," Walsh begins. "McKenzie you will lead your own team. Today, search the home again, and I mean search it! Another group of you will comb the neighborhood conducting interviews, got that? Meanwhile, I will oversee all of this."

"Yes, sir." the Officers, Detectives and Investigators chime in unison.

*

"Hate to bother you for that key again…." McKenzie says to Luke.

"Hey, no problem," Luke retrieves the key and brings it back. "Here ya go."

"You know, any information you can provide…"

"Oh yeah, by all means, sir," Luke assures.

Annie hears the conversation and reacts immediately. She does something Luke has never seen her do. She cries. A couple tears come down her face. She remains silent, but does not feel good about what is going on. She wants to hope for the best but expects the worst. She watches out the window as the police tape-off the house.

McKenzie leads the way into the house, followed by four investigators, guns drawn. He finds the place much the way Ernie described it in his report. He assigns two men upstairs, a man down here with him, and a man to the basement. Upstairs, the investigators hit the first room they get to, the boys' room on the left. They look under the bed, over the bed, between the sheets, in the closets, and in the drawers. There is also a pile of soiled clothes in the corner. They look there. They find nothing.

The next room down the hall is Kat's

bedroom. They perform the same routine search, looking for any sign of a clue. The search upstairs continues, uneventfully.

"Ready for printing, boss."

Downstairs, the officers comb over the entire first floor.

"We are Print-ready!" McKenzie bellows, somewhat frustrated, a little disappointed even, by now.

The Detective down in the basement goes straight to the freezer. He opens it hastily, and sees what Ernie saw; a freezer full of food. It sure is full: Filled almost to the top. He pushes some corn aside, then some spinach. There is a section of meat at one end. After a few photos, he goes to it and begins digging into the pile. He hits what has to be a side of beef. He goes back to the vegetables and digs there. The officer digs until he hits another solid mass: He raises the Sargent on the radio and asks him to come down to witness the potential discovery. McKenzie arrives and the two carefully and dutifully remove and stack the frozen food from the freezer, placing them all on the folding table next to the drier. At the bottom of the box, they discover a wrapped cut of something. McKenzie's Investigator quickly suggests they slice a portion at the end of the package to see what is inside.

After the photographer takes a few shots, the Detective pulls a knife from his belt and hands it to McKenzie. He takes the blade and saws a slice into the frozen plastic outer layer and into the second layer of what seems to be frozen carpet. It is extremely difficult to cut through that wrapper, so they decide to leave the freezer open, off for an hour, and come back to it.

"Call Crime Scene," McKenzie orders his Investigator.

"You got it."

The CSI arrive within twenty minutes. They continue the slice the Sargent began earlier using a heavy-duty, electric mini-chainsaw. Within moments, he is down to frozen flesh, though he cannot yet tell what it is. It has to be unpacked. The photographer continues to snap shots of the scene. Four men lift the bundle from the freezer and place it on the floor atop another spread of tarpaulin from the corner of the cellar room. It appears more obvious by the moment to all what lay within. Baily, from crime, proceeds carefully unravelling the packed meat. Typically, he observes, but this could be sensitive material.

He is beyond all the plastic and is now peeling the frozen blanket back. The smell is unmistakable. The sight that comes next is also unmistakable. A head and a pair of feet at one end, and he bets he sees the same things at the other end. He removes the entire blanket and puts it next to the plastic. There, before McKenzie and his basement team, lay a frozen pair of humans in a head to foot position each. One appears to be male and the other, female. They are both fully clothed and freezer-burned. The Coroner announces easily that they are clearly dead.

The team heads out through the back basement door and load the frozen bodies on a stretcher, then wheel and hoist them into the Coroner's vehicle, which is backed-up and parked at the head of the driveway. At the Coroner's imperative, they will let the bodies thaw at the morgue. All eyes of those neighbor's at home are on the happenings at Kat's house. Annie cries as she watches the police wheel out the stretcher. Police scour the neighborhood a second time for potential witnesses and persons of interest.

"The last man I saw her date," Annie tells the detective, "was a Contractor from where she works."

"Do you recall his name?"

"No, I'm sorry, I don't," replies Annie. "But, he drove a small white Mercedes and was tall and thin with black hair."

"Any difficulties between her and her ex, do you know?"

"They have not gotten along since before their divorce. It's as bad now as it ever was."

"Do you have any details for me?"

"No, just that Kat complained of Stone often." Annie continues, and offers; "We have never thought much of Stone. We've had problems with him in the past."

"What kind of problems?"

"Well he just has an arrogant, nasty attitude."

"He's hard to get along with, then?"

"Yes, that's how I'd put it."

"Thanks, Mrs. L'Italian," The cop stands up. "That is it for now. You don't mind if we stop back by if necessary, do you?"

"No sir, of course not," Annie is relieved and excited at the same time.

He will want to come back to interview Luke. He knows it, but Annie has not a clue. Why, he knows nothing more than she does! Luke has been in the basement, barely able to hear their voices upstairs, but he knew what was going on. He hears it said it would be his turn next. He prepares to psych-up for it, and, take a handful of Valium when that time comes. It will come soon enough, but for now, there is a lot of ground to cover. The Investigators go from door to door interviewing those closest to Mrs. Rossinski.

At the morgue, Doctor Robertson carefully separates the bodies. They finally thaw out. He rolls them onto their backs, though they are still in a fetal position. The first thing he notices is a bullet hole to the head. On a second look down, he sees a second bullet hole in the chest. Both bullets on both victims are in the same place. The wounds enter from the front not the rear – not execution style. There are no exit wounds.

*

There is little residue, but there are trace amounts, which suggest close range with a silencer. The Coroner performs the traditional and typical approach to examination. He opens-up the head and body cavity, and begins with the woman cadaver, simply because she is on the table closest to him. The body is a little more relaxed now, as the frozen state left the body in a temporary rigor mortis. The Coroner saws open Kat's head. Lifting the skullcap, he immediately sees trauma, most likely caused by the impact of the bullet. For now, he leaves the path and bullet alone.

He wants Walsh and McKenzie here to witness the event.

There are no contusions or bruises anywhere on the body, save for the surrounding tissue at the entry wound. She is in fine physical condition, considering… but now it is time. He takes the breastplate pruner and inserts one blade into the incision made moments before. The handle comes down with the familiar crack at the lower end of the sternum, prompting him to keep going upward to the throat. He then spreads the breast, exposing the stomach, chest area, lungs, liver, pancreas and the heart. The trauma here is to the heart. He sees the entry wound clearly, a jagged hole – a direct hit, the trajectory leads straight to her heart.

Walsh arrives within the hour.

"Okay," Walsh asks. "What's going on?"

The Coroner first shows him the trauma to the head and has Walsh watch as he extracts the bullet. Video recording cements the drama into something more evidentiary.

"There is extensive brain damage where the bullet abutted." The doctor drops the bullet from the tweezers into a tray.

"It is a flattened specimen, but maybe the one from the heart will be in better shape."

The bullet extracted from within the heart's Left Ventricle also contributed to the death, but is in nearly perfect condition.

The Lieutenant stays for the entire autopsy of the male. They discover almost the exact circumstances, and evidence. CSI have to test for all possibilities, however, so Walsh lets the Coroner drop the four bullets into an evidence bag. The show there can go on without those.

The Coroner continues his work as Walsh; bag in hand, quickly struts out the big, heavy doors. Next stop is Ballistics. If he were to guess, he would say something close to a nine millimeter. Ballistics will take a day. Autopsy, for what it's worth at this point, another day, as well. It is back to the Rossinski home for now. He needs a debriefing and must prep for the inevitable press conference.

"There seems to be what look like scuff marks barely visible, but clearly apparent from the dining room and living room, to the basement door, Sir."

"Hmmm… They are very faint, aren't they?"

"Yes, we were just barely able to make them out."

"No blood?"

"No blood, Sir."

"Get any Prints?" Walsh asks.

"Yes sir," says the McKenzie. "We lifted plenty."

"There should be trace amounts of blood on the carpet and maybe the plastic, too."

"Yes, sir, those tests are in progress."

"Okay, McKenzie," Walsh asks. "At what time do they expect me to talk?"

"17:00 Sir, it is live NEWS, just so you know."

"Shit."

The Chief shows-up at 16:55 sharp, ready to introduce Walsh to the press and audience. That is his sole purpose there today besides some background considering the missing person phone calls received, and the evidence thus far collected. He delivers a short speech, that of which he has not had to do since taking on Chief of the Borough. He introduces Walsh – the Lead Investigator - to the crowd. Walsh makes the obligatory introductions of McKenzie and other key players on his team.

"Members of the Press, ladies and gentlemen, today we made the gruesome discovery of two bodies in the Rossinski home. Identification of the bodies is pending, but I will release those names as soon as we have them verified. That is all I have for you right now. Thank you very much. We will meet here again tomorrow at three PM. Thank you. That's it."

With that, Walsh goes on to his next place of business: Stone Rossinski's house. Dawna answers the door. Stone is not home yet, she tells the Officer. Of course, she is glad to talk with him. She tells him that they were supposed to meet Kat to deliver the children back on Sunday evening, but she was not there, so the kids have been staying with her and Stone.

"How has Stone been acting lately?" the cop asks Dawna. "Have you noticed anything different?"

"Well, yes, actually," Dawna cannot lie. "He is very nervous and preoccupied, and has lost all interest in things that have to do with me." She is crying now.

"Relax, Miss, just one more thing. What time do you expect him home?"

It is a frozen zone at Stone's, cold as the bodies found acrobatically molded to each other in Kat's freezer. Dawna rushes to the bathroom with nerve-related Diarrhea.

# CHAPTER SEVENTEEN

One thing is clear; Stone Rossinski is not a well-liked man in the neighborhood. The interviews reflect not one positive opinion of the man. Of course, that does not make him a murderer: It does raise suspicion.

"…Ex-husband is bitter…angry, yes, a person of interest." Walsh thinks aloud.

On top of that, he has the affidavit and recording taken during the interview with Dawna. If Walsh is not mistaken, even she seems to hold some disdain for her boyfriend.

He heads back to the office to request a warrant to search Stone's home and property. He has an unconditional warrant for Kat's house and property by association with the crime. He seeks no other warrants for the time being. The judge issues the warrant in the morning, so Walsh goes home to think it off. This is unheard-of in Washington Borough. The press is wild, the neighborhoods are vigilant and the people are talking as the police raid Stone's home with a warrant at 06:00 hours.

The team arrives at Stone's house right on time. There is a heavy thudded knock on the door, but not enough to wake the clan. The cops break the door in with a battering ram. That was enough to wake everyone up inside. The bellowed announcement of a warranted search brought Stone, Dawna and the kids padding from their rooms in their pajamas. Guns are drawn but pointed upward, as Walsh approaches Stone.

"Mr. Rossinski, we have a search warrant for your home, and property."

"And this is in reference to my missing ex-wife, I take it."

"Yes, sir, and is routine. You are not under arrest at this time."

By now, Dawna and the two boys are crying, huddled together at the entrance to the hallway. They said it was routine, Stone tells Dawna. They are both hardly alert enough to have to handle this rude an awakening. They cannot count all the cops they had in their house. There had to be at least a dozen, in and out, sometimes carrying a paper evidence bag out the door with them. They take both computers, which upset Dawna. Why take hers?

The cops tear the place apart, but do not put it back together again. Stone looks at Dawna saying: "I have nothing to do with it."

"I know you don't honey."

"They said it was routine."

"Yes, they did. I'm sure it is."

"Yeah…Think about it."

"Dad," Brian asks. "Why are the police here?"

"They are looking for your mother, kids."

The cops outside look in the shed, and rummage around the back yard. They work with rakes, to get beneath the leaves on the ground. Some wander into the woods off the trail from within the backyard. The boys with the rakes do not miss a spot. Walsh orders Stone to keep his seat during the procedure, please, as he tries to get up to look out the back window. He cannot help but feel like he is already a prisoner.

As the officers rake through the back yard each has taken a square of the grid hastily strung out. It does not take long for one of the officers to uncover what looks to be a small tomb at the edge of the woods. He radios Walsh over, along with an Investigator. The Investigator daintily brushes back the leaves on all sides, photos snapped all around, and then digs into the crevice with a gloved finger. He finds nothing at first, but upon digging his finger a little deeper, he feels a hard abject. He gently brushes the dirt away to uncover a handgun. It is equipped with a silencer. The photographer marks and shoots some more.

It looks a little smaller than a nine-millimeter, but not much. Walsh's hopes are up, but he has learned his lesson on early celebration. The Investigator drops the firearm into an evidence bag and walks toward the wagon. This is a big find, so Walsh follows the Investigator: He signs the piece out for the next two days and takes it to Ballistics. Before he takes the weapon, it is prepped and dusted. He takes what turns-out to be a .380 caliber to Ballistics and asks if the technician can match the bullets from the coroner, with the gun. It will take some time, but yes. Ballistics not only identifies the crushed bullets as three-eighties, they also easily tie the intact bullets to the gun in question. It takes two days, but Walsh gets the answers needed. The gun is evidence.

Walsh has to tie the murder weapon to a person. The hardest part of the job comes with no prints of any kind. All he has are traces of latex. There is no registered owner of the firearm. The last known owner was from

Maine, and he is deceased. The Investigators search for records. A bill of sale could lead somewhere. There are no footprints near the site the gun was found. The leaf cover guaranteed that.

The weapon found on Stone's property mandates a broader and deeper search of his home and belongings. He still holds a multi-hundred-thousand dollar Life Insurance policy over Kat, too. There is motive right there. He meant to change the beneficiary to the children, fifty-fifty, but never got around to it after the divorce. Now, he wishes he had. A circumstantial case is already building against Stone in Walsh's eyes.

Even he could not be that stupid, as he is reputed to be, to think the firearm would go unnoticed. The Insurance Policy is common enough. Post-divorce bitterness is also common. The kids, the poor kids: How could he do this to his own kids? No cause of death issued yet. Walsh did not look forward to that three o'clock presser this afternoon.

"I cannot compromise the integrity of the investigation, so I will tell you all I can, then, that will be it." Walsh is grooming the press and standers-by for an official read-out only. "Yesterday afternoon at approximately sixteen-hundred hours, two bodies were taken from the Rossinski residence on Youmans

Avenue. One body identified as Kat Rossinski, of Washington Borough. The other body is that of Thomas Headley, also of Washington Borough. Pending further investigation, both appear to have died of multiple gunshot wounds. Murder-Suicide and Murder are both under consideration at this time. The investigation continues. That's' it for now."

The killer is loose in the Borough, and word spreads quickly among the citizens. 'It could be anyone' heard aloud everywhere and indeed it could be anyone. It looks more to Walsh like a bitter ex-husband walked in on a date he did not approve-of. Kat worked with Headley at Merck, they were neighbors, what could be more convenient? Stone, for all his faults, cannot stand the thought of his wife with another man. By her own admission, Dawna expressed displeasure with home-life and Stone: Not to mention his recent bouts with nervous tension. Yes, Walsh shall take a good, hard look at Stone.

*

Stone, for that matter, cannot help but feel the squeeze. It comes from deep inside. It makes him ill to know that he slowly becomes public enemy number one in Washington Borough. It does not go unnoticed, as his condition at home worsens. Dawna does not know what to do, or do more of, to help. He and she continue their routine and go to work every weekday, and watch television at night, or read. He sits in his chair and nervously twitches his feet and stares, if not at the television screen, straight ahead. Most attempts at conversation that Dawna tries fizzle and fail. It seems he can only work, and talk about only work. Stone is an Atheist, so he cannot even turn to God, Jesus and the Holy Spirit. This remains one huge difference between Dawna and Stone. She is a faithful, church-going Christian. She prays every night. He worries himself to restless sleep.

# CHAPTER EIGHTEEN

Luke wants a police scanner, without raising suspicion, so he travels to a neighboring county to get one. It takes most of the day, but it is time well spent. He rushes from the driveway, under the deck in back yard, using the basement backdoor to gain entrance to his office. He sets-up the scanner without thinking what it may look like to Police, should they search his home. That thought reminds him that he has more clean up to do, this time targeting his personal computer. Luke has a list of tasks he plans to complete as he marches forward executing his plans day-by-day, in a logical sequence.

First things first, Luke navigates to his hidden Pictures Folder. He drills into it, and reluctantly erases his complete Kat Collection, Martha Collection, and Dawna Folder. Those are critical to the exercise, but other folders come under thought, scrutiny and must go, too, such as the Young and Cute folder, and any other that may cause authorities to look twice. He keeps as many pictures as he believes he can, safely, the criteria obviously of-age and legal subjects, images and videos. The next and final, yet most timely step is browsing within the multitudes of folders in totality. His object is the same, but in these folders the only way he can be sure that any remaining image that whispers or blasts illegal or pedophilia-prone notice to the professional analyst. This takes Luke all evening and into the late night to complete. Moreover, he knows he must go back and double-check before he calls it "done."

Pornography is not illegal in Warren County, where L'Italian lives. Any hint of underage subjects within his personal folders will trigger a nerve in any police officer paying attention. Luke makes significant progress tonight…he is near finished by midnight. He quits then, it being an hour past his typical office hours, for he knows he must take any suspicion of his actions away from Annie. Therefore, that sets him up with a new plan for the next morning.

*

Annie is as stressed and feels the tension everyone else does in the Borough, but no one feels it as much as Luke, at this early point in the investigation, except Stone, of course.

"How can you concentrate on work with all this going on, Luke?" Annie asks first thing in the morning.

"Well, Annie," Luke must explain and make it good. "My work and the activity that revolves around it, does not wait for anything or anybody. So, if I am to keep up with, and not fall behind, I must not let my feelings drive my livelihood." He is satisfied with that: He hopes she is, too. "You know?"

"Yes, I get that now, but isn't it hard?"

"Of course it's hard, but it must be done. I have to stick to my work hours, no matter what is happening extraneously, Annie."

"Yes, of course, Luke."

"Okay, so since I worked an hour late last night, I will quit an hour early tonight! Sound good?"

"Yes. Yes, it does." Annie gets back to her diddling around with Mal. Annie has a hard time making Mal laugh when Annie feels so low and ill. She intermittently breaks-out in tears all through the day. She is even relieved that Luke will work downstairs all day; her bursts will not bother him.

Luke tiptoes and trudges through all his Sample sub-folders – again. Ugh. It is so tedious that, even though he is in a position to have to review every single nude photograph he has, his mind contains itself, he is not turned-on in the least. He simply starts at the top of the file tree and works his way to the bottom: So beautiful…so many! This proves to be a task well worth the time, as he finds many teen-age-looking images; titled "barely legal," they could also raise suspicion. Doink…Gone. Check!

The task takes longer than Luke's plans; it is almost midnight. He is pleasantly surprised Annie did not holler for him much earlier: Oh, thank God for small favors! He opens his notebook and reviews the outstanding steps he recorded before, and confirms he is right on schedule.

*Time for rest: Time for bed.*

Luke wakes and immediately jumps out of bed full of energy, which is typically unheard-of for him. He is not only eager to move-on with his must-do list, he is downright anxious. Annie was asleep when he came to bed the night before and she is sleeping as he gets-up. He makes coffee, grabs a mug and heads downstairs to the office. 'Equity' is clean; His suggestive image folders are clean, but he must scrub his desk drawers, but good... now!

Even if he thinks, there is nothing to hide inside, he searches through all – every single one – from top-left to bottom-right. He knows he has plenty to hide in some of them. Still, he looks through them all; "no turn left un-stoned." Shit, that is backward! Luke must admit he is more nervous than he cares to be, or admit, but the most important thing is that he marches on, minute-by-minute, hour-by-hour and day by day until he is sure – positive – he covers all the bases.

He second-guesses the purchase and ownership of the police scanner. People everywhere use them to keep-up with current events and law enforcement reaction to them, but he has a gut feeling that law enforcement interpretation may trigger suspicions. Given the position, he is in, keeping the crime at the forefront, and always one to follow his gut, Luke decides to return the scanner.

He replaces the packaging and places it in the bag it came in along with the receipt.

*Okay...Now for the drawers.*

The top two on the far left of his big desk contain documentation. The third holds his printer accessories, such as different weight paper packs, envelopes, labels and a few books of stamps. He moves to the next column of drawers. The top two spaces is office equipment storage; staples, staplers, staple removers, erasures, hole punchers, sticky-finger wax, tape, notebooks of all types and sizes, and more. He knows what is in the third drawer down, and it makes him shiver.

There, he lifts from the space, the original photos of Martha, Kat and Dawna, the stolen underwear from Kat's place. In addition, the star of all, his Kat bag of residual specimens from her diaphragm and the diaphragm itself. He takes a sniff of each item and simply cannot bring himself to drop them into his garbage bag. At the bottom of the drawer, below all those items lay the skinny loose-leaf folder that lists all – every single one – of his now deleted and erased personal Sample image directories. Into the trash bag it goes. It is time he takes a ride back to the shop with the police scanner. He stops on the way, as soon as crosses the county border, and dumps the garbage bag from his office in a large, roadside dumpster belonging to a trailer park. He hastily hides away his love charms where they will stay forever.

Luke returns home and immediately continues his basement chore, but finds nothing else in the desk that has the potential to spark interest. It is late afternoon, and he is hungry and tired from the tedious job he performed today. He climbs up the steps and emerges from the hatch, calling out to Annie.

"Annie…Did you make any lunch today?"

"Yes, Luke. Look in the fridge."

Luke is happy to find a couple of roast-beef on dark Rye bread, with butter and horseradish.

*Mmmmm…My favorite, no less!*

He takes both sandwiches and a bottle of spring water, walks over to, and sits down at, the dining room table. He forces himself to eat slowly, savoring the layers of flavor, and sips his beverage every two or three bites. Luke is satisfied with the day's work and calls it done for now. Tomorrow will deliver to him another list of must-do.

# CHAPTER NINETEEN

Without a trace of blood or foreign prints found upstairs in the Rossinski home, and no prints downstairs, Walsh sends a two-man team to carefully inspect the cellar, in particular the dirt floor. He reminds them to wear hazmat boots before entering the cellar, and suggest they enter from the ground-level back door. Upon the prior investigation, when they turned-up the bodies, Walsh knows that the door is and can assume was, forever unlocked and slightly ajar; no lock and key to be had, and a broken hinge at the top.

The officers arrive and park as far down the driveway as possible. Each investigator puts on their booties, and discusses their plan in detail. They stare at the ground before every forthcoming step. The back lawn is useless, as Walsh, McKenzie and the Coroner trampled over it several times and wheeled the gurney from and back to the coroner's wagon. They lift only smudges from the cellar door handle, then, with some difficulty, pull the door open with a creek, a crack and a squeal.

Before stepping onto the cellar floor, they take a close look at it just in front of the doorway where they stand. It is disheartening to see the numerous prints, wheel ruts and scuffs in the dirt, likely due to, and leftover from the last visit by the recovery team. The two walk slowly toward the freezer, looking down to the left, center then right. They spy nothing alarming between the door and the appliance, so daintily step around the freezer, each of the two one taking an end. They both stop. It is clear that they will not garner any footprints of interest between the stairs and the freezer, either.

"Let's stay here for a moment."

"Okay, Sir, what have you got?"

"I am not sure yet. Let me think for a minute."

"Yes Sir."

"Okay...I have what I think may be our only hope."

"What is it?"

"Think of a method, a tool you might use to smooth over, cover up the signs of dragging bodies thru this loose dirt."

"Well, a rake would be too obvious…for that matter, so would a shovel."

"Hmmm…"

"Um, Sir… I think we just might have something."

"What?"

"Look over there toward the far left, and the far right."

"Oh yeah, what do you see?"

"Look closely: There are slightly raised ridges, both nearly identical."

"We might have a 'find' here partner, good eye!"

"What are you thinking?"

"There are also remnants of the same type of ridging about three feet inward on both sides. Those are scuffed-up yet visible. Take some photos, officer."

The photographs taken, both investigators think. They do not know it, but they are each thinking the same thing. They picture a two by four, cut to approximately three feet, with a towrope of sorts fastened to each end. The user simply drags the makeshift device, or pulls it backing away, from wherever he or she needed a cover-up.

"I have an idea," announces McKenzie.

"I do, too," replies Ernie.

"The ridges could be the result of using a leveling board."

"Exactly, Sir, edged along with a pull made of simple rope."

More photos and a report to add-to keep them put for a few minutes, and then they do the inevitable; search the other side of the cellar where the yard-work tools are. They find two by fours and other scraps. They find heavy-duty rope around a roller. Indeed, one of the lengths of wood appears to have a fresher end-cut. The rope looks freshly cut on the end jutting and hanging from the roller.

"Ernie," begins McKenzie. "We have potentially a new piece of evidence apparently used at the scene. We can search all we want here, but we will also widen the search of the area all around Mr. Rossinski's home."

Back at the station, McKenzie briefs Walsh on the findings and suggests a deeper search around Mr. Rossinski's property. Walsh finally feels a little more warmth of promise: The discovery is in and of it-self; something real in what was once a concluded crime scene. He sends McKenzie back out to carry on their suggestion of a broader search of Kat's Ex's home and property.

It took the better part of three days to dutifully search along and into the brush from, the path and trail leading from Stone's backyard to the park and back. McKenzie took one side and Ernie the other. They walked a zigzag pattern on both sides weaving each up into the bush and back. They are both dissatisfied, as they walk back on the trail to Rossinski's back yard. They climb into the police vehicle and just sit for a while… thinking. Nothing need be said, for they know by shear intuition what the other is thinking.

"Okay, Ernie…where else is there to look where we haven't yet?" McKenzie asks.

"I'm thinking," Ernie says.

"I got it!" McKenzie loudly declares. "We can take a long look in the back yards!"

"…And in the creek!" Ernie excitedly cries out.

"Yeah buddy," McKenzie starts the SUV. "We're on our way!"

McKenzie once again parks the police vehicle as far down as the Rossinski driveway goes. Without actually laying-out a grid, the two agree to review it sticking closer together and moving down and back of each yard, heads turning and heads down.

They cover the backyards all the way from the L'Italian's, to Kat Rossinski's, old woman what's-her-name's, the Mahoney's, the new Christian's, and beyond. They searched the entirety of the landscape planned. They are both in the zone, however, and do not want to stop there.

"The creek," Ernie abruptly breaks all thought.

"Jesus, Ernie," McKenzie is somewhat surprised. "Yes! The fuckin' creek is next!"

The creek begins upstream from the culvert on this side of Route 31. They stand now all the way downstream at the culvert protecting Middle Street. McKenzie radios the station to check-in the results of the initial search, and to let the Chief know of his plan to take on the creek behind the Rossinski residence, and beyond. He receives the all-okay.

"Okay, Ernie, we are going to start here with you on the other side and me on this side. Follow routine search protocol and take it up to the culvert at thirty-one. We will deal-with – if we must – the culverts afterward. Are we clear?"

"Yes Sir, we're clear."

They both keep in-step and look into the depths of the creek quite deliberately. Slow as they go, as not to miss a thing, occasionally fishing a sample that turns-out non-evidentiary. Ernie is giddy as they walk the creek; he has a feeling-a gut feeling. Everybody knows that the gut does not lie!

Feeling a bit let down, both men reach the culvert at thirty-one. Now comes the hard part, sweeping the inside of the fourteen inch round culverts. McKenzie guesses that they will find nothing here, as the creek current runs moderately west, which is where they just came from. Yet, this is it. Having presumed this very situation, McKenzie carries a longish hoe-like tool that will make pushing debris from within the culverts feasible, let alone possible, with ease.

Ernie takes the hoe and crosses the state road. He straddles the culvert from the intake end. He feeds it, sometimes having to push rather strenuously to loosen something or another that McKenzie catches at the other end. They repeat the exercise until Ernie is merely pushing water thru even harder a flow than natural.

"Okay Ernie," calls McKenzie. "Let's hit Middle Street."

"Yes sir, boss."

They turn back and stroll slowly on their respective side of the creek toward Middle Street. The cop instinct has them hold a constant glance in the water out of the corners of their eyes. It does not matter that they already searched this leg of the creek just several minutes before.

McKenzie calls Ernie over to him, and says, "Look there, Ernie, across the street. Mr. Rossinski's place is just the third door up Middle."

"Okay, let's see what we can push-through this culvert!"

"Yes, Sir McKenzie."

Ernie straddles the culvert, and once his partner is in place, begins to scrape and push using the long-handle, hoe-like tool. He pushes two feet in and hits what he imagines are clumps of leaves. McKenzie sees a part of them come out the other end and float by. His partner tries it again, this time going hard almost half way into the underground steel tube.

"McKenzie!" Ernie exclaims. "I hit something!"

"Okay, twist the hoe right and left while pushing."

Ernie sweats while following the directions,

but feels the object loosening-up with each twist and push. This drives him excitedly on. He jumps when the objects seems to completely dislodge, and tells his boss to look for it – any second now.

"BINGO!" McKenzie bellows. "Ernie, I believe we might just have something here!"

Ernie jumps to his left and briskly crosses the street – his senses on fire. McKenzie holds with his boot one end of a two-by. He lets the length of cut wood slowly emerge fully from the culvert. Their hearts sink and at the same time feel a sense of accomplishment. The board is approximately three feet long, and more importantly, has a rope pull tied to a U-nail at each end.

"Ernie, go get some gloves, a large black evidence bag and the measurement wheel."

McKenzie measures the board then places it in the bag. He orders his partner to walk the measurement from the culvert to Mr. Rossinski's property. The difference between the length of wood and the dirt trail-ridges discovered in the cellar searched earlier explained away by simple logic: The board did smooth the dirt in its path, yet it naturally pushes outward on either side the ridge pushed aside during the action. He can easily picture it being much like the push-aside of a snowplow.

"Okay Ernie, use the wheel and get the distance from the creek at the other end of the culvert, to Mr. Rossinski's place."

McKenzie writes-out a written report describing the findings. He will augment it upon Ernie's return. He notes the entire day's search actions, but stresses the point of finding the wood board leveler and its potential relation to the case. The distance, Ernie relays, is a short two-hundred-thirty feet.

# CHAPTER TWENTY

Dawna reminds Stone, once again, that it is high time to talk to his boys about their mother. He has put it off, along with having to answer the questions raised with see-through stock answers, such as 'Oh she'll be back soon' or 'don't worry, mom is okay.' Although the children nod with forced smiles, they walk away sadly and hibernate in their room. Sometimes they sob aloud; sometimes they play a game or watch Television.

"Brian…Timmy…Come out here," Stone calls out to his boys. "I want to talk to you about something."

"Yeah, Dad, what is it?"

"Sit down on the couch."

"I have news about your mom." Stone begins to leak tears from his eyes. Just the sight of Dad crying brings tears out from both children, as well.

"What?" Timmy asks."

"Did you find out where she is?" probes Brian. "Where is she?"

"Kids…" Stone has no idea where to go from there.

"Kids…the police found her during a search and recovery effort. Boys, they found your mother dead. She died."

The young children fall naturally into shock, and despair. They have trouble absorbing what Dad just told them. They cannot process it, so feeling defeated and in a world of disbelief, they both break out into sobs – long and loud. Everything is leaking from their faces, from the eyes, noses and their mouths. They are stuck in a moment they cannot escape. All three hug tight.

"I will go to the house and collect all your gear, games, clothes…" In addition, of course anything else they remind him not to forget.

"I will be very busy with the police, but will get to the old house in a day or two for all your stuff."

"Okay Dad," Brian and Timmy reply.

"I will be awarded soul custody of both of you," Stone continues. "That just means you will live with me from now on."

"Well…how'd she die Dad?" Brian asks.

"I do not have any details yet, boys, but as I get them I will be sure to let you know. Fair enough kids?"

The boys turn around, still sniffling, not knowing what to think of the news, and walk to their room…slamming the door behind them. Stone is still in tears, more for his kids' loss than the death of their mother.

Dawna witnesses the scene as it rather quickly unfolds, and sees Stone crying, but she is afraid to say, let alone do, anything to him. She remains seated quietly on the couch, leery of all her choices of action. The crying stops, but the silence otherwise still blankets the room.

"I am going to make a light lunch," she says to Stone. "Do you want anything?"

"No Dawna," Stone replies, then he adds: "How can I eat in this state of mind…and my kids'?"

"Alright Stone…I was just asking."

His state of mind stretches far beyond his children's hardship. He waits day after day for the doors to crash in again, and a slew of cops sweeping his property and all that surround it. His mind remains cluttered, busy and noisy, as he cannot help the thoughts that pop in and out, about what the cops are doing during all this time.

Dawna returns from the kitchen with two avocado wraps, with kale, tomatoes, black olives and a hint of minced onion. She thinks she will have a hard time getting them down, given the circumstances and horrid vibes in the house today, but she is beyond just hungry, and she has a tall glass of iced tea to help. Stone is in what has become his spot and posture, in his recliner, feet up, silent, oblivious and glum. Dawna swears she can see more and more lines, or wrinkles on his face and neck, which have him looking much older than his age.

She is concerned about his state of mind and his non-participatory existence here at home. What is worse is that he cashed-out every vacation day he had left for the year. He sits, he eats little, he remains silent, and he has lost all romanticism and sexual drive – his libido. Dawna has never felt self-conscious, or inferior in her life. Yet, she now feels compelled to look herself over; she knows an attractive girl when she sees one.

She washes her lunch dishes, and then says to Stone on her way to the hall, "I'm going to shower real quickly, Stone, and I'll be right back out." He offers no response whatsoever. None was expected. She goes into the bath side of the master bath. She undresses, and then turns the shower water on. She looks into the full-length mirror, and looks over her entire, nude body. She checks her smile, the firmness of her breasts, the curvy shape of her posterior, her flat belly and tummy below. She takes a long, hard look at her face, both from afar and extremely close-up. She has attractive feet, even, small and cute. Finally, she stares down at her vagina. She uses a hand-held mirror and squats; all looks well, in fact sexy, she stands and separates the lips and let them spring back. She takes a closer look at her genital area. She keeps her pubic hair closely trimmed in a "V" shape above her vagina, but keeps also very close, side burns just to the outside of her womanhood. She is sexy and that is all there is to it. Stone's problem is not her, she repeats as a mantra in her head.

Of course, she understands the discomfort of having the police interrupt his daily life. Yet, something occurs to her that gives her the shivers. Why would he be so nerved-up if he were innocent? She stores that troubling question off to the side, but there nonetheless.

# CHAPTER TWENTY-ONE

Walsh orders McKenzie to deliver the leveling pull to Scene Investigation. The thought he has that their job is cutout for them with this piece...but that is why they make the big bucks. McKenzie takes the time, as protocol dictates; to explain where, how and, when McKenzie and Ernie find it. In the team leader's opinion, what they agree may tie it to the scene. Those are easy – no-brainers. Crime Scene says they will go to Mrs. Rossinski's, with this new evidentiary piece and perform an examination – connect the dots, as they put it.

The crime scene investigators pull into the Rossinski driveway fifteen minutes later. They both walk toward the rickety shed-like backdoor to the cellar. Upon reaching it, they swing and prop open the shaky old entryway. They both stop, intuitively, and professionally, to survey and discuss what exactly they are there for, how they will execute the plan and define their respective roles at this particular time.

The Lieutenant is calling out the orders, or at least facilitating the meeting there in the doorway. The Sargent nods in concurrence throughout the drill.

"Okay partner," the boss begins the exercise. "Look and you can see from here, even, the mess made by the team upon finding the bodies."

"Yes, Sir," the Sargent replies, and takes a few notes in his crime scene evaluation report.

"Fortunately, we have photos of the area taken prior to the search and retrieval."

"I am going to take a quick look in the utility room next to us. I'd like to find wood, nails and rope that match the evidentiary piece we have."

"Excellent." The boss says in agreement.

The Lieutenant very diligently and patiently works from the scenario in his mind. The perpetrator, after storing the victims in the freezer, likely started at the bottom of the stairs, and dragged the makeshift plow behind him. The big investigator continues with his theory. The perpetrator backed his way out toward the door dragging the leveling tool to cover his footprints.

What exactly, intelligently would, in fact produce the desired results? This question is rolling around his mind like mortar material in a spinning cement truck. Like clips of video playing out in the forefront of his mind, he stands almost mesmerized by them all. He gazes into the area, entranced. The Sargent returns.

"Boss," he begins. "I have something for you to see!"

The Lieutenant is almost startled out of his thoughts, but remains composed...calm and rational.

"What'd you find, Sargent?"

"Come on over to the space next door."

In the unfinished lathe overhead, there are scrap lengths of wood, most of them two-by-fours. On the messy workbench, in the back-left corner lay a roll of thick hemp-like twine. At a glance, they both see clearly that it easily represents a match to the length of rope on the bulldozing rake. Finally, the subordinate shows his boss a box of nails that also look unmistakably like the U-nails used to attach the rope to each end of the Two-by.

"It looks like you hit the jackpot!" The Lieutenant enthusiastically says.

"Yep, looks that way…"

"Okay," The Lieutenant begins. "Bag-up the twine. Bag-up the nails. Take some photos of the wood overhead."

As the Sargent follows his orders, his boss returns to the cellar door. The tips of his black shoes are atop the jamb. If it were he carrying out the scheme, how would he approach it? He thinks; then thinks some more while scanning around the entirety of the dirt floor in front of him. Would he start in the middle, or at one end of the room or the other? Sadly, the middle of the floor is by virtue of the investigation that produced the bodies, scuffed. Fortunately, there are photos of the floor taken by Ernie before any one of them set foot on it.

Applying a few rules of logic, the Lieutenant decides the only way to cover the whole floor, without stepping into an already-clean area, would be to start at one end. He plays it out as if he started to his far right. That breaks the straight-face test, as finishing from the opposite end of the room would ruin the smoothly raked lanes already done on the left end. Starting on the right side seems like a no-brainer, now that he scopes-out and thinks of the activity and cleanliness the exercise deserved.

No matter the angle the rake, or how straight, one thing is invariable: The ends of it would create and leave furrows or ridges in the dirt. He pictures a snowplow moving snow around on a winter's night. The Lieutenant does not want to walk on the floor, He is grateful there is another string looped through metal eyes under the joists to switch the light off and on. It is just not enough light! He goes to the patrol SUV to get his flashlight, and instructs the Sargent to belt his, too.

The Sargent finishes-up, stows away in the back, the evidence bags. He moves to put the camera back in its case.

"Keep that camera handy." The Lieutenant says.

"We'll want the handheld bulldozer, too, right?" The Sargent asks.

"Yes and the measuring tape, as well."

It is an unwritten assignment in protocol that the assistant on the case keep the clipboard, pencil and affidavit.

They reach the cellar door together, and the boss lays-out the plan.

"We are going to shine our lights in the

same space for maximum vision advantage. Let's start over in the far-right corner of the dirt floor. We are looking for the furrows or ridges a tool like the one we have might make. I imagine furrows cumulated at either or both ends of the length of wood. That, Sargent, is what we are looking for. You jot down what we see as we see it. We will follow a right to left pattern, using our flashlights to the far wall and back here to the near wall. We will then rest and review what we will have discovered, and talk about next steps. You got all that?"

"Yes, Sir…Got it!"

They point the flashlight rays into the corner and then slowly move them along the wall toward their side of the room. The team did not need so did not take the freezer: It sits lengthwise against the wall just to the right of the doorway.

"…Again." The Lieutenant says. "Do you see it, Sargent?"

"Yes, Sir: It is a skinny ridge that runs the length of the wall."

"Okay…Now move the light to our left the length of the wood. It is thirty-six inches, right?"

"Yes, it is."

"Let's follow the same exercise, slowly, straight-away, and look for the same thing."

They see at the far end of the room, just their side of the staircase, another ridge, but this one is wider and noticeably deeper than the one along the wall. They stop and discuss the logic that fits behind this discovery. The Lieutenant lays out a verbal picture.

"The user hugs the wall on the first trip, which is why the ridge is half the size of the one to their left of the wall. They take a careful walk outside of the newly grated lane made on the floor. Then, they repeat the process. This causes the furrow to double in size at each end of each lane. Watch and see."

They perform their surveillance with diligence, and sure enough, the picture laid out plays out. The area in front of the freezer is scuffed and messy, as expected, but outward toward the stairs, the beginning of each ridge remains quite pronounced. The bulldozed lanes begin to appear again longer and longer until the wall to their left, where they run the full length of it. The Sargent fits-together the scratched-up areas on the cellar floor with his memory of, and made in the course of, the recovery of, and discovery of the two victims.

"Take some photos that reflect what we just did, and discovered," says the Lieutenant.

They are both satisfied that they have what they came for: how the killer used the wooden plow to smooth-out the dirt floor. Thus, the absence of extraneous foot or shoe prints.

# CHAPTER TWENTY-TWO

Luke is exhausted and little Mal, who still has occasional bouts of colic, is crying at the top of her lungs. Annie never has any luck calming the poor child. Luke, however, picks Mal up and carries her football-style all around the first floor. It works every time, but for some reason it is not working for them tonight.

"Annie," Luke calls from the stairs. "I am going to my upstairs office and try plan-B."

"Please…Anything." Annie has lost all patience with this colic problem and cannot wait for it to be over! Mal was born right on time – not a preemie – but her digestive tract has not fully developed yet. It is getting better, but there are times like this when it just takes over the infant…the household!

Luke queues-up four CD's. He and Mal sit back in his recliner. She lays foot-to-head on her belly, over his belly and chest. Her head rests just below his shoulder. Meanwhile, The Allman Brothers and Van Morrison, lull them both immediately to a relaxing nap. Those are Mal's favorites and Luke could ask for nothing better. He loves the Brothers and Van.

The music stops and the room is quiet save for Mal's breathy, purring snores. Annie briefly peeks into the upstairs office at the two sleeping angels on the comfortable chair and she cannot help but smile, her hand over her heart. She decides to make everyone a nice big, warm mid-week meal. She makes Cavatelli with Broccoli and her well-loved broccoli mash with Italian breadcrumbs, olive oil and garlic on the side. Oh, soon the house smells so good of all the layers of flavors that make-up her dinner. She, for some reason, feels better today for the first time since the tragedy next door.

Reflecting on this thought, Annie believes it is a combination of Luke spending more time out of his downstairs office and the overall satisfaction she feels around her marriage; their existence. Why did she doubt Luke when he started his project downstairs? He has become so successful! She likes that. He is the trophy instead of her. That is the way she likes it. Let him have the attention, thank you, and she will be the Italian ma in the kitchen.

Annie's younger sister married a well-off, crooked player, but she and their kids get whatever they want. All of it comes for the small price of his never being home, not for her, and not even for the kids. Of course, everyone in the family knows he is out fucking around, but little sister refuses to admit it, dismissing the very thought with the things he brings home when he does pop-in.

Annie's older sister married up, as she met a wealthy ex-Television star in Philadelphia. They buy a place in Southern California and retire there, in comfort and sunshine. So, Annie feels like she is right in the middle. She is indeed the middle daughter in reality anyway. Daydreaming in her living room chair, she almost overcooks the supper she's making. She gets up and checks in on what she has got going on in the kitchen. Dinner is done, so she puts the pots into the oven to keep them warm. She lets Luke and Mal sleep. If it gets too late, she will wake them.

Annie flips through some channels on the Television and comes across an episode of Martha. She decides to watch her for at least a while. Never before had she paid much attention to the show, even with Luke's interest in it. As she watches and listens to Martha now, however, she begins to gaze and lets the spoken words entertain her. She gets it! Finally, she gets what it is about Martha and why it is that Luke appreciates her as much as he seems to. It is a combination of her looks, and her way of addressing the audience and describing what she has or what she is doing. Admittedly, Annie – outside of her own character – decides the woman is talented, and sexy.

What a revelation for Annie! She feels she finally fully understands an interest of her husband's. They do have something else in common, and what's more, because Annie's honesty with herself is for real, she does not mind. There is one thing tickling her insides. The more she watches and listens to Martha, the more she feels genuinely attracted to her. This is a first for Annie. She has NEVER felt any attraction toward a female before. Not even an innocent puppy-glance in the high school locker-room.

Instead of denial, guilt or self-conscious embarrassment, she experiences liberation. Yes! That is what it is – simple liberation; the kind that Luke had tried so hard to instill in her, even though by now he has given-up. A difference between Luke's attraction to Martha and Annie is that Annie's feelings are a wanton for her husband, not to use the image to masturbate as he does. She does not know, but surmises he does…that…sometimes. Annie's wheels are turning faster and faster reeling. It is but a truth and problem, as well as a simple answer.

Luke's eyes blink as he wakes in his chair and takes a deep breath. The odiferous broccoli and garlic is probably what wakes him. He feels renewed. Mal is still sleeping, but within a couple minutes begins to show signs of wakefulness. She smiles at her Daddy, and Daddy smiles and chuckles. Mal giggles as Luke lifts her high enough for him to give her hugs, and kisses her all over her forehead. He reaches down the right side of the recliner and grabs the footrest lever. He pulls it all the way back to unlock it, and then flips it forward and down all the way. With that, the chair rocks, but as soon as it stops, he gets-up, Mal hoisted up by his left arm and hand. She has her little arms holding on around his neck.

Annie is setting the table as they reach the dining room. Luke places Mal in her special eating table corner to corner at Annie's end of the table, and takes his seat at the other end of the table. The two main dishes are already sitting on trivets on the table. Annie comes in to sit and start dinner. Her seat is to Luke's right, along the side of the table so she can assist Mal, if necessary; and it usually is.

Luke lets Annie plate herself and commence

with Mal's dinner routine before serving himself with a good-sized dollop of each warm dish. Luke's mother made sure she raised him under the use of strict manners, particularly when eating. One may find fault in Luke, but his manners are impeccable. He sits fork in his left hand, and stairs at the plate of food before him. He is taken by the smell of the broccoli, but the aroma of the roasted garlic overtakes all else and reminds Luke of what is inevitably coming.

Luke unfortunately inherited from his father a very sensitive entire gastro-intestinal tract. Therefore, he has to expect and gear-up to deal-with, sweating garlic and suffer through a day and a half of irregularity of all types between his throat and his rectum. Of course Annie is aware of this, but with Luke's okay she continues to serve this dinner every few weeks, or so. Luke chooses to eat the foods he loves to eat, no matter what, and coddle his self through the consequences. That usually includes sleeping in the recliner, typically the one in his upstairs office. Remaining in an upward posture helps tremendously, and, sleeping apart from Annie in their bed relieves her from all the obvious side effects of the garlic going through Luke's system. There is no need to explain the arrangement: It is merely a common occurrence for the sake of all.

That night, and the following couple of days, everything is off for Luke. He remains in his living room recliner all day and sleeps in his office at night. It is as if he sacrifices two or three days of his life for the sake of one night of good food! He is thankful his dad did not pass down the bleeding ulcers he had to deal-with most of his adult life. After giving thanks for small favors, Luke also reminds him-self of the two mantra-like rules that keep him grounded: It can always be worse, and there is always hope.

He realizes that he has been able, even after having to put forth much effort, to keep his mind off the murders and the investigation. Just once, while just spacing-out in the living room did he take and check the inventory of chores he established. All of them will be complete in full and in no time! Drifting off to a rare nap, Luke begins to dream.

He dreams of Martha. The scene is quite vivid, though unlike any of those he has seen before on the Television. This one is somewhat pornographic. There is no active sex acts playing-out in Luke's head, but Martha is clearly nude...all nude. She is maintaining her perennial garden, doing some heavy-duty work. When she bends to weed, Luke has a view of her privates from the rear: They even zoom-in. She lifts heavy bags, then slices them open and shovels the bark material into the garden. During the mulch scenes, the images viewed concentrate around her breasts, as they heave, and wobble and bobble. Luke likes that they are not big ones. He likes her size a lot. Annie notices he is hard in his sleep.

After cleaning everything up in the dining room and kitchen, she gets Mal ready for, and put into bed – her crib. She takes a quick shower, then, with only a robe for cover, she goes downstairs and recalls her thoughts and feelings about her and Luke. She does not have to touch herself to know she is already damp. Annie gently wakes Luke, takes his hand, and leads him upstairs. He is still half-asleep and still half-hard as Annie showers him down with a rather quick warm rinse. She touches him, it, a few times and it turns her on even more.

He is awake now and is surprised at the attention alone, let alone the sensual sexuality pouring out from his wife. It has been a long time and never has she been the instigator, the initiator. Luke decides to let her and follows that lead, because he wants to know what it is like to let her have her way. For the very first time, she takes him in her mouth. Afterward, for maybe the second time ever takes the top. She does not last long up there, so she puts her bottom up and face down and Luke knows exactly what she wants. She has climaxed three times already, yet she pulls away, flips herself over, spreads out, and takes Luke's head and puts it where she loves it the most – a guarantee of the most powerful orgasm she could ever muster up. She is not disappointed, and neither is he, as he takes a few pumps for himself before they both fall asleep cuddling, a first.

# CHAPTER TWENTY-THREE

Dawna and Stone by this time are used to the authorities coming and going, at their whim and need. If anything, it keeps Stone oddly filled with anxiety and makes him nervous every day. The goings-on do not affect Dawna in the least. She lives out her daily and nightly routines uneventfully. Stone once asks her how she manages to remain so calm amidst the endless investigation...magnified under the microscope of tears.

"Well Stone," Dawna says. "Why dwell on a problem that doesn't exist? I do not mean to minimize the hardships and pain, but the innocent need not worry, in my opinion."

"I know all that, Dawna!"

"Then why must you day after day make yourself so sick about it?"

"I have the feeling I am the only one under scrutiny, okay?"

"And when they discover that they cannot bring any charges up against you, they will move-on to their next person of interest."

"So, Dawna, who might that, be? Do you have any idea?" Luke answers for her: "NO, YOU DON'T! And, I don't either."

"Stone," Dawna takes a try at toning down the conversation. "Maybe what I am doing is something you can try to do."

"What is that?" Stone asks her.

"Simply take things day-by-day. Live out your life as it lay before you, and just easily slip from one day to the next – no determinations, no expectations. That's all."

"You make it sound so simple."

"It IS simple, Stone. Just try."

"Okay, Dawna, I will do my best."

"Good." Dawna puts a lid on this conversation for now.

*

Brian and Timmy full-time living with their dad, adjust very well. Their unspoken concern is the endless tension, second only to missing mom. They spend more time out in the living room and outside in the yard, much more than their old weekend habit of hibernating in their room. While the tension upsets them, their presence comforts Stone and Dawna. Having them commingle with the adults helps keep Stone a little less disturbed and a little more upbeat, not much, but a little bit. The little bit helps nonetheless.

Dawna is surprised at how much their diet has changed due to the kids' liking. More times than not, she makes two to three dinners just to keep everyone, including herself, happy and satisfied. Even Brian – the oldest of the two boys – is still quite fussy about what he will eat, let alone Timmy, who is even worse. Dawna has never made so much macaroni and cheese in her life! She finds herself making smaller portion dinners of different simple foods, such as hamburgers and fries, hot-dogs and beans, and other foods – processed – that she swore-off of long ago. The occasional pizza, spaghetti and meatballs or sub-sandwiches are always welcome by all, but otherwise, she makes good, balanced and nutritious meals for her and Stone. Though unmentioned, they all love what she does for them.

Dawna's only wish from their relationship is for Stone to let them have their own baby. She is at her peak, at her age, but he feels like he should be done with it. He has two kids already and went thru the difficult infancy stages with each. For those reasons, a touchy subject is why Dawna is fearful of bringing it up again. You would be hard-pressed to find a woman in her mid to late thirties who does not want children. They feel like "the last call" is on its way. It is sad and self-absorbed for any man, truly committed to his woman, to refuse to give her what she is on Earth to fulfill – the gift and miracle of life from God.

Unfortunately, the dream is real, yet unseen in the short-term future. Dawn remains patient and hopes, thinks about and prays to her God that she receives this gift one day. Maybe she should just stop taking her birth-control pills: She could have an 'accident.' Could she really do that? She does not think so, but the idea runs through her mind with all the rest. It is very tempting. She thinks about it seriously for a moment. She must sit tight until this whole investigation is over and justice served. Then, she can let her thoughts on the subject take-up where they left-off.

The police just left. That takes some weight off the evening. Neither Stone nor Dawna see whether they take anything with them, or did not notice if they did. It does not matter anymore to Stone. They will do whatever they have to do regardless of how he feels. He ponders that thought and relays it to Dawna. She is pleased to hear him rationalize some. It will probably help calm him of most of his anxiety. With that simple little cue, she has her mind on making love, and she means having some SEX, with Stone tonight.

What else is in her favor? Well…it is Friday night; there is no work tomorrow. They both share the same feelings and are in the same moment at the same time. This triggers more confidence and expectation. She will seduce him, and she will not fail, rejected or take "No" for an answer. She feels unstoppable and nothing is going to break that: Nothing!

Stone sleeps in his underwear, and Dawna wears her undies and a tee. After his bedtime routine, Stone climbs into bed and lays there on his back, staring at the ceiling. Dawna slowly strolls out of the walk-in closet and into the bedroom nude. The bedroom light that is on is dim and soft. She leaves it on. Stone does not pay her even a glance. Unlike the past, however, Dawna takes things in her own hands…and plays…while he stares at her face like a boy might his first time.

She lays a big, wet, sloppy kiss on him. He begins to grow. She quickly sinks down with her head in his lap, lets him, and helps him harden in her mouth. She does not hint at or even have any expectation of his, but she will keep going and have her way with him, and she will make sure they both climax together. She can do this! He is hard enough now for her to straddle him, and she fucks him, without any thought of any action from except to enjoy. She could go at any time now, but she will wait until he is ready to, and she will go with him: Yes!

"Tell me when you're ready babe," Dawna whispers to Stone. "I want to go with you."

Through all his heavy panting, responds, "Uh-huh."

She decides to get him off with something that always worked before – for both of them. She takes him in all the way, and she grinds on him. She goes a little faster with each moment. She can feel him hitting her back wall and is ready as she continues to grind her clitoris on his lower tummy.

"Okay!" Stone cries out.

"Oh yes baby! I am coming with you!"

"I love you."

"I love you."

This does more for the relationship, and their individual mindsets, than anything else could have.

# CHAPTER TWENTY-FOUR

"Okay here it is for the day Officers, Deputies," Chief Deckham no longer sounds so nonchalant facilitating the morning case statuses and assignments. "We now have a homicide case open. We have ruled-out a murder-suicide. We have investigators and forensics looking over a considerable cache of evidentiary items. We have an approximate day and time of death. Today marks day forty-eight since the initial discovery of the victims. The house is still taped-off, even though searches are complete and documented. I want the door-to-door performed again today. Walsh, of course, your team will be responsible for carrying out that task. I want you to take it even deeper this time. Everyone else's assignments are on the chart. Most of you go back to your daily shift routines. Finally, we have yet to tie any evidence to a person, but that is where we are going at this point. I will keep you updated. This could escalate at any time. That's it."

Walsh summons McKenzie and orders him to get the team together. "Let's meet right back here in thirty minutes – sharp."

"Yes, Sir: I will take care of it."

Rather than passing along the orders at the search area, Walsh prefers to lay it out here at the station, then all will proceed from there. He sits at a workstation and opens a homicide Q & A and checklist for his search team to follow. Questions and Answers will likely bring forth more information unsaid up to now. The checklist revolves around reading posture, mannerisms, expressions and reactions. Sometimes body language offers more than any word does depending on the subject's ability to hide in their statements all other hidden truths.

Generally, they keep eye contact at the same time, and secondarily hand and leg movements. The officers and investigators trained well in the process, but to insure they follow orders, they will each carry on their clipboards this cheat-sheet. Partner officers take notes; write reports, and possibly, affidavits at each residence. Walsh takes the lead with two additional investigating officers on the west side of Youmans Avenue and McKenzie and his trio take the east side.

It is a Saturday morning, so there is a better chance of all adults being home and available for a conversation. Each team submits to all the households the same series of queries. If any one investigator hears, sees or otherwise notices anything that triggers a concern, then the lead officer reviews it and performs a follow-up, to see where the response leads him next. There appears to be a trend among almost all the Rossinski neighbors: Stone Rossinski is cold and spends more time away from home than at home, and, Mrs. Rossinski is a lonely woman, good mother, and stays busy between work and home.

*

Lieutenant Walsh reaches the L'Italian residence and for the first time this morning garners much more detail with each question. Both Mr. and Mrs. L'Italian agree on all points raised between each other. They took residence in the Borough eight years ago, just after the Rossinskis moved-in. They learn quickly how unfriendly and arrogant Mr. Rossinski is, and how sweet, smart and devoted Mrs. Rossinski was. The L'Italians become familiar with Mrs. Rossinski well, pretty quickly. They even trade house keys with her, and agree to watch each other's houses when either is away. Luke tells Walsh about the maddening interactions with Stone, and the down-to-Earth conversations with Kat. Walsh's scribe is busy as ever, taking detailed notes during the interview.

The team is already aware of both the Rossinski's professional lives. It is a surprise to them however; as Annie raises interest as she tells Walsh how long, Stone's affair had been going on behind Kat's back. She goes on to tell him the story about the sting she and Luke planned, based on the conversations heard over the baby monitors. Luke, caught off-guard, meant to coach Annie on anything he did not want to share with the police, but he does not let it upset him. He remains calm and rational…yes, calm and rational…the ever-reiterative, endless loop of a mantra rolling in his mind.

"What do you do for a living, Mrs. L'Italian?" asks Walsh.

"I am a stay-at-home mom, sir."

"We understand you had a job at Merck, but they let you go for abusing your Internet access." Walsh says to Luke, and then asks, "Please tell me your side of the story."

"Well," Luke is comfortable with the question. "It is pretty simple. I work very hard; I complete the work of four men and consistently finish assignments ahead of time and under budget. After I completed the last assignment, before they let me go, I spent a few days – that I viewed well-deserved – looking up and reviewing different Web Sites, all music-related."

"So, what do you do now…for work?"

"I am self-employed, Sir."

"Okay…Doing what, exactly?"

"I have an S-Corp," Luke carefully begins. "I am the Administrator of an ISP – that is Internet Service Provider – named 'Equity.'"

"Where is your office and data center?"

"Don't laugh…it is right here," Luke continues. "I work from a home-office."

"Where is your office?"

"I finished-off the basement, and then converted it to a data center and office."

"Do you mind showing it to me?"

"No, Sir, not at all. It is a little cramped, but works for now."

They both stand up, Walsh makes a gesture to the team scribe to come and follow, and Luke, by force of habit, leads them to the hatch in the closet.

"There was no entry to the space downstairs

from the inside, so I built this ladder and cut-out the hatch."

"Holy smokes," Walsh exclaims. "This is very nicely done! I like the color of the stain you used."

"Thanks," replies Luke. "Be careful in the rungs on your way down. The ladder is a bit steep."

"Okay," both officers acknowledge together.

All three transport themselves down the magic entrance, and then find themselves standing in the corner of the office. The two investigators look out across the impressive vista.

"Wow, Mr. L'Italian," Walsh is surprised at the sight of this home-office. "Just wow…"

The blue and black Berber carpet is attractive, the oak desk appears neat and clean, and all of the peripheral hardware, such as servers and disc-space sit on risers, made of refashioned pallets raised and placed three feet from the back wall and the long wall to their right.

"So, the devices are placed like this so they can breathe?" Walsh begins the interview, yet makes it come-off more like a conversation.

"That, plus, I need to be able to access each box from the rear."

"Very tidy set-up," Walsh is genuinely impressed. "Wiring through conduits and corner blocks…"

"I run a tight ship," jokes Luke.

"I see. Do me a favor and explain 'Equity' to me, Mr. L'Italian."

"Okay…"

Luke goes on and on for what seemed like an entire afternoon. Walsh cannot get enough of it all. Luke first lays out basic concepts, such as Input-Process-Output and Web Technologies 101. Now that he has told Walsh what goes on under the sheets, he logs into the 'Equity' Portal and shows-off a bit of the 'Equity' User experience. Walsh has heard enough. He jots a note down and passes it to his scribe.

*

Walsh spent a lot of time with the L'Italians, so his team falls behind McKenzie and his. They are already waiting at the origin point waiting for their boss. The white next door are notorious in Washington Borough. It has always been a conspicuous place. Due in no part to the old woman and her dogs downstairs, the family in the upstairs apartment are infamous for trouble-making and voluminous reports to the police

Department from others in the neighborhood. Therefore, Walsh spends a lot of time with them, as well. The men in that apartment are second only to Stone Rossinski, even so as unofficial persons of interest.

The interviews with the last two homeowners on the block appear uneventful, but the team dissects all notes in all the reports when they return to the station nonetheless. Walsh instructs the team to prepare to work on Sunday, that he and they will complete the full debrief and discussion over the information retrieved. That implies without saying that they will all be working late tonight.

*

Walsh is busy creating a project plan for this latest phase of the investigation. He asks McKenzie to order four large pizzas for the team dinner tonight. He also lets the team know to be ready to work at 6:30 this evening, and not to worry about supper; he has got it covered. A patrol officer prepares the conference room – dedicated to this case – for the upcoming sessions. He places flip charts in each corner, makes certain there is plenty of white-board space, dry-erasures, and dry-erase markers of assorted colors. He does not disturb the assorted shallow stacks of paperwork already in the room; he only makes the stacks neat and manageable. He also puts the four piles of paper on the off-desk, which is right next to one end of the conference room, beside the room computer.

Six-thirty rolls by as the team trickles into the labeled on the outside of the door as the Situation Room - Homicide. They all take their places around the table. Each investigator prints their last name on the bi-fold placard at their seat. Walsh opens the door and walks carrying a clipboard, pads of legal size paper, pens and pencils. McKenzie brings in the Case Log Book; a three-inch ARMY green binder, which is almost full. He brings another brand new binder with him, too.

"Okay, now that we are all here," Walsh commences the exercise. "The plan for tonight calls for each of you to take ownership of equal portions out of the reports and all extended documentation we've collected from the residents on Youmans Avenue. I'll pass the paper-clipped reports recorded at each household, and the four of you will each take the first four from the top of the stack."

"Walsh and I will scribe and use the clipboards as necessary as you complete each one of your completely notated reports." McKenzie adds.

"Additionally, in the meantime," Walsh says. "McKenzie and I will decide which methodology template fits this phase of this homicide case best."

Walsh and McKenzie peruse through a book of methodology worksheets and easily pick one. They chat, almost whisper to each other while their subordinates follow through with their orders.

"I didn't get much more than we already know on my side of the avenue, Lieutenant."

"I interviewed one couple that somehow raised a flag," Walsh replies. "I am not sure what color that flag is, though."

"Oh yeah…? And who was that?"

"…The L'Italians."

"I fuckin' knew it!" McKenzie exclaims.

"Yep… I can't put my finger on it yet, but the moment shall come."

"Well, what are you going to be doing first about your inevitably approaching moment?"

"This guy – L'Italian has an elaborate cottage industry that he runs from a basement office: It's an impressive office and data center that constitutes Internet Service Provision! Do you believe that shit?"

"Tell me more, Walsh," McKenzie is genuinely interested. "Tell me about it, please."

Walsh explains to McKenzie what Luke showed him in his cellar room. He says to McKenzie, "I can't wait to hear the read-out on that visit!"

"It was that good, huh?"

"Like I said, I think so, somehow, someway."

"How about L'Italian's behavior; did anything jump out at you?"

"That is what is tickling me about the interview: They were both extremely cool, calm and rational…relaxed, even."

"Boy…That makes it easy doesn't it?" McKenzie sarcastically remarks.

"Yeah… right McKenzie!"

"The Read-Outs should be interesting."

"Yeah…Especially any Common Threads or Themes discovered."

"Okay, Sargent, let's review in total the logical sequence contained in the methodology template we chose."

"Yes, Sir, let's do that."

Homicides are very rare in the Washington Borough jurisdiction, so Walsh coaches and stresses points of interest and actionable line items in the reports. He came from the City eight years ago, and this only the third homicide he has investigated here, even though other causes of death although uncommon, do surface from time to time. His style and strategies fill the rest of his team with intelligence, comfort and reward. He lets them work in their own way and sometimes merely puts a goal out there and then steps out of everyone's way. Everyone likes and respects him. There is an air of mutual trust, appreciation and respect among all in Department, due in large part to Walsh's accommodating, yet effective style of management.

McKenzie is from the Borough. He began as a patrol officer, and has been climbing the ladder ever since. He came on as a Cadet, stepped-up to Patrolman, and is now a Sargent with one foot in the Investigation Tier – an Associate Detective. He strikes a balance between the concentration on his own professional goals and being a respected Team Lead. The Department holds him in high regard, too. He and Walsh work very well together. Perhaps the star of the show is Captain Deckham. He is on top of the latest in crime-related practices and technology.

He remains very accessible, and listens well to everyone involved at any given time. He keeps his eye on those individuals' goals, as well as management of teams, such as Walsh's – currently – with the attitude of the consummate supporter, cheerleader and professional Captain that he is.

Walsh tells the group to break for supper as the delivery boy from New York Pizza walks through the doors, a yellow Pass and lanyard hanging down from around his neck. He slides four large pies out from the insulated carrier and stacks them up at the nearest corner of the table along with four big bottles of Diet Pepsi.

"Here you go," Walsh holds out forty bucks.

"The boss said to comp you."

"Okay then, tell him I said thanks, but break this twenty, and keep five bucks for your tip," Walsh says. "I insist."

"Yes, Sir...I can do that!" The delivery boy is obviously pleased and very happy!

The boy walks out of the room and drops off the Pass when he gets to the dispatcher's desk.

"You take of yourself." The desk Sargent says with a smile and a wink.

"Okay…Thank you."

The team breaks to eat, and the boss orders them *not* to work through supper. That is typical of men working late; they are notorious for this. Walsh is big on upholding his order for the team to have a relaxing time while eating. These little things bubble his work ethic and team Lead competency to the top. He cannot keep them from eating fast, but he can halt the work while eating. Who would not like a pizza party, even if it were in the middle of a work session?

There are a few slices left in a box when the investigators turn back to their work. Surely, those will go-down nicely cold, later. One by one as each team member completes their read-out notes, turn their name placards back upright, name showing, to indicate so. When everyone is finished, Walsh orders the team to work together and a mission of discovery: Find any possible Common Threads or Themes among the neighborhood.

"Alright McKenzie…" Walsh begins. "Please coach and observe, and as each team member sets a report aside, skim it for stand-out statements notes and comments. Thank you."

"Will do, Boss."

"Everyone else, please pass along the completed documents to McKenzie as soon as you are finished with your assignment."

"Yes, Sir," They reply in almost perfect unison.

"Okay, thank you all."

Walsh draws a table of clues on the largest whiteboard in the room, and it spills over onto the second board, as well. The Headers above the Columns he labels with the residence head-of-household's Surname. The table is an array of elementary, if not atomic fact, ordered by Street Address, lowest to highest. Walsh enters the Commonalities at the top of each column first, followed by the stand-alone facts garnered from each Interview. There are rows of common themes about Stone Rossinski, common opinions about Kat Rossinski, and other line items about the observations of the Rossinski's behavior- alone and together. Finally, Walsh works on putting up various red, yellow and green flag statements collected earlier.

Stone is arrogant and cold; Kat was quiet and kind. Stone is an away from home father; Kat took on all aspects of housekeeping and was dedicated to involvement with her children. Stone has been having an affair for over two years; Kat was in the dark, even though everyone around her knew, or felt strongly she had no idea. Stone is never home under the guise of working late, or out of town; Kat was a hard worker but always there at home with her kids. Stone was not involved with family affairs; Kat kept the children busy doing all sorts of fun and interesting things with them. These opposing profiles between each of the Rossinskis soon form a trend that cannot be far from the truth, nor denied.

Clearly, the bulk of their reports are backed-up and reflected by the Rossinski's closest neighbors and supposed friends, the L'Italians. Mr. L'Italian remarked the most on Stone Rossinski, and Mrs. L'Italian spoke of Kat the most. That seems to make sense, and leaves closed any door that may lead Walsh and McKenzie to the idea of envy, anger with, and any other encroaching or immoral dispositions of the L'Italians toward the Rossinskis. Their statements definitely stress the dissatisfaction with Stone Rossinski and the satisfaction with Mrs. Rossinski. They played a key role in her red-handed discovery of her husband and his administrative assistant – in her home – in her bed, no less! A small bell begins to ring in Walsh's mind: How long have, and who else in the neighborhood do the L'Italians eaves drop on? How did that and the related questions slip by him at the L'Italian interview?

He writes a reminder in his own case notebook: "Follow-up with L'Italians i.e., what else have they heard bleed through their baby monitors?" The bothersome reaction he has because of his overlooking that question the first time makes him wish he could jump-up and head over there now! He does not, though; he nervously carries on with the group. They have collected two, chock-full whiteboards of facts about the Rossinskis and the case generally. All the data is valid until proven not. It is approaching twenty-two-hundred hours, so Walsh, with some sense of relief, adjourns the discovery session. He sends all the men home, after setting-up a time to resume tomorrow morning.

At home, Walsh feels the need to take a prescribed Seroquel tablet. He takes two. Sleep will come soon. Without the medication, it will have been a sleepless night. He carries this bag around easily, for he is used to the fifteen-year behavioral issue. He helps himself by using Dialectical Based Therapy he picked-up in a group therapy class recommended by his doctor years ago. The combination of the DBT and the Seroquel always do the trick.

*

"Good morning everyone," Walsh addresses his team. "McKenzie is covering for me while I go back to the L'Italians for an additional follow-up discussion."

"We got it, Lieutenant."

"Good." Walsh picks one of his detectives for an escort and backup, and they leave in Walsh's Department-loaned Ford LTD. He is happy to reach the L'Italians on this Sunday morning. They are not avid churchgoers, he suspects. They are fine with another sit-down with him. He feels so much better, now that he knows he is about to resolve the problem that hit him the night before. He prepares his backup detective for the upcoming interview, with some history and background. The escort reiterates his dismay over the entire baby-monitor uncovered and used by the L'Italians. Moreover, that played a big part in their nailing Rossinski and his girlfriend, not to mention bringing closure to Kat. Now, he silently wonders, why...what for...dead.

*

"They will be here any minute, now, Annie." Luke reminds his wife.

"I know...I know. But thanks Luke."

"Well, I'm going to just sit here and relax until they arrive."

"I am too. Do you know what they want this time, Luke?"

"Walsh just said he had some follow-up questions and told me he apologizes."

"Why would he apologize?"

"He said he should have brought them up yesterday, that's all. Oh, and he apologized that he has to bother us on a Sunday."

"He's here." Luke says.

"They're here," Annie replies. "He's got someone else with him."

"Okay. I'll get it."

*

Walsh drives past the L'Italian residence just far enough to turn his vehicle around, so he can park in front along the curbside facing the proper direction. He silently wishes everyone would practice that simple bit of discipline. Both the L'Italians cars are in their driveway, leaving no room for Walsh to merely pull-in and park right there. He finishes prepping his partner just as they reach forty-seven Youmans Avenue.

"Good morning, Mr. L'Italian, Mrs. L'Italian," Walsh says, and his backup tips his hat. Annie gets up with Luke. She is behind him at the front door way.

"Good morning, officers." Luke greets the

two detectives. Annie says nothing. "Look, you may call us by our first names if you'd like – Luke and Annie."

"Okay, Luke." Walsh acknowledges.

"Please," Annie interjects. "Come right in."

"Yes." Luke says."Okay," Walsh replies as he and the other officer cross the threshold leading them into the living room. "We are here today to follow-up on your statements that introduced me to 'Equity' yesterday. We can start up here, but I think we will probably eventually go down to your office. …Sound okay?"

"Yes, of course," Luke makes clear that he welcomes the idea. "We will both follow your lead, Sir." Luke does all the talking as Annie sits right back in her chair and listens quietly.

"Great," Walsh says. "We'll sit here on the couch, and just go through some preliminary questions."

"Sounds good to me," Luke replies.

"Okay, then…" Walsh begins. "When did 'Equity' first go live?"

"About thirty-six months ago. Hold on, let me give you something to look at." Luke goes to a sizable Shaker Style set of built-in drawers in the back of the dividing counter opposite the lower cabinets and stovetop-oven on the kitchen side. Walsh is impressed at how genuine and authentic this Primitive-Colonial home's remodeling. "I keep some of the corporation legal documentation up here, because I have found that, typically, I prefer to do the paperwork and record keeping at the dining room table."

Luke lifts a three-inch, three-ring binder from one of the drawers, pushes the drawer shut, and holds it out for Walsh to take.

"This is my S-Corp record book and Charter," Luke begins. "For a corporation, the charter document, which essentially creates the corporation, is generally known as the articles of incorporation (although some states refer to it as the certificate of incorporation)."

"Oh, well," Walsh is surprised. "Thanks very much. Do you mind if I take a quick peek right now?"

"That's why I took it out. Go right ahead. You will find all applicable dates relating to the S-Corp, the Charter, Stock, and all the rest. Looking thru that may answer your questions about 'Equity' the company."

"Excellent! Thank you, Luke."

Walsh slowly rifles through the binder, his fingers bringing him to various divided sections. He utters several facts to his partner, acting scribe who quickly and efficiently jots the information down on their report. There is a wealth of data within the binder, and Walsh pours over it all, it seems to Luke. Luke remains silent and just lets the investigators have at it.

"Wow," Walsh declares. "This just answered half of my questions! Thank you, Luke.

"You're welcome. Do you have to take it with you?"

"No, Sir, not today."

"Okay, if you'd like and if you don't mind, I would appreciate being given the opportunity to make a copy of it for you. The articles of corporate are, as you may have guessed, very sensitive, so I would like to be able to keep the original here…if that is all right with you. But, you do whatever you must."

"That makes good sense to me," Walsh says. "If I need a copy, I will let you know, and give you some lead-time in order make the copy."

"Thanks a lot," Luke is relieved. "Just let me know: No problem.

Annie has never heard Luke speak so articulately, and she is impressed, if not feeling inferior. She is, however, smart enough to know that his correctness must be an important part to his line of work. He sounds so…so…professional! She watches and listens to the two officers, as they work their way through Luke's binder.

"Let's go down to your data center, Luke, Okay?"

"Okay."

The three men get up from their seats in the living room and once again follow Luke down the hatch. Walsh cannot help but repeat his impressions of the passageway. He is convinced that he is dealing with an intelligent, smart and capable man in Luke L'Italian. He whispers that to the scribe to make the note. It cannot hurt; Walsh is very good at what he does. Luke leads them to his workstation and describes the purpose of each machine's monitor on it. He then turns facing the right, front corner, which gives him a good view of the entire data center, all the servers and disc arrays.

"What I am interested in at this point in time are your users."

"Well, I can produce a membership report that I can customize, so you will get exactly the fields you're looking for."

"Okay," Walsh is satisfied so far. "That would be great."

"I might suggest delivering you any sizable report you request on hard media, but not paper. ….I can put the entire report on a CD or thumb-drive. That way you can take it to the station and print any part of it as the need arises."

"Okay, I agree. What kind of user-related data do you store and keep in 'Equity'?

"Well, let me pull-up a record real quick for you to look at, then, you can see it yourself. Naturally, you will notice identity-related data: Name; Address; Method of Payment, and so on. Okay, here is the top result of a query ordered by on Sur Name. It happens to be a Miss Lolia Aaleah. She is located in Manhattan. Go ahead, scroll right and back, and check it out. Do you know how to do that?"

"Luke, that much, I can handle!" Walsh Laughs.

"Have at it, Sir." Luke laughs along.

"So, if we have this data on a digital storage device how will it download?"

"I can establish it in my copy of the entities in their entirety for you.

"We like Spreadsheets. We have 'Office'."

"I will download it comma-delimited so the data fills-in the slots on your spreadsheet."

"Do you keep records of usage?"

"I do. I can link each user to their Activity History records which will give you a Joined Entity report."

"Excellent! How far back does it go?"

"Well, Sir, it is a Generational Paradigm. It stores one year of data: Any data beyond a year drops-off, oldest first. So, I have the most recent twelve month's activity stored by Date, descending, going back at the furthest, one year."

"Okay, Luke," Walsh likes what he hears. "You mentioned that your users have the ability to communicate with each other…"

"They have available to them an opt-in or out Email Client and Chat Engine. They can choose Private Messaging or participate and contribute in a public Chat Room. I have Exchange Servers implemented to manage the back-end email functions."

"How much email and chat content do you save?" Walsh is particularly interested in this data moreover all else attached to each member.

"Any Email over and above one-hundred-twenty days old, they are responsible to off-load it to their own devices. Those older messages I delete from the system. The users have the opportunity to off-load Chat history conversations, public and private. I keep that historic content going back six months."

"Shit…Sorry, but is that it; really?" Walsh is trying to understand the logic behind Luke's backup algorithms.

"Oh! Let me clarify. I apologize: This is the next subject I planned to present to you." Luke begins.

"Okay, please…Go on Luke."

"See those two tape drives?" Luke walks over to point them out to the detectives. "Every night a batch operation runs that captures the latest database changes in a first-in, first-out logical sequence. Then, bi-monthly, I transfer the back-up tapes to Stone Mountain underground storage facilities, in Allentown. There they remain for thirty-six months, then destroyed. Every time the carrier picks up the new tapes, they return to me the old ones erased and reformatted."

"Good deal!"

"It is the right thing to do, but it is a pain pulling data back out of Stone Mountain. The wait-time is considerable."

"I'll keep that in mind. You know- I

believe – the span of time we are interested in and why."

"Oh yeah…I sure do! Jesus…I will do all I can to help."

"Well, to be sure, go back twenty-four months."

"Yes, Sir…will do."

"Oh, I almost forgot. What else do you pick-up through your baby monitors?"

"Not much. We hear other parents doing goo-goo – ga ga with their infants. Stone's cordless phone is the only phone bleed we've ever heard."

# CHAPTER TWENTY-FIVE

Stone and Dawna wake together after a night spent truly together; the first time in too long a time. She reaches over and gently caresses his hairless chest, running her fingers across his nipples. As they harden, she moves her hand down to his genitals, increasingly, yet quickly arousing him plenty. He groans a little. Last night remains in his being as an all-over reminder of how keeping sex alive can help keep a couple alive. She does not wait for an invitation. Dawna climbs up on top and slowly rides him—reverse cowgirl this time. By the time she begins to move faster and faster and finally the fastest ever, Stone mutters through the heavy pants he's been heaving for the entire ride, 'I'm ready, babe.' She goes with him, a wonderfully beautiful moment.

It was like last night, only more quickly done and complete. She turns and bends down, gives him a nice kiss on the cheek, rolls away and gets in the shower. Stone lays there drifting in and out of wakefulness waiting, because he wants to shower, too. He will wait. Dawna softly sings a favorite song while she lathers all over and shampoos her hair. Unlike her mate, she wipes and dries herself off in the tub, and then steps out and onto the soft, dry bathmat. She wishes everyone in the household could follow this simple procedure.

"Stone," Dawna yells just loud enough and melodically. "I'm out…it's your turn!"

"Okay." Stone responds barely audible.

"Don't dilly-dally…I am making a nice, big breakfast for everyone."

Dawna goes to the kitchen and gets all her ingredients together on the counter. She interrupts herself, as she realizes the boys may still be sleeping, and shuffles to their bedroom door. She can hear the Television squawking. 'Was it left on all night?' She calls them through a closed door, her voice uncomfortably bouncing back to her. Both boys answer. Good…both boys are awake.

Back in the kitchen, Dawna mindlessly begins to do what she has done a hundred times before; systematically even if she does not have to put much thought into it. She knows what to start first and what to cook last to have everything ready at the same time. That is the trickiest part of cooking any meal, but she knows well what she is doing. Just after calling everyone to the table, Dawna plates it and puts the serving dishes on it.

"Come on, everyone," Dawna hollers to all. "Breakfast is on the table."

Stone comes into the dining room. He is all dressed and his hair is still wet.

"Mmmm," He looks at the presentation before him. "Dawna, this looks so good!"

"Good!" She says with a smile.

The boys come running in, still in their pajamas. They sit at their places at the table, without saying a thing, but their body language and expressions are unmistakable.

"Boys, you both look like you're hungry!"

"Well, let's eat!" Stone starts serving him-self and passes each dish to his left to Dawna, as he finishes with each one.

"Yeah," Timmy exclaims. "Let's…"

It is a big, hearty meal and Dawna eats, slowly, and smiles at everyone in turn. As usual, the boys begin to wolf down their food, and, as usual, Dawna tries to curb them. Oh, when will they ever learn the benefits of eating slow and chewing their bites of food better? She wipes away the thought and enjoys the breakfast. So does everyone else! There comes a point, no matter who she is dealing with, that Dawna feels it's best to just give-up.

"So, did everybody sleep well last night?" She asks.

"I did." Stone replies.

"Yup!" The boys did, too.

When everyone is finished eating, Dawna clears the table and stacks the dirty dishes beside the kitchen sink. She wonders what Stone will do if she just leaves them there. She very neatly segregates and stacks by type: the larger serving plates, the dinner plates, the silverware, utensils and the juice glasses. She even scrapes and rinses each scrappy-looking dish and utensil, so that everything there is ready for washing. She hardly ever uses the dishwasher; neither does Stone. She wonders whether he will this morning, but first questions silently if he even offers to help. He has dismissed his share of the housework – which is not very much – lately, but she will wait and see.

Having taken matters in her hands, last night…this morning…she feels empowered and comfortable embracing what is by far a lead role unlike any other time in their relationship. It has worked so far, even if it is only day two! She laughs inside, as she walks to the living room, coffee in-hand, and sits in her spot on the couch. The boys scatter to their room after Stone asks them to get dressed. Stone sits silently at the table. He leans on his elbows, with his chin in hands, and his head in the clouds. He knows what Dawna would like from him, but he questions whether he will comply. Finally, he lets the thought wash away from his mind. He is on autopilot, his pre-trouble default behavior.

"I'll do the dishes." Stone says to Dawna.

"Aww, that would be so great," she says. "That's very nice of you."

"I'll wipe-down the table and clean the kitchen, too."

"Thank you so much, Stone!"

She is not aware of any plans for the weekend, or the day that Stone might have on his mind, but she waits for him to finish what he is doing, and comes to the living room to relax. Dawna still feels like she must walk on eggshells around Stone, for fear of triggering either backlash from, or anxiety in her partner. One thing is clear to her: She no longer fears him. For the first time since confronting him with the telling message, she received about his online affair, she feels well balanced and at ease.

As she works on a crossword puzzle, he sneaks right by her and sits down with his coffee. He looks over at her; she is deeply engaged on the puzzle. He clears his throat to get her attention. If she has anything pressing on her mind, he wants to hear about it now. She looks over at him and smiles.

"Oh," Dawna says. "I didn't even know you came in."

"I just did a couple minutes ago," he replies. "Do you have any plans for today, or maybe the weekend?"

"That is so funny! I was going to ask you the same, exact thing!" Dawna laughs aloud. "Anyway, no Stone, I don't. So do you?"

"No, I have no plans this weekend. It is the first week that has gone by uneventfully, if you know what I mean. I would like to just be…just relax."

"I think that's a wonderful idea. You really do need a rest. I'm proud of how you're handling the tension." She pumps him up a little with her white lie declaration.

"Oh, well, what else can I do?"

"There is nothing more you can do that I

know of, other than wait and see. You have no need to worry, because you are innocent. Thank you for a nice night and morning. I do love you, you know."

"Oh Dawna, I needed it as bad as you did. You are as lovely as ever. I love you, too."

*

Dawna feels uplifted. She no longer has a thought of anoMan, even though she uses 'Equity' almost every day. She has not seen Stone using his Laptop in ages. Like her and anoMan, go Stone and Sweetlilgreek…Gone! Now that Stone and Dawna have broken the ice, neither one wants anything more than what they already have between each other. They oddly feel the same sense of relief but do not know it, they can assume it, and that is good enough for both of them. It helps that their respective playmates are nowhere anymore.

"You know what, Stone?" Dawna says.

"What?"

"I think I will treat the boys to a movie tomorrow afternoon," she announces. "I will look-up Matinee times for both theaters today."

"I like that idea, Dawna." Stone says. "I

will let you know tomorrow whether I want to go, or not. Maybe you should ask the boys if there is anything playing that they would especially like to see."

"Yes, Stone. That is a good idea. I will do that."

# CHAPTER TWENTY-SIX

Walsh is at his desk with McKenzie in the seat opposite and facing him. They get periodic updates from the Case Situation Room, discuss all notes of discovery, and together dig further hoping to find something deeper into the evidentiary updates. They order-up a membership report segmented by postal code. They agree they appear to, or at least may be on to something. Walsh knows better than to get excited over it, veteran that he is, but McKenzie smiles ear-to-ear at the potential, the chance of something big coming away from the idea.

The next report requested shows Membership Activity History. It is a treasure trove of data, but moreover, information. Walsh uncharacteristically smiles as they begin to discover more and more about the History report.

"Oh, so now you decide to get excited," laughs McKenzie.

"Well," Walsh explains his thought aloud to his second in command. "I just noticed that there are data that reflects the members' chat history. All I see initially is a list of User Names that, according to the column header, are the identifiers of the chat buddy or companion."

"Oh, yeah, I see that now." McKenzie replies.

"Okay then, let's first look through the chat history of Mrs. Rossinski and Mr. Headley."

"Okay…excellent!"

While they wait for the latest requested report, Walsh puts his idea out on the table. McKenzie listens attentively, and nods in agreement each time Walsh looks directly at him, and points out clearly to McKenzie what he expects to find.

"I hope to find trending data as we study the private chat and chat room activity."

"Nice idea, boss."

They receive the report as requested, Walsh having asked for, specifically, the listing discussed fifteen minutes before, but narrows it down within the Washington Borough postal code. This is, they agree, a very logical starting point, and understood by each, that this avenue is standard investigative procedure. Cases like this one usually come down to an identifying clue, be it a witness, an event, a statement, or an outright bombshell for the intelligence team.

"The database dump L'Italian provided is working wonders!" exclaims McKenzie.

"Not to mention our own 'Equity' User ID's, too."

"First," Walsh begins. "Let's look at Mrs. Rossinski's habits and chat buddies. After we have exhausted the analysis from her records, we'll do the same for Mr. Headley's records."

"Okay. This should be very interesting."

"We're not here for our own interest, McKenzie, so keep your investigator's hat on."

"Yes, Sir…No need to get antsy: I understand completely."

Walsh wipes the perspiration from his forehead. McKenzie, by power of suggestion wipes sweat from the back of his neck. Mrs. Rossinski spent more time surfing the Web, than in private conversations with anyone in particular. However, she visited the same chat room most every woman in the neighborhood does. They decide to log in to the 'Equity' portal, and navigate to the room in question.

"L'Italian set us up pretty well, huh Boss?"

"Yes he did. We should have no trouble since we have a site map, and relational database report."

McKenzie cannot believe what he is reading. Walsh can. He becomes almost saddened, as he delves into the personal lives of those on pages spanning the report on the desk before them. Their user names are invisible to all other users, so there is no chance of, or fear that, random members messaging them. It is good to know, however, that with a simple phone call to Mr. L'Italian could grant them any authority necessary. For now, Walsh and his assistant detective engage in eaves dropping in the chat room.

"Wow, this room is sexually charged!" McKenzie says.

"You bet: You are not that surprised, though, are you?"

"Well, not really, but it's not often I watch the sexual behavior of others"

"I know; just keep your eye on the ball. We want to garner the general and maybe specific nature of the room and its visiting members."

"Right; I've got it."

They continue to peer into the chat box of rolling sexual innuendoes and direct imperatives and invitations. They can also see the 'red-line' messages and conversations, which reflect in most a triple-X theme between two members. The open activities in the room are for the most part just a little cooler in nature, with the periodic and extremely suggestive outburst between the room guests. It appears as though the motive behind it all is merely sexual related sharing, discussing, playfulness and watching.

"Okay," Walsh says. "You keep an eye on the room, and I will keep one on the red-line messages."

"I got it!"

"Let's see if many or any members arrange face-to-face meetings with one another from within this room."

"Right...okay."

They watch, waiting for an instance of meeting plans arranged. After a half-hour, walsh sees one before his eyes. Two members engaged in cyber-sex seem to wind down, yet eventually lead to one member suggesting they meet. The local member at the other end of the wire messages an affirmative response to the idea, but does not commit to it. Still, this is proof that at least some of the folks do intend to get to the next level, somehow, sometime.

"I've got a hit," Walsh exclaims. "A local

is entertaining the idea of meeting her chat partner!"

"So it does happen," McKenzie replies. "It is no surprise, but what this impromptu and wide area investigation of this report illustrates that there could be one of these events happening every half-hour, or so. I smell danger in all that."

"Yes…exactly. Let's see if there resides any data regarding the content of private chats and email between members."

McKenzie peers at the entity-relationship map. It takes him some time to find the source of chat history in full. They want to see content. After a fifteen-minute exercise in relational database analysis, he finds the table they want to look at. Now, Walsh is very glad and relieved he brought in an Information Technology man, deputizing him as an extended team member. His priority is to support the team in whatever they request extracted from 'Equity.'

Walsh did not tell Luke about his plan to bring in the expert, but it is of no consequence to Luke anyway. After getting the gist of the messages that fly back and forth, Walsh decides to look for Kat's and Headley's activity and content data. Understandably, neither has current, up-to-date data. All their activity ceased the very day they are murdered. Mrs. Rossinski frequented several 'Equity' chat rooms, but the only private chat is between Headley and her.

Every entity devoted to them is marked as obsolete and for eventual deletion. Walsh shares that Mr. L'Italian sure is on top of things. It does seem odd that Mrs. Rossinski had any dialog with anyone except Headley. They also are among a small subset of members that registered relatively recently – Headley six weeks before Mrs. Rossinski. They both worked at Merck. Even though they worked in different departments, they worked virtually together for a number of years.

It is a well-established fact that Mr. Headley had an affinity and interest in pornography. The team completed dusting his and Kat's machines shortly after the grisly discovery. Mrs. Rossinski, for that matter, appears rather innocent: She browsed the Web for different work related articles as well as home and garden sites. She also took college courses in online Physiology. Her email recipients include family and old friends, all of whom clear of interest for now.

Headley maintains several online handles, and one in particular he used often the six weeks before his demise. During that time span, Headley, known as Sweetlilgreek hits Walsh right over the head. That is Stone

Rossinski's online fantasy 'girl!' Headley is no innocent bystander, McKenzie!

"BAM!" escapes McKenzie in a loud voice.

Headley has a second computer, but it is still in the process of crime-related scouring. The latest word on that one is that he seems to have been an amateur software enthusiast. Beyond that, forensic investigators must decrypt the abundance of programs and data that reside on that system. Word should come soon on the nature of the software. The files, encrypted over and above typical executables, or machine code, make discovery difficult.

Walsh and McKenzie are aware of the implicit suggestion that Headley may have been involved with one of two things: private illegal pornography, such as pedophilia, bestiality, etc., and, hacking others' machines for some personal gain. Discovery will prove either or both within the week. That is the latest word from the forensics technology team. It is clear that Headley and Mrs. Rossinski were actively into some sort of relationship. The day of the murders, he urged her to let him visit with her.

He announces in two ways, email first, chat finally, to her that he had something important, vital and relevant to tell her about and show her, too. The investigators discover that the content in question are the most recent and last correspondence between the two neighbors. If there is more from him on that mystery machine, Walsh will soon find out. He also decides he wants to revisit yet again, Mr. L'Italian in person. Walsh is making sure they are retrieving all the data that is stored regarding content.

*

"Hello there Mrs. L'Italian," Walsh sounds friendly. "Is your husband at home?"

"Yes, he is."

"I hope we are not interrupting anything."

"Oh, no…He is just downstairs working, that's all."

"That is we prefer to speak with him. May I go knock on the hatch door?"

"Of course you can. That's all I would do if it were me calling on him!" she laughs as she lies.

"Okay, thank you."

Luke waits at the bottom of the office ladder for Walsh to climb down. As Walsh steps down into the large room, Luke welcomes him warmly. Walsh thanks him and walks toward Luke's workstation. Unlike Walsh's first visit to the office, Luke follows *him* across the floor. Walsh lets Luke know that he only has a few questions for him at this time. Luke invites the detective to sit in the recliner, as he sits at his desk.

"So, what's up, Sir?"

"Okay, Mr. L'Italian, how far back do you keep the membership activity data? Is it the same as the other membership entities?"

"No, Sir. That is a good question: I keep membership activities online for twelve months. Anything older will have been shipped off to Iron Mountain."

"Oh, I see. Do you keep an eyeball on registrations?"

"Yes, I do with almost every new entry at first. However, early on, I kept a real keen eye on the growth of the database, and everything related to new registrations… users. 'Equity' was so new to me back then."

"Well, that makes sense, but I have a question. I apologize if it seems redundant. I have to confirm we are finding data in our shadow database that you, as the expert over the system would expect. Does that make sense?"

"Yes, it does make sense…No problem…Let's just drill into it now. Just ask me what you need or tell me what you are looking for, and we'll submit the appropriate queries right here – right now."

"That sounds great, Mr. L'Italian! So, if when we do not find activities or other data for any member or individual within a twelve period, it is an indication that they registered less than twelve months ago, right?"

"Yes, detective, that is correct–if I understand your question. Let's see what I can do to help."

"There is probably an easier way, so let me know if there is one, okay?"

"Okay, I am performing a look-up of the root entity for the users in question. Who are we looking for?"

"Mrs. Rossinski and Mr. Headley are the subjects currently."

Luke retrieves the results of the query within seconds. Walsh asks Luke if it is normal for look-ups to take longer on the shadow database the investigative team is using. Luke tells him that going directly against the hosted database is always faster than retrieval of data that resides elsewhere.

"Okay then, here are the two membership records. What we should do is this: And this is the better way to access child entities of the parent membership entity. Watch this. Take notes. I will do this slowly."

"Okay, thanks a lot Mr. L'Italian."

Luke joins the child entity named 'membership_times_and_dates' with the membership entity by primary key 'member_id.' The query returns the member ID, the member name, and any time and date information attached to the user in question. The very first date and time displayed is the date and time of registration, followed by other miscellaneous records, such as member obsolete, member last access and several more that Luke treats as referential time stamps. He prints off the query for Walsh after pointing out the fields that are of interest to him.

"Whoa! This is much easier! I like that the column labels are at the top. Did I say that correctly?"

"Yes, that function comes for free with the database."

Walsh skims the query results and sees right away that Mrs. Rossinski registered nine months ago and Mr. Headley registered eleven months ago. He asks Luke what the entity name for message content is. Luke states that there are separate entities for message types, but a join query, similar to the one they ran a few minutes ago will do the trick. He writes the multi-join query for Walsh then prints it off and hands it to him.

"Is there anything else I can help you with?" Luke asks.

"Not just yet, however I hope that we can continue this open dialog if I have more questions at a later date. We do appreciate all you're doing Mr. L'Italian."

"Sure, Sir, it is no problem at all. We are usually here every day, although Annie takes the baby to Grandma's and other places occasionally. I am here either working in the office or lounging, if I am not doing some household chore." Luke laughs."

"Alright then, I will call or drop by if we come across anything we can't figure out." Walsh laughs back.

"I'll walk you to the door. Oh, do you need a drink – water or anything?"

"No I don't but thanks any way."

Luke walks to the fridge after closing the door behind Walsh. It is late enough in the day that he can afford to have a New Castle Brown Ale! He sits in his recliner in the living room and thinks through what he believes could be happening at the police station and what more he can expect to hear from Walsh about 'Equity.' Luke begins to sweat as Headley comes to mind. Luke does not know what, if anything Headley stored on his home computer system. Luke is certain that Kat did not have the time or the expertise to jump over the limited access granted her at registration. There is not a reason for her to go out of her way documenting anything about her online goings-on with Luke.

# CHAPTER TWENTY-SEVEN

Annie suggests to Luke in a question that it seems too early for him to be drinking. He almost snaps back at her. This is the first moment of discomfort he feels, even throughout the interrogation by Walsh. He does not, though: He simply tells his wife that one bottle of Ale does not constitute 'drinking.' He adds that he is almost done for the day, anyway. Annie takes a deep breath and exhales slowly. Luke does the same thing. He realizes that he saved up this anxiety until Walsh left the house. He must let it out now, so he goes out the back door onto the deck. There, he sits, bottle in hand and he alone. This is all he could ask right now. He is good.

Luke wonders what, if anything could go wrong as the investigation continues. The police have access to virtually all the data stored under 'Equity.' They do not have yet, but could ask for access to Luke's personal computer. He bides his time thoughtfully, in his mind's eye, looking at his file system. All references to 'Equity,' all instances of suggestive and pornographic data files and anything that could in any way raise questions and suspicion toward Luke. He realizes he has to revisit his personal file system. Right after that, he plans to look-over 'Equity,' as well.

Luke heads back in after Annie calls him for dinner. He feels considerably better, and enjoys the meal sitting with his small family. Mal babbles and slurps food with only a little bit of help from her mother. Luke comments that her development is seems to be improving faster and faster by the day. Annie agrees. She is surprised to hear that coming out of Luke. She knows he cares, but he does not mention Mal often. She must give him credit for all the crying spells he squelches and his direct interaction with Mal.

"Annie," Luke begins.

"Yes?"

"I am working in the office for a while after dinner tonight."

"Oh, okay."

"If I end-up working any additional nights, I am taking an extra day next weekend."

"You really should, I think."

"Yeah, that's what I am thinking."

"So, what did the officer want, Luke?"

"Oh…I provided him with a copy of the 'Equity' database, and he came with questions about how to drill into certain areas. I wrote a few queries for him to take back to his office."

"Does it bother you when he comes over?"

"No, it doesn't…not really. A call ahead of time would be nice, but I know he has a full plate. He cannot cover ALL his bases. You know?"

"I don't know how you do it, Luke. You always seem so calm and collected. How do you do that? I would be a complete wreck!"

"Well Annie, it's not altogether easy."

"What time will you be done tonight?"

"Oh, I only plan on being down there for two or three hours."

"Oh Good – that sounds good – not too much…"

"Right, I am not going out of my way. I just want to clean things up a bit."

*

Luke performs this exercise as methodically as he did the first time. He knows where to begin and what to expect. This is not anything new coming at him, it is a double take he decides for himself to do. He is careful to leave all instances of innocent and unrelated files of his alone. Having a presence on the personal level is to be expected; he will delete only elements that he foresees being potential attention-grabbers. He starts at the top of the file tree and works downward and to the right, manually looking through every subdirectory belonging to the root folder.

He finds that even in haste, he cleaned real well questionable or suggestive files and content the first time. Still, he again works slowly through his documents, pictures, and all folders. He leases online backup systems and storage, so every time he deletes a file locally, the backup system deletes it remotely, as well. Lastly, for now, he scours email messages received and sent, saved etc., and realizes he has yet to tackle the exchange email server with the same objective as all other files, using the same or similar tasks and logical steps.

Finally, at nine-thirty, he notes what he has left to do. He must scour specifically the 'Equity' file systems and database entities. It feels so nice reclining in his comfortable chair in the living room. Annie asks if is done, and he lets her know he is done for the night, but must work on the 'Equity' systems tomorrow. They together enjoy the ice cream sundaes Annie brought in from kitchen. This is Luke's favorite part of their evening routine. Annie already put Mal to bed: She is thankfully sleeping quietly. Luke misses kissing her good night, but he does not beat himself up. These are not his average days, lately.

He is so tired his mind is mush, so Annie has control of the Television remote control. Luke could care less. He watches whatever she settles on but inside he cannot stop thinking about the chores he is set to do tomorrow on 'Equity.' Before he knows it, time takes him to eleven-o'clock, as Luke announces bedtime for around midnight. Annie's concentration on the Television show blurs, as she thinks about the possibility of another night of fooling around.

Luke always sleeps nude and Annie in a tee shirt and undies, but tonight, she climbs into bed nude, as well. Luke gets the hint and somewhat regretfully lets her know he is much too tired to make love tonight. He stresses to her that he hopes she will touch him awake and aroused in the morning. Annie is fine with that: She already knows, of course, that the wee hours of the morning have Luke waking terrifically aroused already. She falls asleep with a smile on her face, as Luke tosses and turns for forty-five minutes before sleep comes to him.

Annie dreams of random sexual encounters, with men, with women, strangers and by herself. Luke once again dreams the reoccurring dream he lives with night after night. The crime plays repeatedly until he wakes briefly, sweating. He tends to fall right back asleep, but the dark dream always picks-up where it left-off. Eventually, in R.E.M., the dream puts him beside Kat in a big fluffy bed and canopy of lace.

It is three-forty-five in the early morning when Luke inadvertently rolls over into a spooning posture with Annie. He is oblivious to it, but he is fully aroused already and he is poking his wife in the rear end. She eventually wakes to it, reaches around and takes shim in one hand and slowly strokes. She lets her other hand travel to her pubis and discovers that she is already soaking wet. Without breaking their position together on the bed, she guides Luke into that warm, wet place. She commences with the movements and does not lose tempo. Finally, Luke wakes, catches-on and finds he is participating already. He will now actually contribute.

They both easily fall back asleep at

five-o'clock: It feels more like a nap after the ninety-minute escapade they just shared. Annie wakes first hearing Mal's morning cries. Luke wakes in an empty bed. Silence finally comes to the home, as he slowly rises out of bed. He heads straight to the shower and turns on the water. Luke's routine is shaving while the water comes to a comfortable temperature. In the shower, he slowly becomes more and more grounded and ready to dress and take on the day. Annie is downstairs, still in her robe, feeding Mal and having a light breakfast of her own, when Luke walks-in dressed.

"Good morning," She says to him.

"Yes…good morning, Annie."

"After this, I have to take my shower. I have already bathed Mal."

"You do that, Annie. I know I needed a shower badly when I woke back up!" Luke smiles at Annie and she smiles back. "I will put Mal in the romper-chair for a little while. She can watch her favorite video and I will make myself a little bite to eat."

"Thank you, Luke."

"Okay, Annie, you're welcome."

Luke pours a coffee and begins to make his breakfast, as Mal giggles at the video. He hears the shower running as he sits down at the table with his bagel with cream cheese. With all the thought behind his eventual actions today still clear in his mind, he finds that he is on autopilot. He goes through the motions without much thought yet manages to find comfort in his actions nonetheless. When Annie returns to the first floor, she is dressed for the day. She picks-up Mal and they sit together in Annie's recliner as Annie enjoys a second cup of tea.

"I am going to work now," Luke says.

"Okay," says Annie, and asks: "How long is your work day today?"

"Oh, I'll be down there for about four or five hours."

"Well, don't work too hard."

They both exchange smiles, as Luke opens the hatch. He descends the ladder, steps into the office and stares at his creation. He strides to his desk and logs-in to the 'Equity' servers before he has the chance to slip into any daydreams. He opens his day planner and reviews the task list he entered last night. He looks it over and knows he can plan to spend almost an entire day on 'Equity' after all. He begins writing query after query that bounce against the databases and return results indicative of each inevitable next step to fulfill the requirements noted last night for 'Equity' today.

He begins by targeting first the membership database and painstakingly pours over every entity, every element and every entity relationship. Luke finishes his priority with only a dozen instances shown in the query results from the membership tables. The next step is crucial in that it involves digging down into the system-related files and operating-system application programs. He intends to download into a private, hidden directory each utility script that could raise a red flag, especially those he wrote himself to clean-up the data space after the incident next door. All the commercial, generally available applications do not stand out, buried deep under the covers of the operating system.

All the homegrown utility scripts become small, tar-balls, or compressed UNIX files that Luke extracts and writes to a compact disc. He spends almost forty-five minutes merely coming-up with a hiding place that convinces and makes him comfortable, in the event of a search. He heads to the vegetable garden. The thought of the police tearing up his home and office is enough to make him ill. He runs upstairs to visit the washroom.

Back in the office, Luke leans back in

his manager's chair, puts his fingers to his forehead and brows, closes his eyes and thinks. What more could there be? What is he missing? He has a tickle in his gut similar to the common sensation people generally have when they feel like they are forgetting something, but they do not know what it is. He stays put and concentrates.

Luke stays right there, still and anxious, until it comes to him. He does not care how long it may take. Discovery is paramount! It occurs to him that it might be something that entered the system remotely. He thinks back to his days at Merck. Did he ever send anything to 'Equity' from there? He may have. Think. Damn it. Think. He comes up empty. There is nothing.

Luke has an idea. He remembers keeping an online log of database and system events in a custom spreadsheet. Records formatted feed an automated sub-system that ultimately writes them to the spreadsheet. Very seldom does Luke ever augment the file manually. He knows where it is, and he navigates to the all-telling log. It is a very long, large report that drops records to the backup system by time – every month after the first eleven.

He begins with the oldest records and works his way to the current ones. Unfortunately, the only way to be sure of the content, every bit of it, is to review the report manually. It contains source of the event, target system file and database entities, date and time stamps, IP addresses, and messages from every targeted element that describe the nature of the action. It all comes back to him as he pages through the report: a hacker penetrated 'Equity' just a few weeks before K1tty invited DrJMrJ over for the meet and greet!

He goes straight to the line items that reflect the actions during the invasion and those following: The source should be the same for all. He laments over his own dangerous loss of sight over this security breach. He forces his mind to snap out of it and on to the analysis at hand. He finds several records and notices that the sender tried to gain access with a hidden IP address. Luke is no man's fool. He has a security and authority firewall that can rebound unidentifiable requests, infiltrates the hacker machine and ultimately returns control to the host security system with the alien IP.

Taken aback and pained, he remembers analyzing this breach the moment he identified it, alerted by the firewall and internet security software. He cannot remember tracing it, but he does remember making a note of his discovery. If he can just remember where in the notes, he will be one-step closer to system cleanliness. That is paramount, but also very important to his cleanliness. He discovers the notes taken in the margins of a hard-copy printout of the online tell-all.

He retrieves the report from the file cabinet he keeps these system-related reports, brings the stack of paper to his desk. He drops it in front of him and rifles through it. He finds the page that he wrote the notes on, and looks. In big, bold hand-written block letters is the name 'HEADLEY!' In the margin where Luke documented 'ACTION PLAN', he sees what he did in response to the attack.

# CHAPTER TWENTY-EIGHT

The team of detectives gather in their case study room, Walsh and McKenzie included. Walsh takes the floor and asks for individual discoveries from everyone, and shares his and McKenzie's team lead discoveries and perceived next steps with the rank investigators. The I.S., extended team members are due to arrive soon, probably right after lunch, to read-out their own points of interest.

Walsh and McKenzie learn, or confirm earlier read-outs, concerning the victim on-line activities. Mrs. Rossinski was indeed an innocent user. Yes, she visited the questionable chat rooms occasionally, but sent and received private chat and email messages, as well. Those recipients and senders are noted being family, co-worker or personal-related. The last duo of detectives raises a potential bombshell. Headley contacted Mrs. Rossinski for the first time just a couple hours before the approximate time of death.

"He writes that he has something of importance to discuss with her." The spokesperson says. "The prose is not verbose, although it reads impatient, urgent and is worded with aggravation. He states that he must speak with her about something extremely important, but says he cannot do it online: He must see her in person."

"Hmmm…Interesting," Walsh replies. "Is there anything else on the victims' activities?"

The I.S., team files through the door and take a place at the conference table. Walsh welcomes the interruption, a little ahead of schedule; they could have something else very telling.

"Walsh…McKenzie…Everyone else…" the lead I.S., man begins with a greeting, "We have for you several topics of interest documented, as discovered, on the hard-drives on Mr. Headley's home computer, as well as his second computer."

"Oh, okay, go right ahead." McKenzie gives up the floor on behalf of his boss and teammates.

"Okay," The team I.S., representative begins. "What we know: Mr. Headley seems a lonely man: His machine is filled with pornography. He particularly enjoyed young girls; the images, be they photographs, video-movies, or historic and bookmarked links clearly illustrate the deceased man's demons. We can go so far as to relay, as the forensic evidence reveals, he did little else on his computer. The exception is his intimate chats, posing as a woman from the city, with Mr. Rossinski. This continued until Mr. Headley's death. This plays along with the variety of the other sexually related articles found on the physical searches of his home, of which you are all clearly aware."

"Right…okay then. Tell me about Mrs. Rossinski's hard drive." Walsh quietly orders.

"Yes, Sir…well, she barely made a dent in her available storage. There does not appear to be stored anything we can honestly introduce as evidentiary. The only exceptions are the messages she received and sent to Mr. Headley leading to their respective demise."

"Have you scoured the second machine taken from Mr. Headley's home?" Walsh asks.

"We have, Sir, although that investigation cannot at this time be regarded as complete just yet."

"Okay, just give us what you do have as of now, please."

"It appears that Mr. Headley was also into computer programming, or at least purchasing or downloading shareware, that indicate he was an amateur hacker. We are finding one black-hat occurrence after another, and still looking. What we have found thus far are malware and viral worms designed to hack into machines that he was indeed trying to attack. That is, the inherent behavior of the cache of applications is to sneak into the targeted system through back-door means and security holes, if he is lucky, through other weaknesses of the target systems."

"Can you tell us, in the simplest terms, the typical modus operandi based in his black-hat attacks?"

"Yes, we can. First, it searches for specific I.P., addresses. Once returned to his system, he used the addresses as key input parameters that open a slot in the targeted system's memory. By nature of the initial access, the network packet creates an open network thread connecting the attacker system and the target system. Finally, but likely ongoing, is the interaction between the two systems that begins, continues and ends by virtue of command-line entries provided by the attacker from the sinister machine."

"What kind of commands have you found?" Walsh asks.

"That is exactly where we are as of now in our analysis and fact-finding tasks, Sir."

"Please call me when you are ready to turn-over that information and whatever else you find that raises interest."

"Yes, Sir, we will do that, of course."

"Thank you very much. You can turn in the written report upon completion of your efforts. Thank you both very, very much."

Walsh continues speaking to his team, thinking aloud for the most part. "That was certainly interesting, huh? I wonder which network or networks Mr. Headley attempted to attack."

"All good questions, Walsh," McKenzie says. "They did say that was their next step, so it shouldn't be long till we find out."

"Right you are, partner."

*

The Information Science team continues to scour Headley's black-hat machine. It becomes apparent to them that Mr. Headley bought and loaded the machine just several weeks ahead of the murders. What is also clear is that he used the illegal applications to obtain entry into one network, only. Oddly and queer, however, the I.P., address of the attacked network cannot be found anywhere in storage or cache memory. This not startling by any means, as I.S., know that owning the black-hat software and proving it is used to attack any specific network are two different beasts. They will scour until they are convinced that the data never was, or no longer exists.

The next logical step in their methodology sequence is to tie any data co-existing between the personal computer systems and the activity and other entities found in their query results against the 'Equity' database. They have discussed and commented on briefly the cooperation Mr. L'Italian exercises. They are thankful for the favor, and can only sense that he may justify it all quite simply. He would obviously want to ward-off any deep searches and-or confiscation of his personal computer, let alone the 'Equity' hardware.

They cannot blame him: Nobody likes their domain all torn-up by the authorities, especially when that search includes aspects of their livelihood…their living, too. Mr. L'Italian has nothing to worry about; at least, not yet. I.S., continue walking through Headley's machine, in search of any field, semaphores left-over in memory, saved parameters related to the hacking sub-systems, and then take the search wider. They have searched the depths, and now it is time to expand the breadth.

They find several text files that each contain an erotic story in one vein or another. It immediately occurs to them that he may have used these dialogs while eliciting cyber-sex over the 'Equity' membership. They turn to the 'Equity' database and query the activities data stores, using non-key parameters taken from the X-rated text files. They find a good number of occurrences, some within the same record, and some in separate records. Bingo!

In moments, they realize that Mr. Headley used several, many different chat handles while employing these sexually charged scripts. All of them smell of suggestion, in the phraseology or word(s) used to formulate each handle. This raises eyebrows and interests between the two-team members.

"So, Mr. Headley was a busy guy, huh?"

# PART III
## EVER AFTER

# CHAPTER TWENTY-NINE

Dawna knows...knew about Stone's online affair with Sweetlilgreek, painfully read the sexting shared between the two. Dawna easily dismisses her own follies simply because anoMan never took her all the way. Each time, they always seemed interrupted with one issue or another. Maybe, that is an unfair view, to a degree, but clearly, Stone spent a lot of energy and sexuality on his electro-girlfriend! Dawna wonders if they ever met in person. She rids herself of the ugly thought immediately.

There is a knock on the door that sounds familiar...the Cops. Stone sleeps through it, and Dawna opens the door a crack. Yep...Cops! Officer Walsh and McKenzie trade pleasantries with the young redhead Dawna, then ask if Stone is available. As she lets them through the door, they see he is asleep in a recliner.

"Ma'am," asks Walsh. "Would you mind gently waking him for us, please?"

"Um, no...I can do that Sir."

Dawna lightly places her hand on Stone's shoulder and whispers to him, "Stone, honey, you have company. Stone, did you hear me?"

"Yes, I am awake now, Dawna." Says Stone with his eyes still closed. "Who is it?"

"It is officers Walsh and McKenzie, babe."

Stone wakes in a start and flips his seat up straight. "Oh, I'm sorry. I must have dozed-off."

"No problem, Mr. Rossinski. Once you get your head together, would you mind coming to the station to answer a few questions?"

"No, I wouldn't. So, you have questions about what?"

"Let's keep it that until we get to the office."

"Should Dawna come, too?"

"No. Let's keep it between you and us for the time being."

"Okay, I will be right back. I would like to wash my face."

"Go right ahead, Mr. Rossinski...we're not going to a wedding, though."

Everyone laughs at that, though deep down

Dawna feels queasy. Stone returns, washed-up, brushed hair and a change of shirt.

"We should have him back soon, Dawna," Says Walsh.

Dawna kisses Stone on the cheek, saying, "Bye Babe."

"Bye Dawn."

The three men file out the front door; McKenzie has a hold on Stone's bicep.

Dawna runs to the bathroom.

*

Walsh leads Stone into a rather small interrogation room, and motions him to have a seat across the table opposite him. Walsh, then, without a word, turns to go out the door. The two lead investigators sit watching the camera images and through the one-way glass at Stone's body language.

"He's sweating, Walsh."

"Profusely, I'd say."

"He is fidgeting, too."

"That, he is, McKenzie."

Stone sits and waits, elbows on the table and head in hands hiding his face. His knees bounce up and down on the balls of his feet in ferocity. Fifteen minutes pass and Walsh announces, "I am going to start on him now."

There is no wall clock in the interrogation room, so the fifteen minutes seems more like an hour to Stone. Walsh enters the small room and sits down. McKenzie watches closely the body language displayed by Mr. Rossinski. Walsh stares into Stone's eyes for several seconds that of course pass like minutes to Stone.

"I suppose you might be asking yourself why we brought you in, eh, Mr. Rossinski."

"Well, yes, of course I am."

"Let's talk in general terms about your activities over the weekend your Ex-wife was murdered...Please, go ahead."

"I picked the children up at our agreed-upon time – six-thirty – that Friday evening. We spent the night at home. Dawna was there, too, of course. We planned on surprising the kids with a trip to Sesame Place on Saturday."

"And how did that work-out?"

"We booked a room between Sesame Place and Battleship Cove."

"The kids were excited about our trip to Sesame Place, once they quickly discovered, or more extracted the plan out of us!"

"But, they had no idea about Battleship Cove?"

"No they did not – none whatsoever. They were ecstatic, however, once we had no choice to give-in, pulling into the parking lot!"

"Did anything happen out of the ordinary, Mr. Rossinski?"

"I remember the day being so excruciatingly hot that we were all soaking in sweat and dragging along for as long as we could. The standout thought is that Brian could not get enough of meeting all her favorite characters, regardless of the heat. Timmy however was terrified at the characters – their being so much bigger than they are on the Television."

"How did you handle that?"

"We explained to Brian that we could do one more ride, then we had to drive back home. He was fine with that, if not a little relieved to know he would soon be in an air-conditioned car."

"What time did you arrive home?"

"We were there by about two o'clock. Dawna had to wash all their weekend clothes – sending the boys and their clothes home spic and span was a rule upon which we agreed. I bathed the kids while she did the laundry."

"So, your habit was to have them back to your ex-wife's house by six-fifteen – six-thirty in the evening?"

"Yes...always."

"Mr. Rossinski, do you have ticket stubs and credit card receipts reflecting your activities and hotel room?"

"Oh gawd...I am terrible at keeping up with anything financial in nature. I cannot be sure right now, but I think I would have, or probably handed them all over to Dawna."

"I will ask her when I bring you back home. I am switching gears now, okay"

"How did your Ex-wife make you feel when she caught you?"

"I reflected an arrogant and aloof reaction, but truthfully, I felt humiliated, embarrassed and angry. I still have no idea how she knew we were there."

"Mr. Rossinski, what does the name Sweetlilgreek mean to you?"

"Ugh! Please!"

"Is there a problem Mr. Rossinski?"

"I met her on the Internet. I was separated, eventually divorced from Kat, but I had a girlfriend living with me."

"Do you know where she is from?"

"She told me New York City."

"What happened to her?

"Well, Dawna caught wind of the affair in a Private Message from 'Equity'."

"I kept my online activities very limited after that happened, but when I did go back to look for her, she appeared to have disappeared."

"Do you remember hen that was?"

"Yes, the weekend of the murders, Sir."

"I think you've had enough, and I want you to know we all appreciate your full cooperation. Thank you. Let's get you back home now."

Walsh gets out of the car with Stone. He has to question Dawna about the receipts. Stone forgot all about them. Dawna is troubled; she has no idea what she may have done with them. She looks in all the obvious places, as well as a few obscure spaces. She feels she is letting everyone down.

"I am so sorry, officer, I can't seem to find them anywhere."

"Don't be upset Ma'am, it was a shot in the dark – nobody saves receipts anymore! Ha!"

"Thank you so much for understanding."

"Finally, Mr. Rossinski, I am obligated to read you your Miranda Rights.

- Anything you say or do can and will be used against you in a court of law.

- You have the right to consult an attorney before speaking to the police and to have an attorney present during questioning now or in the future.

- If you cannot afford an attorney, one will be appointed for you before any questioning, if you wish.

- If you decide to answer any questions now, without an attorney present, you will still have the right to stop answering at any time until you talk to an attorney.

- Knowing and understanding your rights as I have explained them to you, are you willing to answer my questions without an attorney present?"

"Why?" Stone asks.

"We have information and evidence that potentially tie you to the murder of Mrs. Kat Rossinski."

"But…but…I…"

"Be quiet, Stone!" Dawna says. "I will call

for an attorney, referenced by your divorce lawyer. I am sure he has a colleague that will be willing to help you."

"Okay...okay." Stone is breathing hard and heavy and the perspiration is dripping down every part of his being. He is trembling.

"Calm down honey," Dawna tries to soothe her man. "Everything will be fine."

"You will face the Judge in the morning for arraignment, Mr. Rossinski. Walsh continues. "It is your choice to continue to cooperate, or, to layer-up before we are entitled to ask you anything. Do you understand your rights, clearly, and what I just explained to you?"

"Yes I do, Sir."

# CHAPTER THIRTY

"Will the defendant please rise?"

The attorney and Rossinski both stand up. The Judge reads the charges to Mr. Rossinski.

"Do you understand the charges, Mr. Rossinski?"

"Yes, I do your Honor."

"And what do you plea?"

The Attorney standing with Stone whispers in his ear, "Say, 'Not Guilty, your honor'."

"Not guilty, your Honor."

"Very well then, you will receive a date for the Grand Jury Hearing in the mail soon. Court adjourned!"

*

The Court releases Stone on his own

recognizance. When he returns home, Dawna wants to hear all about it…everything!

"Dawna, it's been a tough day, please read for yourself the packet I received that covers every aspect of the procedures."

"Okay honey. I'm sorry."

She reads, not skipping or skimming a single subject.

Intake

The Criminal Division of the State Superior Court manage criminal complaints from the time they lodge to their resolution or "disposition." The accused, or "defendant" is charged with an offense because of a formal complaint issued by a law enforcement agent or a citizen who believes an offense has been committed against their person or property. It can also result from an "indictment" by a panel of citizens gathered to consider evidence, called a "grand jury." Arrests can occur at the scene of a crime or based on warrants or sworn statements ordering a court appearance. All arrests must be based on "probable cause," or reasonable grounds to believe that an offense has been committed, and the defendant may have committed the offense. Complaints state the reasons for the charge, and refer to offenses listed in the "New Jersey Code of Criminal Justice" (Title 2C) that includes all of the

Criminal offenses are heard, or considered in Superior Court, and are more serious than non-criminal charges heard in municipal courts where the offense occurred. Defendants found guilty, or "convicted" of crimes face more serious consequences, with punishments spanning probation supervision and fines to the loss of liberty through confinement for a year or more. Crimes are classified by degree. Degrees range from first to fourth degree offenses. A First degree crime carries the potential penalty of 10-20 years in prison. A Second degree crime carries a potential penalty of 5-10 years. Defendants who are convicted of first and second-degree crimes face a presumptive term of incarceration. It is assumed that they will be sentenced to serve time in prison. A Third degree crime may result in 3-5 years if convicted, while Fourth degree crimes carry a potential penalty of up to 18 months in jail. There is a presumption of non-custodial sentences on third and 4th degree offenses.

Complaints heard in municipal courts are "disorderly persons" offenses or "petty disorderly persons" violations, which carry less restrictive punishments upon conviction. Disorderly person's offenses may be sentenced to up to 6 months in a county jail. Petty disorderly convictions may render up to 30 days in jail.

First Appearance

Once a complaint is issued, defendants are either arrested or issued a summons or notice to appear in municipal or Superior Court on a first appearance. If they fail to appear, a warrant may be issued for the accused's arrest by a judge if there is proof of service, or evidence that the accused received the summons or notice and failed to appear. At the first court appearance, defendants are advised of their rights. Their bail is reviewed.

Bail

Bail is required to be set within twelve hours of the issuance of a complaint. All defendants have a right to bail under our state constitution. If bail is posted, defendants are released until the charges listed in the complaint are resolved. Defendants can be required to post funds or property to assure that they will appear in court in the future. They may be required to deposit funds or property in exchange for a promise to appear. If defendants have significant ties to the community, or no criminal history, they may be considered for a Release on Own Recognizance or R.O.R., which is an affidavit certifying that they are aware of the charges, levied against them, and will appear in court to face them. Defendants may also be required to give a personal bond, which is a promise to appear or face a judgment, whereby a specified amount of money is forfeited. Some defendants pay a bail bondsman to post funds on their behalf. These defendants may be ordered to post a higher bail, or have no bail set. They will remain in jail until the charges are disposed. If they are released and appear in court as required, bail money may be refunded in full upon case resolution or disposition. Once defendants are released, bail is discharged to the surety.

Bail Investigations

A Superior Court judge of the Criminal Division may order bail investigations. Criminal Division bail investigators or case supervisors collect information on the defendant's ties or standing in the community. Identifying information is collected, including the names, addresses dates of birth, employment, criminal record, mental health and drug abuse history. Professionals working for the court conduct these investigations. They investigate and report on a defendant's amenability to bail. Bail investigation reports consider the seriousness of the offense and the severity of punishment upon conviction, as well as the defendant's family ties and financial status. All of these factors are considered in light of the probability that the defendant will appear for trial or other court events. Case supervisors or bail investigators report to the judge, who hears evidence from the defense and prosecution and decides the amount and form of bail to be set, if any.

Right to Counsel

At their first appearance, defendants are advised of their right to counsel. This means that they are entitled to have an attorney represent them and answer the charges. If they indicate that they are unable to afford an attorney, Criminal Division staff is assigned to conduct indigence investigations. These investigations consider defendants' assets and liabilities, and recommend that cases be assigned to a public defender if a defendant is unable to afford a private attorney. Private attorneys are usually either self-employed or work for private law firms who charge an hourly rate for services.

In making indigence determinations, Criminal Division staff considers defendants' ability to post bail, the amount of bail posted, the willingness of friends and family members to pay for an attorney, and any factor related to a defendant's claim of impoverishment. They review tax returns, credit and wage records and any other relevant information regarding the ability of defendants to hire their own attorneys. If a defendant is declared indigent, a public defender or "pool attorney" will handle the case until it is resolved, by a "plea", "downgrade," "dismissal, or Pretrial Intervention", or "trial" through a sentencing process. Some downgraded cases are ordered, or "remanded" back to the local municipal court for disposition. A local public defender may be assigned to the case by the magistrate.

If an investigation reveals assets or it is determined that a defendant has some means to pay for an attorney, the criminal case supervisor will recommend that a defendant's application for indigent defense services be denied. A Criminal Division judge may rule on the recommendation, ordering a defendant to hire an attorney, allow "pro-se" or "self" representation, or order a defendant to consult attorneys who may take their case at a reduced rate. Over 85% of all criminal cases have a public defender assigned.

Substance Abuse Evaluations

According to state and federal estimates, up to 70% of all persons charged with a criminal offense are impaired with drugs during the crime. Substance abuse evaluators interview defendants charged with drug and property offenses to determine the extent of their involvement with addictive drugs. Working within the Criminal Division's Treatment Assessment Services for the Courts (TASC), these professional evaluators interview defendants, subject them to urine screening to identify current drug use, and prepare drug assessments or reports for criminal judges, detailing drug abuse histories, identifying treatment needs and recommending counseling at local drug and alcohol treatment centers when support is needed to overcome addiction. Judges may order defendants into drug or alcohol treatment as a condition of their bail or probation. This program is resourceful to judges when determining appropriate community support systems for defendants who are released from jail. Failure to complete treatment may result in sanctions, including bail or probation revocation with a loss of liberty. For some defendants who suffer from severe drug addiction, receiving treatment arranged and mandated by the courts becomes not only a choice between jail and community living, but one of life or death. The program is expanding and has provided judges with an option to interfere with a cycle of arrest and drug abuse that threatened to smother the judicial system in 1989-90 with a colossal backlog of drug cases.

Pre-Indictment Events

Trial Case Dispositions

Downgrades & Dismissals

Following the filing of a complaint and the first court appearance, the prosecutor's office in each county determines whether to pursue a criminal complaint. Prosecutors determine if cases have merit and sufficient evidence to pursue a conviction. In most counties, the prosecutor's Case Screening Unit reviews police reports and interviews victims and witnesses to determine if the original charges will be prosecuted. If there is insufficient evidence, the charges are downgraded to disorderly persons offenses and "remanded" or sent to the municipal courts for a hearing or dismissed. In some counties, prosecutors pre-screen potential Superior Court filings before a complaint is signed.

Plea Bargains

In many cases, the prosecutor and a defendant's lawyer will negotiate a plea bargain. In a plea agreement, the prosecutor may offer the accused an arrangement where s/he will recommend a reduced term of incarceration or probation in exchange for a guilty plea. In some instances, the charges are reduced or dismissed as part of the plea bargain. Maximum sentence terms may also be part of negotiated agreements. Criminal Division individual judge teams, managed by team leaders, coordinate court dates with the prosecutor and the defense attorney regarding the plea agreement and establish a court date for the plea to be entered.

Defendants entering a plea must sign a statement certifying that they understand the plea and are entering into the agreement voluntarily and without pressure from the prosecution or their own attorney. They also acknowledge that the Criminal Division judges are not bound by the agreement when deciding and rendering sentences. If a judge perceives that the plea bargain is too lenient, the judge can reject the plea and order the prosecution and defense parties to renegotiate, or order the matter set down for trial. 30% of all complaints are settled through pretrial programs and negotiations. After a criminal case is indicted, over 70% are resolved without proceeding to a full trial.

The Criminal Practice Division of the Administrative Office of the Courts tracks all criminal cases in all counties from the time a complaint is issued to its disposition. If some courts have persistent backlogs, an analysis of the system can be made through the division's statewide criminal case computer network known as Promise Gavel. Methods for reducing backlogs can be formulated by the Conference of Presiding Judges and Criminal Division managers, or local speedy trial coordinating committees led by criminal presiding judges.

Defendants pleading guilty because of the plea agreement must acknowledge their plea in open court. Defendants who plead guilty after plea negotiations do not surrender their right to appeal their convictions to the Appellate Division of Superior Court.

Defendants pleading guilty to crimes are subject to a Presentence Investigation, conducted by probation officers or case supervisors on the judge's team in the Criminal Division.

Pre Trial Intervention Program (PTI)

Criminal Division Case Supervisors conduct investigations on adult defendants who apply for Pretrial Intervention. This is a diversionary program that permits certain defendants to avoid formal prosecution and conviction by entering into a term of court-supervised community living, often with counseling or other support. Criminal Division Managers direct this program. Case supervisors prepare reports to aid the Criminal Division Manager and the prosecutor in deciding whether to recommend approval and for criminal judges determining if defendants will be admitted. Defendants opting for this program apply directly to Criminal Division Management. Case supervisors conduct investigations into the history of all applicants, to ensure their eligibility. Admission to the program requires the consent of the prosecutor, the Criminal Division Manager and the criminal judge.

Defendants charged with violent offenses generally are not admitted. Probationers and parolees are also generally excluded, since they have prior convictions. Persons accused of racketeering or organized crime are generally not admitted, as well as public officials who are accused of abusing their positions for personal gain against the public trust. Prosecutors must be consulted before an applicant charged with a first or second-degree crime can even be considered for PTI.

The objective of PTI is to provide an incentive for first time non-violent offenders to rehabilitate. Conditions attached to judicial orders for pretrial intervention may require defendants to obtain a substance abuse evaluation from TASC, participate in substance abuse or mental health counseling or community service, submit to urine testing, pay restitution and fines, or give up a firearm or driver's license. Participants have criminal charges formally suspended for up to three years. Once a participant completes the program, charges are dismissed. However, if defendants fail to complete special conditions attached to their term of PTI supervision, the participant can be terminated from the program, triggering a resumption of the formal criminal process. These defendants may face indictment and trial, and if convicted, face the penalties prescribed by the criminal code. The Administrative Office of the Courts maintains a computer registry of all PTI applicants, to ensure a person is not admitted into PTI more than once.

For More Information, Contact Your Local Superior Court Criminal Division.

The Grand Jury

If a criminal case has not been, downgraded, diverted or dismissed, the prosecutor will present the case to a grand jury for an indictment. The grand jury is composed of a group of citizens who have been selected from voter registration, driver's license and tax lists. The grand jury considers evidence presented by the county prosecutor and determines if there is sufficient evidence to formally charge defendants and require them to respond to the charge(s). An indictment is not a finding of guilt. Generally, neither the accused nor their attorneys are present. Witnesses normally testify regarding the crime. After considering evidence, if a majority of the 23 jurors votes to indict defendants, they must face further criminal proceedings. The return of an indictment is called a true bill. If a majority finds the evidence to be insufficient to indict, the grand jury enters a no bill and the charge(s) are dismissed. The jury may, however, decide to charge defendants with a less serious offense, to be downgraded or remanded to the municipal court. The accused must appear in municipal court to face a disorderly persons or petty disorderly persons charge.

The Indictment Process

If a criminal case has not been downgraded, diverted, dismissed, or pled out the prosecutor will present the case to a grand jury for an indictment. The grand jury is composed of a group of citizens who have been selected from voter registration lists. It is their civic duty to serve. They consider evidence presented by the county prosecutor and determine if there is sufficient evidence to formally charge the defendant and oblige him to respond to the charge(s). The indictment is not a finding of guilt or a conviction. Neither the accused nor his attorney is present. Witnesses may testify regarding the crime. Defendants may testify, however, if they are requested to attend and elect to surrender their right against self-incrimination as guaranteed by the constitution. After considering the prosecutor's evidence and the testimony of witnesses, if a majority of the 23 jurors vote to indict the defendant, he must face further criminal action. This finding is a true bill that triggers further proceedings in the Criminal Superior Court. If a majority finds the evidence to be insufficient to indict, the grand jury enters a no bill and the charge(s) are dismissed. The jury may, however, decide to charge the defendant with a less serious offense, to be heard in municipal court. In this instance, the offense has been downgraded or remanded. The accused must appear in municipal court to face a disorderly persons or petty disorderly persons charge.

The Pre-Arraignment Conference and the Arraignment

Within twenty-one days of the return of an indictment, a pre-arraignment conference is held. Criminal Division Staff schedule this pre-arraignment conference. Defendants may wish to apply for public defender representation at this point, if they are not yet represented. Prior to this conference, discovery or evidence is available to defense counsel. This exchange of evidence provides the defense with an opportunity to review the evidence the prosecution intends to use against the accused prior to the conference. After reviewing the discovery provided prior to the pre arraignment conference, defendants may decide to apply for Pretrial Intervention, or to enter plea bargain negotiations. Defendants may also indicate their intention to plead guilty to the charge for which they were indicted.

## Arraignment/Status Conference Standards

A formal arraignment occurs no later than 50 days after an indictment. Upon notification by the Criminal Division, defendants must appear and face formal notification of their charges. They may plead guilty at this point, either to the charges listed in the indictment, or to revised charges resulting from plea negotiations. If plea negotiations are ongoing, the parties may review the status of the plea offer. Defendants may also opt to apply for the Pretrial Intervention program at this juncture, or be admitted into the program if they have not applied prior to arraignment. If a guilty plea is entered at the formal arraignment, Criminal Division judges order a presentence investigation to be conducted by Criminal Division case supervisors. Sentencing will follow the presentence investigation, generally 4 to 6 weeks after convictions.

Status Conferences and the Pretrial Conference

Defendants who have pleaded not guilty at this point may continue plea negotiations or preparation for trial. Pretrial case resolutions may occur at a status conference, where a defendant may decide to enter a guilty plea with or without a negotiated plea bargain.

At Pretrial Conferences, defendants may enter a guilty plea to the charges. At the Pretrial Conference, there is a plea cutoff date, after which no further plea negotiations can occur. If no agreement to plead guilty is reached, the matter will proceed to trial. Criminal Division staff track conferences to ensure that cases are moving without undue delays. The Administrative Office of the Courts evaluates statistics entered by Criminal Division staff in each criminal court to stay abreast of overall case movements statewide. The Criminal Practice Division assists local court staff to address backlogs if they should occur.

Trials

Defendants have a constitutional right to a jury trial, but may opt to forego this right in favor of a trial by a judge in the Law Division of Superior Court, Criminal Part. Once a case has been decided, there are two outcomes. Defendants are found either guilty or not guilty by a jury or judge. Normally, an acquitted person has no further obligation to the court, unless they face new charges. Prosecutors have no right to appeal acquittals, and defendants may not be charged twice for the same offense. Defendants who are found guilty or convicted face sentencing, where the judge who tried the case renders punishments. Once a trial is concluded, criminal judges order a presentence investigation by the Criminal Division on all defendants who have been convicted. Judges set a date for sentencing.

## Presentence Investigations, Reports and Sentencing

Criminal Division case supervisors perform presentence investigations for criminal judges who render sentences on all convicted defendants. The presentence investigation report is designed to assist a judge in weighing the circumstances of the crime and a defendant's criminal and juvenile record and overall life situation to the severity of the sentence. The investigative reports provide a uniform assessment of a defendant's overall family, medical and criminal background. Offense circumstances are summarized, as well as statements received from victims and their families. Assessments of drug abuse history and the amenability to probation supervision and treatment are addressed. Financial conditions of defendants are considered, since most sentences involve a fine, penalty, restitution or reimbursement to a victim. Assessments of defendants' situations and their suitability for probation are also discussed. Reports generally recommend either prison or probation. Judges are obviously not bound by their advice, but their insight is essential in the criminal sentencing process.

Judges consider the degree of harm and hardship imposed on victims and their families. Mitigating factors or reasons explaining the crime in the light of a defendant's past or present circumstances weigh against aggravating factors, which are elements that speak to the severity of the crime. Prior criminal record weighs heavily, and is an indicator of a defendant's potential for rehabilitation based on his history, as well as the risk posed for another crime if probation is ordered.

In most cases, sentencing judges have some discretion or choices on how they will sentence convicted criminals within the parameters of the Criminal Code. This discretion may extend to whether a defendant must serve time in prison, or receive a term of probation. Of course, a judge's discretion may be limited if there is a plea agreement which contains a sentencing recommendation. Some crimes, such as convictions for using a gun during a robbery, carry mandatory prison terms, where, the judge must sentence a criminal to prison for at least a minimum term.

Post-Conviction Motions

Defendants who are convicted of crimes may appeal their cases to the

Appellate Division of Superior Court, which reviews trial records and decides if decisions made by judges in the Superior Court are fair and equitable. Defendants may file motions, or requests to their sentencing judge to have sentences modified, or for other relief.

## Teams in Criminal Division Case Processing

Some Criminal Division offices are organized into "teams." There are individual judge teams, where each criminal judge is assigned a team leader with a team of clerical staff, a court clerk, a group of case supervisors and investigators who perform all the work on the cases to be heard by the team's trial judge. Each team conducts calendar management, or scheduling of all court events for that particular judge. The team also performs pretrial intervention and presentence investigations for one judge, as well as courtroom support, computer data entry,

Manages active court files and records and coordinates court dates with prosecutors and public defenders, who are assigned to their judge. Team members work in unison, and one member can generally perform the work of any member within that team. Their familiarity with each other's work and their judge improves efficiency and reduces wasted time. The team process helps to ease the anonymous and crowded nature of a high volume judicial system, as members become accustomed to working in harmony and are accountable for all cases.

*

"Oh my gawd, Stone!" exclaims Dawna. That was a headful of information: 'No wonder he is snoring-I am about to doze-off, too!' She is surprised at how poorly the rules of grammar are in that document. It just adds to the convolution and legalese, and takes away from the readability! In addition, she thought she was going to read it twice through…to get a complete and better understanding. Hah! There is no fucking way. She gets the general idea and stress points, which are the most important to know, necessarily for now. She worries that, on top of all else, reading that guide will make poor Stone's head explode into black confetti!

Dawna leaves Stone to sleep in his chair: He looks so comfortable there. She hates to wake him. She creeps down the hall to get ready for bed. He is still asleep in the recliner, but she is sure he will crawl into bed should he awake in the night. Jumbles of legalities ride a death cage around her mind. She cannot sleep. She does not know how he can, either, but he sat through an interrogation and everything else, so this well-deserved rest comes easier than one might think it would…or could.

Dawna wakes alone in bed, does her morning thing, and goes out to the living room. Stone looks as though he had not moved an inch since last night. The poor man…he looks dead. Why did that thought have to come to mind? She is careful to make as little noise as possible in the kitchen while she makes coffee and puts the clean dishes away from yesterday. She will let him sleep as long as he will. He needs it.

Sitting in her corner spot on the couch, it finally hits Dawna like a hammer on head. He is the prime suspect, even though she has not heard anyone announce it in that way, yet. Tears leak from her eyes and she whimpers like a young, hungry kitten. At the same time, she cannot help but wonder…what if? She reviews life in their home since the discovery. He has turned into a new person, and not in a good way, either. He quakes with anxiety, he has contracted essential tremors, and he has become low, down low and lethargic.

Dawna feels scared…afraid…it came from

nowhere. No, it came directly from the fear she holds inside. It is finally escaping from the denial that has been hiding behind the walls of her mind. It is like a severe case of vasculitis, the white blood cells stuck leaving no immune system. The guilt sets-in for her even entertaining these thoughts. Nevertheless, her parents taught her long ago the benefits of being a realist.

Should she be scared? Should she run? Should she stand by her man? Should she do and say anything to save him? Does he need saving? Does he need prayers? Does he have a price to pay? She is sobbing now, sniffling and her head is throbbing. Stone sleeps on. Dawna slowly shuffles back to the bedroom, all of a sudden feeling haggard and confused. She huddles all the pillows around her and falls asleep within moments. Her deep dreams let her fall with them. She wants to float gently down like a feather, but she is in a freefall and sees only ugly reflections on her way down.

# CHAPTER THIRTY-ONE

Annie makes sub-sandwiches while Mal looks on from her table, and Luke works as hard as he has ever had sweeping his office. He is certain he never hided anything outside the desk drawers. The desk-drawers are a complete mess, though, and it is up to him and him alone to sweep them out impeccably. Of course that will come only after he empties each one and either brushes the page off, or shreds it.

He hears the hatch open, and unlike the usual beckoning, Annie tells him in a subdued, quiet way that it is time for lunch. Instead of feeling annoyed at the interruption – no matter the soft-spoken mode – he feels relieved and soothed. He needs a rest. He needs to further plan. He needs to think. He needs to be.

"Oh, Annie, these are great subs!"

"Thanks Luke," she replies. "Let's see how Mal does with it!" Annie laughs.

"Annie, I would like to take a short nap, and then go back downstairs to finish-up for the day. Will you wake me in about an hour and a half?"

"Sure – where will you nap…upstairs or down here?"

"Living room, I think."

"Okay," Annie sounds a little challenged. "I will keep Mal as quiet as possible."

"Thanks, babe…that would be great!"

It takes mere moments for Luke to doze-off, feet up and arms folded across his chest. He begins to dream. The dream is of him cleaning the office – exactly what he had been doing before lunch! Even in the dream state, he realizes how weird it seems…weird it is. A big difference is that he dreams of surprisingly finding what appears to be something crucial to the crime. It just will not come to him! Damn it…Come on! This hurdle is strong enough in sleep to make it nearly impossible for him to rest at all anymore. Yet, he remains there, eyes closed and head open.

Annie comes to wake him, and he is more than ready to get up. She wants to know if he slept well, and he lies and says, "Yes-Okay."

"All ready for work, now, Luke?"

"Yes…As ready as I'll ever be." He laughs.

Luke walks slowly to the hatch and pulls it open. Annie does not notice that he accidentally slid down the ladder. He could have been hurt, but is not. He shakes it off and sits at his desk, still bothered by loose strings hanging in front of him. They tie to balloons and he is as nervous as he has ever been. Terrified of the balloons exploding… popping! He is losing it. There is something left hanging, something of importance…but what? Damn it all: What is it? The feeling is so strong he believes he actually sees to strings hanging don all around him from the floating balloons.

*THIS…is NOT good!*

He draws one blank after another, due to his nervous tension. He remembers going through the entire desk, the file cabinet. Wait…Did he go through the filing cabinet? He is certain he must have. Besides that, the cabinet is all and nothing more than paperwork he is required to save for different lengths of time depending on the content. He falls into his chair, almost falling all the way back over to the floor. He starts yet but just for a moment. He talks himself into knowing he covered all his bases.

He goes upstairs and sneaks through the hatch. He steps into the living room.

"Is Mal napping well?" Luke whispers to Annie.

"She is out like a light, Luke. Why?"

"Let's go upstairs for a while."

"You mean that you want to fool-around?" Annie cannot help but smirk and smile.

"Shall I spell it out for you, dear?"

This time, Luke takes the lead. He turns her around – back to his front. He disrobes her slowly, and by the time he is done, he fingers her nipples until they are hard and firm. He then runs his hands up and down her legs. On the way up, he spreads her cheeks and runs a finger from pussy to neck – through her ass crack and up the middle of her back. She moans. He blindfolds her and cuffs her hands above her head, before giving her a little shove onto the bed. He ties the cuffs, but leaves her legs loose.

He has wanted to break out his new box of toys for her forever. The time has come today. He is horny, and she definitely is now. Luke takes his feather and does a light full body treatment. Then, surprisingly so, begins to lightly strap her…her tits, her ear end, then goes back to caressing her with his hands. He kisses the longest soul kiss ever while he gently runs a finger up het slit. He touches her clit very now and again, which elicits a moan of pleasure from Annie. He works magic with his mouth over her nipples and fingers. Finally, what she waits for comes.

Luke takes the entire vulva in his mouth, sucking it all in. He uses his tongue to dart and massage her puss and tongues her pee hole. It drives her mad – for this is a first for her! Finally, he gives it to her. He muckles onto her clit, and sucks and tongue-flicks, slow, then fast, and then fastest as Annie shakes and quakes in climax. Luke puts two fingers into her and finds her G-spot. He wastes no time building up speed and sucking on her clit. Before either knows, what happens, Annie is screaming, and then… not just a little… freaks them both out by squirting. It goes on repeatedly accompanied by a scream each time. They and the bedding are extremely wet. Luke begs and urges her not to be embarrassed: That is what he was after.

The noise in Mommy and Daddy's room wake Mal. She is making impatient noises, which also signal she is near the point of crying. Annie takes a rinse – the fastest she ever has. Luke strips the bed, then, once Annie has a hold on Mal, follows Annie into the shower. He plans to carry the sheets downstairs after his rinse. He did not climax in bed, so without much thought, jerks-off in the shower.

*

Luke and Annie remain quiet about the exotic episode they experienced earlier. He simply waits for her to make the first mention. She is still recovering from the incident. Unlike her usual self, she does not feel freaked-out by it or embarrassed. She feels sexier than she had in months: So does he. Ever since Martha being put away, and Kat's disappearance, sexuality has finally returned to the L'Italian home, and neither partner could be happier!

Luke's sexual confidence and experience does not surprise Annie at all – that is, his ability to please. Luke wonders how far Annie will go with it all. He decides he will take her up degree by degree to the point where she has no inhibition left in her. He will strip her of her shyness and timidity, slow and steady, and make her know it is not wrong to look, to talk, to direct, and most of all, let it all out…let it go!

That is the kind of sex life he wants and needs. She will soon discover the pinnacle of pleasure it all can bring. She does not know about the collection of toys he bought for her long ago. Nor, is she aware of the bag full of movies. Each or one of each will periodically make an appearance to raise the mood. A movie here may be what they enjoy.

A toy there may do the trick. Maybe both at once will one day be in order! He wants to try mutual masturbation, but plans to wait until Annie loosens up just a little bit more.

They do both agree that skin-to-skin is the best, but they also realize the fun they can have with their sex toys. She learns quite quickly that a blind fold and cuffs above the head turns her on. Therefore, every third or fourth night, he positions her that way. That is when he finds it best to try out the different toys. She likes the Rabbit a lot! She also likes his dick-chin toy. He takes it slow. He has plenty of time and plenty of toys. However, his fantasy is to double-penetrate her. He is positive she will hit the ceiling. In due time, he is sure… in due time.

# CHAPTER THIRTY-TWO

walsh begins to lose patience waiting for more forensics from Mr. Headley's second machine – in light nicknamed his 'sand-box.' Headley's personal computer reflected the sinister acts of deceit between him and Mr. Rossinski. There were much more; mostly neighborhood women, but Rossinski is the man of interest for now. They carefully plan time to spend together, and never a conversation goes by they do not text to climax. It is quite odd that Mr. Headley usually plays 'the woman' in the fantasies.

The investigators dissect messages from members of 'Equity,' each as long and mischievous as the next. Most appear to be typical hetrosexual online affairs for the sake of relief and not much more. There are clean conversations, as well, but even they ultimately lead to sex. All those around walsh's table agree that there are some pretty lazy and veiled men out there! It is the same almost everywhere and almost everyone. Love lives thrive in newlyweds, but once childbirth and rearing all but destroys mother's body, men sadly, lose all interest in them.

There are examples that differ. Some of the younger generation take seriously fitness, and are quite athletic. They obviously do this to keep their partners satisfied in hopes there is some reciprocity. Simply stated, it is all about the sex. The elder generations continue to fulfill their respective manly or womanly duties no matter what. This may be love – of a sort.

"Rossinski's girlfriend is clean as a whistle, if we go by her computer usage and habits." Walsh says.

"None of my boys came-up with anything, Sir." McKenzie says.

"What could have happened to Sweetlilgreek?" Walsh asks no one in particular. "She comes up on no reports extracted from 'Equity.' I do mean NONE. No initial membership or any activity at all, outside of her exchanges with Mr. Rossinski."

"Well, sir, you know there plenty of nerds out there that like doing nothing more than to hack into compelling and perilous networks, no matter the pay-off."

"Yeah, McKenzie," Walsh looks up. "I know."

*

Walsh calls Ernie into his office. Ernie is just outside it so just has to turn the corner to enter. They exchange greetings. Ernie asks Walsh how the case is coming along. Walsh wishes he had better news, but admittedly, they are getting somewhere. The evidence is coming in slow. Nevertheless, it is coming. In addition, they have yet to hear the read-out on the sandbox!

"Hey, Ernie...I need to talk to you. It has to remain between us *only* for now. Can you handle that?"

"Yes, Sir," replies Ernie. "Of course I can!"

"Good. This is case-related, but it is a hunch. The kind of hunch that feels like a bug in your pants, you know?"

"I assure you that you can count on me to help...whatever it is."

"Okay now. This is on the sly – got it?"

"Yes, Sir...Go ahead."

Walsh explains to Ernie what he wants done. He wants a tertiary search of Mrs. Rossinski's bathroom and bedroom. Any disruption, under the sink, in the hamper, in the linen closet;

report it. Walsh asks Ernie to look into Mrs. Rossinski's drawers, particularly her underwear drawer. Both eyes open, Ernie is to bring back on a report of any sign of disarray. Finally, Walsh asks Ernie to look closely inside the bottom nightstand drawer. He is to look for *anything*; hair…flakes of dead skin or whatever…anything and everything.

"Consider it done, Sir!"

"Okay, bring anything found directly to me in plastic, inside paper."

Ernie drives easy down the couple of blocks to the Rossinski house. Key in hand, he slips through the front door and following orders, walks straight up the stairs. It is no easy feat to judge whether a hamper has been rummaged-through or not, and likewise no easier identifying anything out-of-place in an underwear drawer.

He imagines the type of disturbances Walsh is looking-for. Ernie, painstakingly sorts through the hamper. This is worse than a math test! Eventually, he is able to ascertain that laundry was a twice a week chore. With that denominator identified, he realizes what could well be a telling clue bubbling to the top. He writes on his report that there appears to be one pair of woman's underwear missing.

Ernie carefully counts the underwear and

bra combinations. The apparent evidentiary thought is that she recently bought two new sets each of tops and bottoms. The bottoms are there, but the bottoms are not. He drives back to see Lieutenant Walsh, carries the rather small bundles in, and talks through his experience and the notes he took in the house.

Walsh is satisfied with the job Ernie performed...happy. Another memo comes up from the coroner. Mrs. Rossinski was not wearing her birth control diaphragm at the time of death. One of two things, more than likely, is that it got old and she disposed of it or either it is missing or lost. It is an even further stretch to play-out the missing pair of new underwear.

*

Mr. Rossinski and Sweetlilgreek certainly kept each other hot and sexually charged and active during the few weeks leading to the crimes. At Walsh's age, he can't help but wonder...how, why he would wrap himself up in what seems like a seedy and nasty online fling with someone as cute as Dawna at home. She is so adorable!

# CHAPTER THIRTY-THREE

It truly seems that the good old days between Stone and Dawna are finally back. Well, at least they are not clear off or away from them anymore. The department has evidence against him: He has yet to see how they plan to use it against him. He thinks often about it all. He cannot believe the piece they have that would go way – the most – is the messages between him and Sweetlilgreek.

What drew him to her? What was it about it about her? Dawna is so perfect a younger woman for him. Making love is slowly creeping back into their lives, and for that, he is thankful and relieved. Dawna is clearly happier with home life lately, too. She has nary a thought about anoMan, and adores the love life Stone and she share. They make love, typically, three or four times a week. Sometimes they will even more than that!

Life has come back around in full. The only

adjustment they both continue to work out, or work with, is a household with full-time kids. It sometimes seems that Stone has a harder time with it than does she. The only nagging question in her mind is how having two kids at home impacts Stone's and Dawna's chances of having one or two children of their own. She sometimes thinks she already knows the answer. It is a sad answer in her mind, indeed.

She gives him her whole, day in and day out: She wants to give him...have his babies. She is quite aware of how self-absorbed he can be...he is. She is purely a giver, and he is much more a taker. Naturally, she learned all this and more back when they first started seeing each other. She puts down two notes 'To: Self:

1.) Is he all over with the NYC chick, in addition, what drew him to her to begin with?

2.) Will we ever have our own babies?'

She will not hit him with these questions until the time is right. Moreover, she will recognize when that time arrives. The routines are good. They are good for everybody. The boys will at times continue to cry at their loss, but even these sad episodes have all but ceased. On the weekdays, it is boys out of bed, showered, fed, and out the door-lunches in clenched fist. On the weekends, the boys hang out in their room playing or watching Television, until that magic moment when Dana calls them out for breakfast.

Stone and Dawna are once again enjoying more and more of their 'sexcapades'; in the morning, in the evening and every other chance they get. She knows it is not just her: It is getting better, too! Like this lovely, slow-loving Saturday morning…

BAM!

BAM!

…Instant flaccidity overcomes Stone, and the tears of a young woman fall, saddest of all.

"Police! We are in your living room. Come out…NOW. Do it NOW!"

They throw on their robes and slowly trudge up the hallway.

"Let me get my boys, please."

Stone sits in his chair and the boys sit close together and snuggle against Dawna. All four of them are trembling terribly. Walsh steps up to the front from behind.

"Sorry folks, but we have the County Sniff Hounds. We have a search only they are talented enough to do."

The hound handlers have their backs to

the household. They are rubbing a bunched-up handful of items in the hounds' noses and issuing commands that certainly, only the hounds can understand. The handler lets the hounds go. One runs down the hallway, one remains in the living room, dining and kitchen areas and the third run into the boys' room.

Stone and Dawna both choke down the question they want to know: "What are they looking for this time?"

By the time the thoughts fleet by, they pack-away source items brought back to the SUV.

"Are you going to tell me what you are looking for?" Stone asks.

"No." Walsh simply and sharply replies.

*

"Well, it WAS a good morning, Stone Daddy." Dawna uses Daddy. Stone loves that.

"Yes, Baby," Stone replies knowing her hearing him refer to her, as Baby would dampen her. It was that simple. "...More later, Dawna..." Stone finishes.

They stop the whispering and merely wait... and wait...and wait.

# CHAPTER THIRTY-FOUR

Walsh expects non-eventful day in the situation room, although the day before offered-up viable information. The most promising indicator is the discovery that Mr. Rossinski's online sexting partner from New York City – Sweetlilgreek – actually lives on Mr. Headley's hard-drive. This hardly seems coincidental; however, Rossinski would certainly find it surprising.

"Hey McKenzie," Walsh calls across the table. "The two home computers are complete, for now; correct?"

"Yeah, and all the slightest evidentiary incidentals about each are documented."

"Okay...thanks. So today we should have some news about Headley's black box."

"The Information Sciences team is due to visit sometime mid-day, Sir." McKenzie offers.

"I expect an update regarding Headley's black box."

By noon, the team has before them a neat, clean, clear and concise case log. As impressive as it is, they still have nothing that carves-out a suspect, beyond a reasonable doubt. A strong circumstantial case can win, and often, do, but they are risky…Double Jeopardy.

The Information Science team arrives just after lunch. They talk through the software discoveries and analysis. None of the information sums-up anything of substance, except that it is all black-market and hacking utilities. This is, without a doubt, a black box. Machines like this perform one thing: wreak havoc on another targeted machine or Network.

"Lieutenant Walsh," the Information Science spokesperson begins. "We can prove that there is one, single target this machine and the software within hit."

"Let me guess…Mr. Rossinski!"

"No Sir. It's not that easy at this point."

"Talk to us."

"One more fact is that there a register where the target I.P. Address is stored."

"Well?"

"This black box targeted a single environment, yet the address of that target was somehow wiped clear from within the register. Our concern is that only very intelligent security software would be able to back track to this internal register, remove the data and any footprint that may identify the target. The better news is that if we have the target machine, we can recognize it as such."

*

Walsh asks his two small teams to brainwash, and tells them that McKenzie and he will do the same. McKenzie follows Walsh to his office. The door is closed and they pull the shades shut.

"McKenzie," Walsh says. "I am not giving-up, naturally, but I may ask you to work with me on an alternative path of evidence."

"Sure Walsh, no problem. Whatever it takes… right?"

Walsh explains the technique and approach to the investigation he has on his mind. They find themselves with a mound of evidence, supposedly pointing to Mr. Rossinski, but they so far cannot connect the dots. "Yes," he fully admits to McKenzie, "I am talking a possible set-up."

"I have not ruled that out at all, either, walsh."

"If Headley weren't dead, he would be at the top of my list!"

There is one more thing walsh has to say. He knows it is an unorthodox practice, but he must put it on the table.

"McKenzie," walsh begins. "I want to perform a blanket sniff-out. I want the hounds to run the length of Youmans and back."

"Really…that's bold."

walsh explains a hunch that has been eating away at him. Ernie came back with a few items that walsh wants to use as source scents with the hounds.

"I am going to feed the hounds…a pair of soiled panties from Mrs. Rossinki's hamper. I am also getting a vaginal swab from the coroner."

The entire team has a singular question that if answered could crack the case. Who was Headley spying-on? Whom was he hacking? Sciences also delivered another interesting fact. Headley used his black box against one and only one Network or computer. Typically, the black hat software saves the target address somewhere in memory, or other spaces and registry entries. This, Sciences points out, suggests that Mr. Headley's target has extremely sophisticated Internet Security software and firewalls.

The team has ruled-out Headley for all the obvious reasons, however, continued analysis of his computers and content might surface additional clues. Sciences suggest they get back to their lab to perform more scrubbing, data lifting and scraping. The team resumes their work; running queries against the 'Equity' shadow database Luke created for them.

"Okay guys, McKenzie and I are going to escort the sniffers and let them loose on Youmans." Walsh says.

"We are working on a hunch that our boss has jabbing his gut." McKenzie adds with a chuckle.

Walsh instructs the team to continue until he returns, when he will debrief.

*

The two team leads work on gathering the sniffer team. Walsh does the legwork, such as reserving the K9 unit and trainers and lines them up for an A.S.A.P., exercise. The K9 team has two SUV vehicles and a large loot of other necessary items for the hounds' sake. Pallet-cleansing chews, reward bones, command

and discipline clickers, and more. While the trainers prepare the hounds and gather the gear, Walsh explains his objective in general terms but stresses the importance of, and the break their afternoon could bring if his idea pays-off.

"The paper work is done, Sir," McKenzie says to Walsh.

"Excellent! The K9 unit will be ready within thirty minutes."

"In the meantime," McKenzie asks. "Why don't you describe to me your objective and reasoning...rational?"

"Okay...I hope to get a pointer to someone in the off-chance they may have taken personal items belonging to Ms. Rossinski, like underwear, the missing diaphragm, and so on."

"Oh, I see. Good idea."

# CHAPTER THIRTY-FIVE

Another of a series of court dates come. Stone's case is at nine-thirty in the morning. Dawna, of course, wants to accompany him. He argues with her for a few moments, and then lets the numbness, anxiety and fear settle in. He runs back and forth to the toilet suffering through nervous diarrhea. He has little discussion with his court appointed attorney. They meet thirty minutes early. Dawna tags along and keeps her mouth shut. She will not speak, unless someone asks her to.

"All rise!" The Bailiff commands.

Stone stands, but oddly cannot hear anything for a few minutes. He is in a surreal moment. He has no idea who the Bailiff introduces as the Judge of this case. He sits only because he sees everyone else is.

"Mr. Stone Rossinski," the Judge begins. "Please rise."

Stone, glued to his seat sees his attorney stand up.

"Stand up, Mr. Rossinski." Stones attorney whispers in his ear.

The Judge begins to speak in a booming voice. Suddenly, Stone wakes, which is good, but a feeling of intense mania has him quaking in his suit. His diarrhea is killing him. Waves of pain and the feeling that his anus is on the verge of explosion is almost unbearable. He is afraid to ask to go to the bathroom.

"Mr. Rossinski…Mr. Rossinski…MR. ROSSINSKI!"

Stone comes-to and responds. "Yes, your Honor?"

"Please recite the pledge with the Bailiff."

"Okay."

The Bailiff asks Stone to put his hand on a bible and raise his right hand.

"Do you solemnly swear that the testimony you are about to give is the truth, whole truth and nothing but the truth?"

"Yes."

"So help you God?"

"Yes."

All the questions in this phase of the trial come from the judge.

"Please state your full name for the court."

"Stone Rossinski..."

"You have no middle name, I understand. Correct?"

"I have no middle name."

"We have your current address. What is your previous address?"

"45 Youmans Avenue…"

"What do you do for a living? Where do you work?"

The preliminary, by rote questioning drags on. Stone learns that he is here to establish whether the judge decides to grant him bail. The questions continue and grow more case related. The judge calls for an hour-long recess. When the recess ends and all parties return to the courtroom, the judge sternly and confidently announces his decision.

"After careful consideration of all-encompassing evidence collected to date, bail is denied."

Dawna bursts out from her belly uncontrollable sobs. The judge calls for order. This does not silence Dawna, but it keeps her cries down low enough for the hearing to continue.

"Objection, your Honor!" Stone's lawyer stands and shouts out. "If Mr. Rossinski can get bail, why can't he use it? I do not understand the rationale behind your decision to deny bail."

"Approach the bench," orders the judge. To the prosecution and defense, he simply states, "This is your only suspect to date; we have enough fairly strong circumstantial evidence to justify my decision; He is a flight risk..."

The judge goes on even further with his sermon that will put Stone in jail. Both parties understand and agree to play nice over this. Stone learns his fate for the day. Before walking strong-armed by two court officers, the judge allows Dawna to hug Stone on his way out the door. Like some black and white, slow motion creepy vanishing act, Stone disappears: Poof.

*

There are additional cases in the same room following Stone's, but Dawna cannot move. She feels frozen onto the bench, as if she stood layers of her being would stick to the wood as the fiber rip and tear from her back and back side. The only warmth she feels are the tears rolling out of her eyes and down her cheeks. Logic tells her there are visiting hours for the inmates and their loved ones. That softens the rock hard pain in her heart, yet she thinks of all the other hours, without him at home with her. She also begins a lengthy thought process that considers the reality pointed out this morning. She begins from the start and performs a life review of her relationship with Stone.

She drives home and goes straight to bed. The kids are at school. 'The kids…'what is she going to tell the kids? Dawna lies in bed, on her back, legs and arms straight down and still. Her eyes are wide open. She must calm down first; formulate what she says to the kids; make a dinner. Her thoughts begin to lean toward the possibility of Stone's guilt. Considering his behavior since they were caught in Kat's house, Dawna asks herself, 'What if he did indeed kill his ex-wife and Headley?'

Dawna dozes off with that thought in mind. She dreams deeply down in the throes of sleep of opportunities presented to Stone in order to commit the crime. Her eyes pop open, wide-awake, big and round, like a black-faced burlesque actor of yesteryear. Her skin has sheen from perspiration head to foot.

The boys are home: that is what wakes her up. She goes to greet them and give them a hug. They follow their afterschool routine of TV until dinner, and then to their room to play games. Many afternoons they play out in the back yard, as well. Dawna can only hope she is able to conjure up the right wording, timing and delivery of the message she knows she must pass on to them.

She and Stone try repeatedly to get the boys to finish any homework, if any, first, but their efforts have thus far failed. The boys wait until late – too late in Dawna's eyes – to finish their homework. It often encroaches beyond their bedtime. Tonight has to be different. She does not intend to stretch this situation out with phony excuses and untrue explanations. Dawna decides to bring it up over dinner. Then, afterward, there is plenty of time to further the discussion if it comes to that.

"Where is Dad tonight?" Brian asks. Both boys stare at Dawna as she takes a deep breath.

"Your father has been asked to stay at the police department to help them find out what happened to your mom." There…she said it. It is no more than a white lie, and she feels comfortable with it. What a relief! It is not over yet, by any means, but she is off the proverbial hook for now.

"How long is he going to be there?" Timmy asks.

"We are not exactly sure, right now, but we both hope it is not too long. If there is ever anything, you want to ask or need, you can come to me. I love you guys, too, you know."

# CHAPTER THIRTY-SIX

Walsh is acutely aware of the notion that even when you have mountain of evidence, circumstantial or otherwise that he cannot tie to their only suspect, it could mean that they are holding the wrong person. The classic 'Frame-Up' is today at the forefront of his mind. He calls McKenzie in and talks through the concept. McKenzie gets it. On one side of the coin, you realize it, but the side of that same coin; it virtually represents a new case. That does not nearly outweigh the fact that they will have actually made giant steps forward...or worse case could have.

McKenzie drives his boss to the western end of Youmans and parks their unmarked cruiser on the right, just past the stream culvert. Walsh expects the K9 unit to be there immediately behind him, but they have not yet arrived. McKenzie is excited about the coming sniffer search, but Walsh is literally bouncing his knees up and down off the balls of his feet. His mind is already on the thought: "What if…?"

After what seems like forever, the two K9 SUV's drive up the street. They park together behind Walsh, just before the culvert. The officers get out and go to the rear door to get a hold of their hounds and supplies. They have the hounds stay in the vehicle while and groom them for the task. This is a five or ten minute procedure to both calm the hounds, and, to ready them for the task. By instinct, the hounds excitedly understand what is before them, but the K9 unit officers know they must bring the hounds from a fever pitch to react promptly to their commands.

The hound masters harness the handsome canines, and then put a leash on each of them. The hounds jump out of the vehicles and heel their masters as they walk up to where Walsh and McKenzie stand. On command, the hounds sit and stay. The K9 unit officers want a final confirming talk thru of the plan before priming the hounds and letting them loose. Walsh reveals the scents and the plan to walk the length of Youmans Avenue and back. He says if the hounds get a hit, that he would like a pointer, not an audible.

Everybody is ready to go. The K9 unit presents the scent bag to each hound. Walsh holds one scent bag back. The bag with the clean underwear, he is certain, will trigger too many false positives. The officers hold the bag of soiled panties and vaginal swab under the hounds' snouts, as their respective masters issue a short series of unintelligible commands. The hounds stand, almost like standing at attention, but Walsh and McKenzie can see they are both clearly ready to get started!

Walsh believes the swab in concert with the dirty panties will offer enough difference between their target and other dirty underwear in other homes. The difficult part of this will be the following interrogations… wherever they receive a point from either hound. Walsh and one hound and its master walk up the avenue. They note the address of each hit. That is as far as Walsh cares to take it today. He is still thinking about it. He decides he will return to the station with – hopefully – a page of addresses from Youmans Avenue.

*

The hounds point out several homes, but something peculiar happens at the L'Italian residence. The hound points, and then – coming as a surprise to the handler – barks once. Then the hound runs around the house and points to the door that leads to L'Italian's basement office. Again, the hound issues a single bark, and conveys something to the handler

"What is your hound telling us?" Walsh asks.

"Well Lieutenant," the handler says. "It is as simple as what you are probably thinking. It is indeed the strongest hit today."

"Very interesting…" Walsh says while writing several notes on his report.

"I can tell you one thing, boss," the handler says. "There is something behind that door and whatever it is; my hound tells me he finds a hit. The fact that he also barks, especially only at this location is indeed interesting. I did not issue a command to bark."

"Let's head up to the end of the avenue, for official sake. Tell your hound to move-on."

"Yes, Sir: Here we go."

# CHAPTER THIRTY-SEVEN

Neither L'Italian notices the police activity. They disregard and dismiss the two barks. Annie is in her living room, napping...dozing on her recliner. Mal finally falls asleep for her own afternoon nap. Luke is in his office and has not a clue the bark he hears is just outside the rear basement door. He is in deep thought about his completely general cover-up and framing steps taken. He is certain that his personal computer is squeaky-clean. 'Equity' appears clean thus far, and Luke continues the process to make damn sure it remains shiny new, as well.

He takes his analysis and cleansing down to the kernel level in every server. He must next scrape the disc arrays to make sure there is nothing suspicious. This is his third visit to each 'Equity' system component. Bob Dylan writes, '...to be an outlaw, you must be honest...' Luke applies the simply complex principle to every task he takes-on. 'Equity' is so large a system by now that he feels like he is forgetting something every time he moves from one action to the next.

As hyped-up as Luke is, Annie sleeps deeply, head back, mouth wide open. She twitches intermittently as she dreams. It is a good dream: the family sitting on Jumby Beach on St. John, USVI. She and Mal play in the white sugar sand while Luke snorkels in the coral reefs. Mal eventually dares to wade in the perfectly aqua ocean that fills this cove. The water is perfectly warm and the alcove bottom as all soft sand, until it gets deeper and the coral magically appears. Luke is still diving underwater admiring the tropical fish that live among the coral. Annie takes Mal for a walk along the water's edge and wading a little deeper whenever Mal pulls her mother into it. They hear rustling to their left at the top of a small drop-off. It takes a few seconds, but Mal spots two large iguanas chasing each other. She tugs Annie's hand and says, in her language of infancy, "Mommy look at the lizards!" Two things strike Annie: one is that she completely understands well what Mal is saying, and the other thing is the magic moment she and her daughter share. Annie can clearly see the two iguanas playing in a small tree, but Mal sees them first. They watch the show the lizards create with each chase given, one then the other.

A bizarre sea creature he observes mesmerizes Luke. He does not know whether it is a sea plant or a creature of some sort. It is lightly colored and tubular shaped. It moves just slightly with a nearly nonexistent current. The top end of the thing blooms outward reminiscent of a flower beginning to bloom. It freaks Luke out when he sees a fish slowly swimming over the strange thing he watches. Lash looking feelers, almost like jellyfish tails shoot out lightning fast. It grabs the fish only to quickly draw its prey down into the tube. It scares Luke to some degree, but he wants to see it feed itself again. He cannot take his eyes off it. He has to see it do its thing one more time. He spies all around at the purely natural compound that all these creatures own. He keeps that spooky grabber in the corner of his view. Ah-ha…here comes a pretty, little fish. It swims toward the tubular thing and sure enough, Luke witnesses another horrid-looking grab. The beauty of that little fish makes it sorrowful so easily taken down.

*

Annie suddenly wakes only to realize the combination of qualities, shapes, colors, and form so pleasing in her sleep dissolves. She blinks and looks around for anything that pleases the aesthetic senses, especially the sights just taken away from her. Her head finally wraps itself around reality. Her nap turned into a longer sleep than she planned. Mal is still quiet upstairs. She looks to her right and notices that at some point during her dream, Luke is napping. He never naps, but he is now. Then from upstairs come the cries of Mal. Luke does not dream, but he takes a well-deserved rest.

It is time to start making dinner. Annie feeds Mal first, right away, to give the whining infant what she needs. After only a few bites, Mal quiets and enjoys her pureed dinner. It is a special treat whenever Annie and Luke can enjoy a meal together without the interruptions of a noisy child. Mal finishes her food, as Annie is mid-way through preparation for Luke and her. She puts Mal in the infant's round roller seat and puts a video tape on for her.

The odor of garlic and onions fills the rooms, and is strong enough to wake Luke. He relates the scent of the onion and garlic to the price he will pay for eating it for the next couple of days. He eats and enjoys, but pays the inevitable consequences, by choice, rather than disallowing those ingredients. He knows he inherited his father's stomach. Annie makes a very good plate of fresh Pasta Bolognese, and includes meatballs. She puts the plate in front of Luke, and he waits for his wife to sit down at the dinner table before eating. He was brought-up by parents that cared about manners.

Luke does not feel like working anymore downstairs tonight, so he volunteers to do the dishes, clean the kitchen and wipe down the dinner table. Annie turns on the Television and channel-surfs: There is nothing on, but she leaves it set to the local news. No sooner than Luke sits and kicks up his feet, a news announcement centers on Stone in jail, without bail. He is the lone suspect at this time. Luke, however, knows the authorities may hold Stone for a limited amount of time. There is no arrest made to date…yet.

# CHAPTER THIRTY-EIGHT

The court has no option other than to release Mr. Rossinski, but the judge warns, or rather orders him not to leave his Washington Borough residence. He may go to work, other places around town, but nowhere else until further notice. Walsh and his team are not happy with the release, but understand the system – of course.

The crime teams meet in their situation room, as usual, and collectively place all the current documents in chronological sets of several piles and document type. Today, Walsh announces, he intends to scour the evidence – all of it – in the familiar connect the dots exercise. With minimal assumption, based on fact, they convey each evidential item to Walsh and McKenzie. Around the table, investigator-by-investigator presents verbally each item to the two leaders.

"Rossinski still has access to the home

left to his ex-wife. This is how I want this done, precise but not verbose. Starting on my left, go on and begin." Walsh starts them off.

"We find a gun buried in Rossinski's back yard."

"No prints lifted off the gun or anywhere else that cannot be explained-away."

"Ballistics reports the gun is tied directly to the crime."

"Yes, by virtue of their analysis of the bullets the coroner recovers."

"Mr. Rossinski makes several phone calls to his ex-wife; all after her death."

"Perhaps he is trying to establish a false alibi."

"Rossinski has an online sexual affair with an unidentifiable person."

"Rossinski's girlfriend describes his erratic, moody behavior."

"Yes…that as well as his anxiety and odd behavior at home."

"Forensics and the coroner agree on trajectory and range of each shot fired."

"That would be straight-on from approximately a yard…three feet away."

"The coroner reports the cause of death is the shot to the head of both victims."

"Another bullet is found in the heart of both victims."

"A silencer fit to the murder weapon is used."

"Due to the strength necessary to move the bodies – especially big Tom Headley's – we assume the suspect will have been male."

"The perpetrator performs a considerable and significant clean-up effort."

"Assumed, as well, the suspect is familiar with Ms. Rossinski's home."

"Mr. Rossinski is declared a person of interest."

"We find the tool used by the suspect to grate the cellar's dirt floor at the crime scene."

"It is found stuck inside the length of the Middle Street culvert that supports the stream."

"The elements used to build that tool come from the utility side of Ms. Rossinski's basement."

"The victims and Mr. Rossinski register in the local ISP 'Equity' within a very close time frame."

"Mr. Rossinski's girlfriend has nothing that can be called evidence found in her personal computer."

"Mr. Rossinski's computer is littered with smut and pornography, along with the sexual encounters aforementioned."

"Mr. Rossinski's activities – the questionable behavior – on 'Equity' are concurrent with the victim's time of death."

"Mr. Rossinski's girlfriend, as well as a host of persons in the neighborhood admits that Mr. Rossinski is cold, distant and unfriendly."

"Mr. Rossinski's girlfriend repeatedly and fully admits her boyfriend's odd, nervous and detached behavior."

"That behavior begins very shortly before the murders."

"Mr. Rossinski appears aloof when we pick him up and at the bond hearing."

"He has no alibi indicating is location the night of the crime."

"His girlfriend submits that he phones her in the late afternoon that he had to work late."

"Our suspect gains easy access into Ms.

Rossinski's home. He either has a key, or is invited…expected."

"That about does it, huh?" Walsh asks the team.

"As far as solidity, yes, sir, it does."

"We must gauge or measure our level of confidence that the prosecutor can build a case based on what we have. McKenzie, I would like you to pitch what we do have to date to the county prosecutor. I am interested to hear his opinion. Let us hope we can bring charges to Mr. L'Italian. I have something unrelated to Mr. Rossinski that I must follow-up. Our K9 unit, upon reaching the L'Italian home point and bark their signal. I am submitting a request for a search warrant based on that. It should be delivered to me by tomorrow morning, so all of you please prepare to shift gears and put on your search hats on."

"What was the bait?" asks an officer.

"Items I had Ernie pull from the crime scene, based on a hunch. We used a soiled pair of Mrs. Rossinski's under-clothes and a vaginal swab from the coroner. Everybody take the day when your discussion is complete. I will take care of the warrant."

# CHAPTER THIRTY-NINE

Stone calls in to the university and requests the day off, as vacation. He relaxes at home feeling at ease and thankful for a night back in his own bed after nearly a week away. Dawna spent bedtime caressing Stone gently… soothingly. The boys are happy to wake-up for school knowing their dad is back at home. Dawna, with a sense of purpose, decides not to raise conversations revolving about anything. When Stone is ready to talk, he will. Meanwhile, they enjoy their morning coffee together in the living room.

Luke is sleeping-in and Annie is in the living room when a hard, loud knock on the door comes. It startles her out of her recliner and she walks to the door. She is surprised to see Detective Walsh on the door stoop and several other men in suits close behind him.

"Good morning officer Walsh." Annie begins a cordial greeting and welcome.

Walsh and his team have no patience for that.

"Mrs. L'Italian, is Mr. L'Italian home?"

She realizes that, unlike the previous visits, Walsh is addressing them by their proper married surnames.

"Yes, I will go get him right now."

She climbs the stairs on legs that feel like rubber. She trembles all over.

"Luke, I am sorry, but Walsh is here asking to speak to you."

"I will be right there."

"Please hurry, honey."

Luke jumps out of bed, washes-up, gargles some Listerine; his hair looks okay. He descends the stairs leisurely.

"Hi, Officer Walsh…" Luke is playing nice, like Annie when she answered the door.

"I have a search warrant over your home, home office and property." Walsh is serious; there is no doubt. Yet Luke replies again.

"After all the cooperation and help I have contributed?"

"Please step aside so we can carry out our search."

"All I ask is that you do not tear up my home, moreover, my livelihood, 'Equity.'"

"I will say one more thing before we come in, only because you've contributed greatly to the case we continue to solve. We do not have a need to look at or in the actual components that constitute 'Equity'. Listen Mr. L'Italian; the K9 unit indicated a positive hit on this location. I cannot disclose any more information. Now…Please step aside."

"Thank you, sir."

The group of detectives gathers in the living room. Walsh issues assignments for each of them: two on the first floor…two on the second floor…two in the office area, who will accompany Walsh. He suggests that one of each team member, in each team, begin at opposite ends of the home and meet in the middle.

"Mr. and Mrs. L'Italian please take a seat here in the living room. Be prepared to issue statements and answer questions."

*

Walsh is not concerned with 'Equity' since Luke gave the Walsh's team and the Information

Science unit unlimited read access to his system. He is interested in the objects that indicated presence by the K9 hound. Anything else found today is a crowning accomplishment.

"Mr. L'Italian, please give to me the padlock key to your rear ground entrance to your basement space. We could always gain entrance using excessive force, so I am doing what I can to concede – when we can – to your request. Better yet, please tell me where I can find it."

"It is on one of the two key rings in the top tray of the gentleman's valet in the Master bedroom."

The upstairs search carries forth with ease, but the two detectives up there are working in Luke's office. This room appears to be where the L'Italians manage their household related bills, payments and balance their budget. The detectives are not especially conforming to the request from Luke not to 'tearing up the house'. They empty every drawer space and look at every piece of paper in each; they look through the small trash receptacle.

The first floor search carries forth with relative ease. Mal sits on her mommy's lap. There appears to be no standout items of interest. Then, they open the coffee table drawer and retrieve what looks like a house key. Annie discloses, thus confirms what they already know, that the key is to Kat's front door. She adds that they both traded keys and kept an eye on each other's places as needed. The key drops into a baggie, and the baggie then falls into the brown paper bag.

Walsh orders one detective to search the utility area that abuts Luke's office. He and the other subordinate begin their search of the office. The entrance from the other side is a small foyer-like space. They look using flashlights at the four sides of the area. They perform that type of generic and initial exercise before taking on the hidden spaces. The man working in the utility room finds four boxes of Playboy and Penthouse magazines. There is also a much smaller stack of Hustler.

Other boxes in the utility area appear to be Mr. L'Italian's computer hardware vendor shipping cartons. He looks into each one of them. There a couple boxes with the word 'obsolete' in black magic-marker that hold smaller devices and documentation. He walks toward the office, stops at the entry and requests permission to enter. He shows Walsh the inventory list.

"Mr. L'Italian holds a penchant for smut magazines, I see," says Walsh.

"Well, Information Sciences found traces of, and a few directories of nude photographs."

"So, there are no big surprises within those boxes…"

"No Sir, nothing: He has a standard work bench, but not many tools, and storage cartons, mostly empty, except for the four containing the magazines, and finally, several vendor packages that L'Italian's hardware came in."

"Go back in there and look again."

"Okay."

Meanwhile, Walsh and his partner begin to look through the desk drawers. The center drawer is where Luke keeps his small office tools, such as a stapler, scissors, paper clip, scotch tape, post-it notepads and other typical workstation items.

"Okay…you take the left side stack of drawers, and I will take the right."

It looks to Walsh like Mr. L'Italian uses the 'David Allen' method of document and communication management. Each of the three stacked drawers from top to bottom has labels just above the drawer pulls. The top-drawer label reads 'Current,' the second one 'Action' and the third one 'History – Keep'.

All the opposite end of the desk-drawers has

a label, too: 'Supplies,' 'Paper & Labels,' and 'Saved Miscellaneous.' The top two drawer's contents do reflect the respective label above the pulls. When the detective opens the third drawer down, he sees that it is relatively empty. He looks at the few sheets of paper within. Something odiferous hits the young detective. He admits to himself that he smells pussy. He invites Walsh to step over and asks if he can smell anything… anything familiar.

Walsh immediately declares in a booming voice, "That is what we are looking for. Smell these."

"They smell the same." After he puts the bait baggie up to his nose and sniffs.

"I am not ruling-out coincidence, but this tells me that something or things, once resided in there. Go start on the filing cabinet in the corner, over there."

Walsh takes the drawer from its chest, wraps it in cellophane and puts it in the evidence box. He checks the odors again. Indeed, he believes that the scents between the bait and the drawer are identical. At that, he walks to the filing cabinet and gets a status from his partner. Each of the five deep drawers held in the vertical filing cabinet, stuffed with hanging files, have labels, as well. The labels have written on each the current and four prior years.

As Walsh's partner rifles, if even very deliberately, through each folder in each file hangers, Walsh takes a time-out in Luke's comfy chair to collect some thoughts about the possibility of finding more. He decides to let his partner complete the tedious search through the filing cabinet, and tells him so. In the chance that anything he finds of interest, may not necessarily tie Mr. L'Italian to the murders. It does warrant interrogation and discovery that L'Italian is involved in this case, or open a second case involving entry to Ms. Rossinski's home unlawfully.

"Fucking BINGO Walsh!" the detective searching the filing cabinet bursts. He is looking into the last hanger's folder in the last, fifth cabinet drawer.

"Whatever it is, don't touch it!"

# CHAPTER FORTY

Captain Deckham reads the debriefing binder. He, thus far, already has a thought that Walsh builds a strong case – circumstantial as it may be – with the evidence against Mr. Rossinski. Walsh knocks at the door and sticks his head in. I have something for you Captain.

"The K9 search hit on the L'Italian home."

"Yes, I remember reading that – you requested a search warrant."

"The search of their house turned-up suspicious items."

"What did you find?"

"A woman's diaphragm a pair of soiled underpants and a clean pair of them, as well."

"Okay, thank you. Have forensics prove a match before taking this any further."

"I am already on it, sir, just thought I would give you this development first-hand."

"I appreciate that, Walsh. It may lead us to a second suspect…as you know. Let's be intelligent handling this newfound evidence."

"Okay. We will at least know if it is ties to a victim. It may not prove Mr. L'Italian committed the crime we are investigating. I plan to interrogate him as soon as I hear back from forensics. He may be guilty of another, standalone crime we do not know of yet."

"Fine…dismissed."

In the course of three days, Walsh and McKenzie spend questioning Stone. They cannot break him, but Stone cannot talk his self from remaining the primary suspect in the case without a reasonable doubt, either.

The two lead detectives sit tight waiting for the verdict from forensics confirming or rejecting the objects taken from Luke's office.

"I debriefed the Captain this morning," Walsh says to McKenzie.

"So we wait for the word from forensics…"

"Yeah, but in the meantime we can still pull together a list of questions for Mr. L'Italian."

"Yup…just in case."

"Well, there has got to be something going on with him, given the intimacy of the objects."

"Yes sir," McKenzie begins. "I will pull his profile: There could be something there to help us start or end our interrogation with L'Italian."

"I was just getting ready to ask you to do that! We are on the same page."

"Well, I am on it, boss!"

"Knock, knock," A detective from forensics is at Walsh's office door.

"Well 'Hello there! We have been waiting for you right here, on Truth or Consequences.' Okay, so give it to me…give me the news, buddy."

"We have a match, sir."

"Is that undeniably and positively?"

"Yes. There no doubt…Zero."

"Excellent, man, you just made my day!"

"…Just doing my job, sir."

*

Walsh and McKenzie get ready for the short drive to the L'Italian residence. For their part, neither has any idea what they yielded in that search, except for Kat's house key. The hope is for ongoing cooperation from Mr. L'Italian. If he refuses, they plan to put him under arrest for suspicion.

Walsh knocks at the door. Luke is taking some time away from the office and 'Equity' today. He gets up and answers the door.

"Hello Officer Walsh...McKenzie..."

"Mr. L'Italian, we would like to have a conversation with you."

"Okay, come on in."

"We would prefer to proceed at the station, if you don't mind."

"Oh...alright...am I under arrest for something?"

"No. We would just like to have your thoughts or answers about the case with you, preferably in private. Please come with us." Walsh is making a beckoning gesture relaying to his request.

"Can I please tell my wife I am taking off for a while?"

"Sure, go ahead."

All three get in the unmarked cruiser, and Walsh drives to the station. There is nothing beside complete silence on the way.

Luke cannot escape the vehicle by virtue of the conventional back seat locking mechanism in most all police cars. McKenzie tells Luke to wait: He will open the door for him. Both cops are outside, as Luke sits patiently inside.

"He sure doesn't think there is any issue," McKenzie says.

"Not a clue. He is very calm and rather aloof. Maybe we'll see some success with this first round of questioning."

"I hope so…let me get him out of the car and we'll walk him to the interrogation room."

"Great."

Walsh plans to steer the conversation toward the double-murder in this first round with Mr. L'Italian. He starts light, and builds the inquiries hotter and higher as the interrogation proceeds. That is just his way. Luke carries in him a tremendous and intelligent kind of confidence. Walsh sits Luke at the table in the sparse and tiny square room and asks Luke to wait a few minutes.

"I will be right with you, Mr. L'Italian."

McKenzie confirms that both of them will attend and he will act as scribe as Walsh facilitates. They both enter the room and take seat. Walsh sits directly across from

Luke, and McKenzie takes a seat at the head of the table.

"I see you have two firearms registered…" Wash begins.

"Yes, I do."

"What do you do with them?"

"I used to like to go to the local shooting range."

"Why don't you do it now?"

"Well…Ever since I started on 'Equity' I have no spare time."

"Your computers take that much time to maintain?"

"Yes, sir, you would be surprised."

"Where are they now? We did not see any firearms during the search."

"I threw them away at the dump. I don't want guns anywhere in the house, now that we have Mal."

"I see. That is a smart move, but why didn't you sell them?"

"That is too much of a hassle."

"Did you own any unregistered weapons?"

"No."

"Okay." Walsh throws caution to the wind, as he reaches into an evidence bag. "We did find these items, though."

"Uh huh…" Luke farts as he takes a breath to wrap is head around the surprise…I threw those out, didn't I? He says, "Excuse me. Please do not disclose this to my wife. Please…"

"We won't unless we have to."

"Kat and I had an affair last year. We were together for about seven months."

"Why did you break it off with her?"

"It was a mutual agreement. We both knew that it just was…not… right: Especially considering Annie and I being married."

"When did this affair begin?"

"It started very soon after her divorce. I do not know the date."

"How did you come to acquire these items?" Walsh holds up the soiled panties and the diaphragm.

"Um…this is a little embarrassing. When we broke-up, I begged her for the souvenirs so I would have a part of her close by me."

"She agreed to that…Really?"

"Yes. We were quite close, so yes, she

gave them to me the last time we…um…uh…made love."

"It seems odd that the panties are virtually quite new."

"I do know she bought and wore this type of underwear the entire time we were together. She told me once that when she tried a pair on the first time, she knew they were 'her kind fit and comfort.'"

"Did Mr. Headley seem like a threat to you?"

"No, not particularly, but admittedly, I tend to be possessive when it comes down to close belongings of mine."

"Did you have any idea he and she were possibly seeing each other?"

"I had no idea they were, if they were."

"Maybe Ms. Rossinski broke it off with you to free herself-up to be with him?"

"At the time, I thought nothing more than how and why we broke up, really."

"Where were you the weekend Ms. Rossinski 'went missing' – was murdered?"

"I can safely say with no doubt that I was home and likely working."

"You are pretty diligent about keeping the system up, huh?"

"Yes, of course. I support, as you know, a very large membership. You have to keep things up-to-date, and moreover, up and running."

"Just one more question for today," Walsh announces.

"Okay."

"We discovered a black box PC in Mr. Headley's home. He had an affinity to Internet hacking. Did you know that, by chance?"

"Wow!"

"Have you ever been hacked, Mr. L'Italian – 'Equity.'?"

"Hackers are coming out of the wood work these days, and my firewall statistics reflect that I am hit-on, literally, hundreds of times a day, but no one has ever been able break through the wall, that I am aware-of. It is a constant worry of mine."

"Our I.S., team discovered that he hacked only one target."

"I'm glad it wasn't me!"

"Of course…we also know that his hacking system includes a register in order to store the address of the current victim."

"That makes sense, I guess. I do not have time to deal with 'all things hacking'."

"Even though he broke down somebody's wall, the IP address is not in the register."

"It could be faulty software."

"We know you have an Internet Security package installed."

"Of course I do!"

"There is an option you have that bounces back to the potential hacker and wipes-out the offending IP Address. Such as exactly what is missing from Mr. Headley's black box. Do you have any ideas? Can you do some analysis in 'Equity'? I would be interested to know if that Security package of yours is configured to do that bounce back, etc., ? In addition, can you offer proof that 'Equity' has never been assaulted?"

"Sure, I can do that."

"Okay, Mr. L'Italian, I will give you a ride home now."

"I am ready…" Luke matter-of-factly mutters.

*

Walsh and McKenzie review the notes and rebuts McKenzie scribed in the L'Italian interrogation. They discover holes in L'Italian's story. The prosecution breaks the news to Walsh that they had an internal investigating detective from State. The three men spend all day pulling evidence, thus, a case against the guilty. Once Walsh and his assistant detective hear the additional evidence they believe, they do indeed have a much stronger case against L'Italian than they have against Rossinski.

The three plow through the administration policies and procedures involved, such as file the charges with the Court. They get an Arraignment for tomorrow morning. Walsh gathers McKenzie and three additional back-up officers to escort and cover him as he places under arrest the guilty party.

They rehearse the plan and coverage, which includes two officers in the back yard. Therefore, Walsh will make the arrest with McKenzie by his side and an office behind them.

*

Luke is startled out of a fantasy that had him playing with himself in the living room. Annie is not home; she took Mal somewhere…a child-related event. He answers the front door.

"Please put your hands behind your head. Please state your full name."

Luke obeys both commands. Before he has any chance at all to speak, Walsh cuts him off.

"You are under arrest for the murders of Ms. Kat Rossinski and Mr. Thomas Headley.

You have the right to remain silent.

Anything you say can be used against you in a court of law.

You have the right to have an attorney present now and during any future questioning.

If you cannot afford an attorney, one will be appointed to you free of charge if you wish.

Do you understand your Miranda Rights?" Walsh asks Luke following the Miranda warning and rights.

"Yes."

# CHAPTER FORTY-ONE

Luke is strong-armed, hands cuffed behind him, into the station. They process him: They fingerprint, take a photo from the front and one profile. Walsh offers him one phone call. Luke calls his lawyer. Luke, surrounded by police officers, walks down a short hall. They escort him to a single cell. Everything is steel and bolted down.

"Here...put these on!"

An officer hands Luke an orange jumpsuit and he orders Luke to surrender all his belongings.

"I will bring you to the designated prisoners' phone."

The officer orders Luke to put his above his head and be still. Another officer shows-up at the cell, gun drawn. The officer in the cell with him now shackles Luke at the ankles. The officer cuffs Luke's wrists to a thick belt.

The two officers strong-arm Luke to the telephone. With one hand temporarily free, he calls his lawyer and tells her that he needs to retain an attorney right away.

"I am already in jail."

"Mr. L'Italian, do not speak to anyone but me or my designee. I would like to handle this personally, if I can make the time. Nonetheless, a designee or I or will be there as soon as possible."

"Okay…I have to go now."

*

Luke spends the night alone. His lawyer did not show-up. He lays awake on the cot all night, eyes wide open. He reviews his cover-up repeatedly in his head. What evidence could they possibly have? Luke trembles and is nauseous by the wee hours of the next morning. He finally falls asleep at four-forty-five in the morning. Nevertheless, he is woken-up by an abrupt and loud breakfast call from an officer carrying a service tray at seven o'clock. Luke forces the food down and immediately has a bout with diarrhea. It continues for the next four hours.

His attorney arrives around noon to review the latest developments with Luke. They both speak in barely audible, whispered tones.

"Luke" begins the lawyer. "The Grand Jury met this morning. It is not often that it occurs so quickly."

"Really...What does that mean to me?"

"The judge handed down an indictment, and the prosecution plans to charge you with two second-degree murders."

"Motherfucker," Luke cannot help spitting that nasty a word. He usually does not use that kind of language.

"Yes, Luke, you will called-in this afternoon at three o'clock to hear the charges against you."

"Is that it?"

"No Luke. You will be called-upon to plead – guilty, or not guilty. Not guilty can be expressed in several different terms, such as guilty due to insanity, or under special circumstances, etc. We will discuss that tomorrow. I will be here in the morning, about nine."

"Oh, yeah...Okay."

"Did you do it, Luke?"

"No," Luke lies.

"Okay, I am not going to ask again. Let's discuss your plea to the court."

"I say 'not-guilty'," Luke replies. He truly does not and cannot believe they have enough to prove him anything, otherwise. He believes the cover-up he performed to point to Stone will rise up again.

"Do you have an alibi?"

"I was at home alone," Luke replies to Ms. Vincenzo. He likes his attorney. She is cute.

"Can you prove that, Luke?"

"Well…I can prove I was in my office most of the weekend. Maintaining 'Equity' is a sixty to seventy hour a week job."

Ms. Vincenzo pauses to write notes on her yellow paper legal pad. Luke waits in silence. Finally, she says, "Announcing your plea is all you have to do today. There will be short back-and-forth between the prosecutor and me. A few minutes afterward, the judge orders you to stand-up. I will stand-up with you. The judge then asks for your plea. You must say it first; I will echo it after you do."

"So, that will indicate that we go to trial?" Luke asks her.

"It does as of today, once you plead. Keep in mind that between this preliminary court appearance and the trial to defend you from the prosecutor's charges – you and I will discuss your plea and options, and I will be in close contact with the prosecution team. Are you okay?"

"Yes, I am. I will follow your lead as we discuss further my options, given all you tell me."

"Alright then...I will be in the court room by two-thirty this afternoon. The two court-ordered police officers must escort you from here to the courthouse at about the same time – two-thirty...give or take. You remain shackled...I am sorry, but there is nothing I can do about that as long as you remain in custody. They walk you to the defendant's table. I will be there. Sit on my left...on the inside. I remind you: Do not say anything except your plea when asked. I will address any necessary responses and replies on your behalf. I'll see you there this afternoon. ...Do you understand?"

"Yes, Ms. Vincenzo," Luke's tears roll down his cheeks.

*

Two officers of the court drive Luke to the courthouse. They circle around to the back lot, secluded by a tall, opaque fence. Beyond that is tree cover. One officer leads Luke to the rear entrance of courthouse. The other officer shifts from the second in line to the first. The lead officer stops, and with a firm grip pulls Luke to the side. The second officer moves ahead and unlocks, then opens the courthouse door.

All three walk slowly, with Luke sadly shuffling along; all extremities restrained. They come to the assigned courtroom and walk in. Luke sees Ms. Vincenzo. He swaggers, quaking inside, as both uniformed escorts seat him. Each of them marches to their respective sides of the courtroom. Luke notices that there are multiple officers standing at their assigned posts. Ms. Vincenzo puts a hand on Luke's shoulder.

"Are you alright, Luke?" The attorney asks.

"I think so. I feel scared shitless, though."

"Try to relax. You cannot plead not guilty and body language that does not match your confidence, okay? Please, breath, relax and listen. You will be okay. This hearing is very short."

"What happens after?"

"I will meet you at your cell."

At precisely three o'clock, the bailiff stands in front of the judge's bench, and announces to the entire court.

"Please rise," he bellows. "Case NU812 is

now in session: The honorable Judge Francis Dellaur presiding."

Upon reaching his bench, the judge stops and insists that the court be seated, and then sits in the most comfortable chair in the room.

"Case NU812 is now in session. The Grand Jury released their petition to prosecute Mr. Luke Anthony L'Italian. Upon reviewing the evidence and witnesses' general role and testimony for the prosecution, I have a unanimous decision among all involved. Will the defendant please rise…?"

Luke and his defending attorney stand straight up.

"Will the defendant please state your name…?"

"Luke Anthony L'Italian is my full name, your Honor."

"Mr. L'Italian…You are charged with two counts of Second Degree Murder. Do you understand?"

"Yes, your Honor."

"How do you plead, Mr. L'Italian?"

Luke coughs, and then declares, "Not Guilty sir."

"I understand you have chosen to plead Not

Guilty against all charges. Is this correct, Ms. Vincenzo?"

"Yes, your Honor. I would like the court to grant bond or bail for my client."

"I OBJECT!" yells the lead prosecutor. "This man is a flight risk and is considered a threat to others."

"Sustained…The defendant shall remain in the county jail until and through the imminent trial."

Ms. Vincenzo whispers, "I am so sorry Luke." Then she requests the prosecution provide an inventory of evidence and their witness list.

"Mr. Prosecutor?"

He responds, "We concede to the request."

"May the Defense reserve the right to change plea between now and the start of the trial, your Honor?"

"Yes, Ms. Vincenzo. The trial is to be held in this courtroom in exactly ninety days…"

"Objection, your Honor. The prosecution requests a more assertive and expeditious lapse of time to trial, and therefore, suggest a trial date within sixty days."

"Sustained. The court accepts the request and documents proceeding at that time. Both teams will receive correspondence via the United States Postal Service announcing the exact date, as well as all other communication from the court."

"I am not going to argue this one, Luke." Ms. Vincenzo whispers in Luke's ear.

"Court adjourned until the trial date," the Judge announces.

"All rise!" The Bailiff bellows again, as Judge Dellaur stands and walks into his chambers.

# CHAPTER FORTY-TWO

There is no time to waste. Ms. Vincenzo forms a small team of associates that begin to put a defense case together for Luke. A letter from the court reads that jury selection begins next week. She plans to keep two associates on the job at the office, and she and one other associate take jury selection. She prompts two of her team to formulate a questionnaire for each potential jury member. Meanwhile, Luke's attorney spends as much interview time with her client as she can before they go to trial.

"Tell me what we have, Luke. We have to build a defense case for you. First do you have an alibi?"

"I was home the entire time. Annie can corroborate with that."

"Okay, what else…"

"I have a service on 'Equity' that will

reflect and indicate that I was online performing maintenance during the hours that Annie is not home."

"What about sleep time…night time?"

"I sleep at home every night."

"Can the prosecutor prove any motive you had for committing these crimes?"

"I doubt it. My relationship with Kat was a close one. I admitted to Detective Walsh that Kat and I had a brief, yet illicit affair"

"What about the personal items belonging to Ms. Rossinski found in your office?"

"I said they were a gift from Kat…When we decided to break it off, mutually, I asked her for a couple souvenirs for me to remind me of her. She gave me those."

"Can they tie the gun used in the crime to you?"

"No."

"What about a make-shift hoe found that was used to grate the Ms. Rossinski's cellar's dirt floor?"

"No."

"They plan on calling many neighbors and users of 'Equity' to the stand. Does that worry you…concern you?"

"No."

"That is the only physical evidence and witnesses they have listed…so far."

"I see…okay."

*

The Jury Selection phase was rather short and uneventful. Most all the candidates called to appear have the same or similar answers to all questions asked. Everyone in the jury pool knew about the crime. No one in the pool was close enough with the L'Italians to offer bias to any degree. No one is aware that Luke owned and operated the ISP 'Equity,' yet all are registered users of the ISP. A few candidates knew Kat from dance class, or from Merck. They all agree she was a sweet woman. Mr. Headley is widely unknown to any of the jurors, except the two called that coincidentally reside on Youmans Avenue right there in the Borough. Twelve jurors and four alternates are selected and uneventfully agreed-upon by the prosecutor and the defense counselor.

Ms. Vincenzo visits with Luke for an hour before she returns to her office.

"Luke...We have selected a jury. I believe all are fair and free-minded of the characters of you, Headley, Kat, and Stone."

"Can you offer-up any character witnesses at all? I am talking about family or friends that can, to the best of their knowledge, reflect you and your character as anything but positive."

"You can call on my entire family, and I can give you a few friends: I don't have many, admittedly."

"Why is that?"

"I believe it is because I have my head and my time wrapped around 'Equity.'"

"I see. Well, let's get the names down on paper. As we go through the list, tell me all you know about them, like their address, phone number…anything at all."


Luke's attorneys only have six weeks to pull-together Opening Statements, the Defendant's Case, Possible Rebuttal and Closing Arguments. To prepare an opening statement, attorneys must organize and outline the entire case they intend to prove at trial. A good opening statement:

Explains what the attorney plans to prove and how they will do it. Presents the events

of the case in a clear, orderly sequence. It suggests a motive or emphasizes a lack of motive for the crime. It is not argumentative.

They tell the story without arguing what the case is about in one or two statements. It also summarizes the story. Ms. Vincenzo must be creative: Use adjectives "It was a dark and quiet night" to give jury a picture of what is going on in your case.

The Defense presents one to three pieces of evidence that the jurors are going to see or hear. The Prosecution explains what they intend to prove. The counsel for the defense repeats their theme. Attorneys usually begin their statement with a formal introduction:

"Your honor, ladies and gentlemen of the jury, opposing counsel, and my name is Ms. Mary Vincenzo, representing the defendant – Mr. Luke L'Italian in this action." That is the easy part of opening. The attorneys then turn to the jury and begin their statements. Opening statements often include such phrases as; the evidence will show that...the facts will prove that...etc. This is a little more difficult. It must be clear, concise and believable. They must have a list of witnesses, by name that they plan to call to the stand and testify – given the evidence; they may call others to stand behind particular evidentiary items.

Ms. Vincenzo's team must also be prepared for cross-examination and rebuttal. Finally, in formal presentation for the lead attorney her team must anticipate the plaintiff presentation of its closing argument – no longer than five minutes. Then, the defense will present its closing. The plaintiff (because it has the burden of proof) has up to two minutes to present its rebuttal closing. The outlined prose takes sixteen days to complete. They review at least three times, and sometimes play-act it out as if in the courtroom. They note the typical remaining sequence of events of the trial.

Testimony of witnesses: Plaintiff calls witnesses first. The order of witness presentations are determined by strategy, i.e., chronologically into overall story. Direct examination of plaintiff witnesses includes cross-examination by defense and redirect examination by plaintiff. Defense case-in-chief then proceeds with direct examination of witnesses called by defense and cross-examination by plaintiff, etc.

# PART IV

## THE TRIAL

# CHAPTER FORTY-THREE

Courtroom and participants include the judge, attorneys, witnesses, jurors, bailiff, court reporter, media observers and attendant observers.

The bailiff announces, "All rise. The High Court of Warren County in the state of New Jersey, Case NU812 is now in session, the Honorable Judge Charles Dellaur presiding."

Everyone remains standing until the judge enters and sits. The judge then asks the attorneys for each side of the case if they are ready to begin the trial. Both sides reply that they are.

The State's Attorney rises and introduces herself, "May it please the court, ladies and gentlemen of the jury, my name is Mrs. Wendy Sprong, counsel for the state of New Jersey, on behalf of Ms. Kat Rossinski and Mr. Thomas Headley in this action."

Ms. Sprong delivers his/her opening statement. It could not have been any longer than five minutes. She very handily and practically claims that she will prove, beyond a reasonable doubt that the defendant is guilty as charged, as well as an implicit mention of a charge to follow...Lying to Police.

Defense attorney Vincenzo gives her opening statement immediately after. She claims to be able to prove that there is reasonable doubt and that Mr. L'Italian has a reasonable alibi.

*

Plaintiff calls witnesses first. The order of witness presentations is determined by a strategy: In this case, a combination of chronological and a layout into the overall story. Direct examination of plaintiff witnesses includes cross-examination by defense and redirect examination by plaintiff.

"The State calls Coroner Peter Gozinia."

The Bailiff swears-in the coroner and waves him to the witness stand.

"Please state your full name for the court," Directs the D.A.

"Peter Gozinia, Coroner for Warren County, New Jersey."

"Please describe to the court how you found the victims initially."

"I was called to the crime scene to assess and ultimately determine both persons – a man and a woman – were indeed dead."

"Did you perform the autopsies on both of the deceased?"

"Yes."

"Can you please describe the procedures implemented?"

"Yes. I used standard procedures, which include a look inside the head and under the sternum and rib-cage."

"Please tell us about your findings?"

"In both the male and female, I found bullets in the head and heart."

"Are you able to confirm the cause of death?"

"Yes. They both expired with the gunshot to the head. Secondarily, the gunshot to the heart is deadly, but the shot to the head came first, and in both cases, that is the shot that killed them."

"And that is your official and documented finding, Mr. Gozinia?"

"Yes."

"That is all I have for you sir. Thank you very much."

Ms. Vincenzo stands and says, "No further questions at this time, your Honor."

"Witness is dismissed at this time." Judge Dellaur says.

"The State calls Warren County Ballistics Examiner Jack Mahogov to the stand."

He is sworn-on and seated. The D.A. asks for his name and role in this case.

"Please tell us the condition of the bullets delivered you from the Coroner by way the Chief of Police?"

"In each case, the bullets retrieved from the heads of the deceased were crushed, but the bullets from both the deceased were in near perfect condition."

"Were you able to match the bullets found in the heart and the head, even though the head-shot nearly flattened it?"

"Yes, all four bullets were of the same caliber."

"You were given a fire arm and asked if the bullets matched the gun allegedly used in the crime?"

"Yes, sir and I provided a positive match in all four bullets with the weapon."

"Thank you. That is all, your Honor."

"No further questions, your Honor." The Defense has nothing to dispute regarding the weapon found or the ballistics report.

"The State calls Mr. Maxwell Littlefield to the stand."

Mrs. Sprong asks Mr. Littlefield to state his name and complete address for the court.

"You are an unlicensed gun dealer; is that correct?"

"Yes, Ma'am that is correct."

Mrs. Sprong picks up the firearm, shows it is not loaded, and asks Littlefield if he recognizes it?

"It looks like one I had. I sold it almost three years ago."

"Do you have a record of sale for the transaction?"

"I do. Yes."

Mrs. Sprong puts a transparency of the record on the overhead projector.

"Let the court record this evidentiary note of sale of three firearms; a .22 Long Barrel Revolver, a .357 Magnum Long Barrel Revolver, and most importantly and pertinent to this case, a .380 Caliber Semi-Automatic pistol."

Sprong hands Littlefield the .380 again and asks him to compare the make and serial number on the weapon and if his note of sale record match. Mr. Littlefield replies that yes, in each case, make and serial number are the same.

"Let the court note those facts." Then, the State's Attorney asks Max Littlefield if he recognizes anyone in the courtroom as the individual that privately bought the firearms.

"Yes, I do."

"Please point that person out for the benefit of the court."

That is him over there; Littlefield points directly at Luke.

"Let the court note that Mr. Littlefield picked out Mr. L'Italian, the defendant, out of the approximately one-hundred or more that fill this courtroom right now." She excuses herself from the Direct Examination with this witness.

"Defense requests cross-examination, you Honor."

"Proceed…"

"Mr. Littlefield…Do you know if this bill

of sales has been shared with a handwriting expert?"

"I do not know."

"May we all understand – correctly – that you are not licensed to sell guns?"

"Yes. That is correct."

"I am compelled to disregard testimony from an underground criminal: Is that a fair understanding of your credibility?"

"The other side doesn't seem to take issue over it."

"No further questions at this time, your Honor."

Ms. Vincenzo walks to her table, and then appeals to the Judge. "Due to credibility issues, I request a motion to disallow Mr. Littlefield's testimony."

"Objection, your Honor," Mrs. Sprong begins. "The State intends to prove the validity of the document by testimony presented by a forensic sciences expert, as well as present a professional, expert handwriting analyst."

The judge looks at both attorneys and orders them to approach the bench. He whispers to the plaintiff attorney, "I intend to reserve judgment on the defense requested motion until the State is finished with your witness' testimonies. Is fair enough for you, Ms. Vincenzo?"

"Yes, your Honor," the Defense agrees, somewhat reluctantly.

"For the record, I too am satisfied with your decision, your Honor." The State prepares to call their next witness.

"Let this ruling be noted for the record that I reserve judgment on the defense requested motion until the State is finished with their witness' testimonies." The Judge has spoken! "You're your next witness please, Ms. Sprong."

"The State calls Dr. Daniel Cyr to the witness stand."

"Please tell the court what your expertise involves, or what your job is, primarily."

"I am a forensics scientist. I am paid by the state."

"Thank you. Now…regarding the testimony of Mr. Littlefield, please testify in simple terms to satisfy the Defense's issues: 1.) what is the age of the paper and ink that constitute this bill of sales we put up on the projector?"

"The paper is very old; I could not pinpoint in exact terms of date or time, but that paper is at least twenty years old…It comes from a letter-sized tear-off pad of paper."

"And the Ink…?"

"The ink I am able to prove is thirty-six months old."

"We have a folder of these facts in no uncertain detail the common law reports that forensics is required to keep and share for official and court records." Mrs. Sprong says, holding up the plastic sleeve in which the forensics documents reside. She brings them to the witness stand. "Dr. Cyr…Can you verify that the every occurrence of a signature on the documents is in no question, your own?"

"Yes, I can, Ma'am – all the signatures are mine."

Holding up an autumn jacket or coat and walking toward the witness stand, Mrs. Sprong asks Dr.Cyr, "Do you recognize this article of clothing, and if so, tell us the significance it has in this case?"

"I ably identified gun oil in the right jacket pocket that matches the firearm I examined."

"Let the records reflect that this jacket belongs to, and was retrieved from Mr. L'Italian upon a warranted search."

Holding up a gallon-size clear evidence

baggie, the State asks, "Dr. Cyr, do you recognize these items and if so, tell us where they originated and how old they are? Start with the underpants, and then tell us about the diaphragm."

"Well, all three come from Ms. Rossinski's home. The soiled underwear is sixteen to eighteen weeks old; the soil melded in the crotch of this pair is about ninety days old. They originate in Ms. Rossinski's bathroom hamper. The woman's diaphragm is approximately twelve to fourteen months old. The residue recovered from it, and around it consisted of her secretions, and the semen of an unknown man, but I proved it was not Mr. L'Italian's.

The clean pair of underwear is the same age as the soiled pair; proven by fibers and dust matching those that remain in Ms. Rossinski's bedroom drawer."

"Were you told where these items were found by any police investigative officer?"

"Yes…they were found in a hanging folder in a file cabinet in Mr. L'Italian's basement office. I was able to prove that, as well."

"That is all for now, your Honor."

"No further questions your Honor," Ms. Vincenzo announces.

"The State will now call witnesses regarding

motive. The State calls Mrs. Redding to the stand."

She is sworn-in, and then Sprong requests, "Please tell the court the position and role you given your job description."

The tall, woman with flaming red hair replies, "I am on the Information Sciences unit at Merck on Route 75. I am the manager of Information Security."

"Were Ms. Rossinski and Mr. Headley both employees at that same location?"

"Yes. Ms. Rossinski worked for me, and Mr. Headley worked in the Facilities unit."

"Are you aware that Mr. L'Italian worked in the Merck Information Sciences unit, but was asked to resign from Merck?"

"Yes, I was aware of it before he even became aware of it happening."

"How is that, Mrs. Redding?"

"His Manager asked me to assign someone to watch his online actions during business hours. I assigned the task to Ms. Rossinski. She noticed, by way of a packet tracking security application that he was visiting sites unrelated to business. They were not found to be illicit in any way; they were for the most part music-related."

"When you run that snooping software, is the target aware?"

"The target is not supposed to be aware, but understand that Mr. L'Italian is incredibly gifted in his field. He had anti-spyware running invisibly within his desktop client's operating system. That kind of talent made him; it is fair to say, 'The Star of the Show' in our department. In fact, not only did he write the aforementioned invisible anti-spyware, he also had running on his machine another piece of software – home grown, as well – that was able to bounce back to the offending target, in this case. He was running his own show, and Ms. Rossinski was his target. Mr. L'Italian was actually able to break through our very tight and solid fire-wall and reach Ms. Rossinski's PC."

"Wow! How do you think he felt when he discovered that his own neighbor was on a project defined to identify him and return suggestive or questionable work ethic results to his manager?"

"He never lied about what he was doing, but at the terminated employee exit meeting he was clearly upset and anxious. He did not have much to say, because he knew anything he offered would be moot and in vain, but we all read the story in his eyes. He was very upset."

"Thank you, Mrs. Redding."

"The State calls Mr. Henry Burke to the stand."

"Recalling the weekend in question – in this case anytime between Friday night and Sunday morning, do you recall seeing Mr. L'Italian outside of his home?"

"Yes, in fact my wife Sharon – he points toward her – saw him in the walkway of Ms. Rossinski's home on Saturday evening. I forget the exact time, but it was not late. She called me and asked that I look. I saw him at her door…knocking."

"Do you have any thoughts or opinion of how Mr. L'Italian felt about Ms. Rossinski?"

"They appeared to be friendly and a bit close, I would say."

"What about Mr. Rossinski?

"He was widely disliked, not just by Mr. L'Italian, but nearly all of us on Youmans Avenue."

"Did you or your wife notice anything odd about your online files or scripts you saved from your 'Equity' ISP?"

"Yes, it appears that certain scripts vanished somehow. We noticed right away after we saw the police at Ms. Rossinski's home. In particular, the scripts with a fellow user of a very specific kind of illicit seductress or seducer were the only ones that disappeared."

The State continues to call neighbors and ask them all the same questions. All of them gave the same or very similar answers to the testimony of Henry Burke. The next and the final three witnesses will complete the State's case.

"The State calls Miss Karen Mahoney to the stand."

In through the courtroom double doors led by her mother Deloris walks the oldest Mahoney girl. She is sworn-in. The Judge allows Mrs. Mahoney to sit beside her daughter and hold her hand.

"Thank you Mrs. Mahoney and Karen. Thank you so much for coming in and helping us today, Karen. I just have one question for you. Okay?"

"Yes Ma'am."

"When was the last time you ever saw Mr. L'Italian at Kat's…Ms. Rossinski's front or back door?"

"My two sisters and me, we saw him walking from the back of his house because we were on our back porch. We ran to the front and saw him standing at her front door. I remember it was a Saturday night, because right after that, my mom called us in for our favorite T.V. show."

"Thank you Karen. Thank you Mrs. Mahoney."

The State calls the Information Sciences designee, Miss Kim Gilford for this case to the stand."

"What was your role in the investigative process for this case?"

"I was asked to identify the software in or last deleted from the 'Equity' ISP."

"Did you find anything peculiar or outstanding?

"I did. I recovered a program written in a low-level language – meaning it was as close to machine code as we can get so far – that has the sole function of fooling the system into behaving as though Mr. L'Italian is online doing things…like artificial activity. Therefore, he could run this software and actually be in another place, but if anyone were to look at the CPU statistics, they would see activity, supposedly initiated by Mr. L'Italian, even though he is not truly there taking part in any activity at all."

"So, Miss Gilford this means that he could run the software and go out for a ham sandwich or something, but his presence still appeared online...active...is that correct?"

"Yes, Ma'am, that is correct."

"...Anything else in 'Equity raise a red flag to you during your investigation?

"One more thing did. That is, even though there are pre-sequenced, commercial sub-systems in place to take care of file back-ups, updates or deletion, there is an off-the-market program to reach into any computer connected to 'Equity' and manipulate the target directory trees and file systems. I scrubbed the CPU Stats and did notice the last time this program ran was the Sunday midafternoon, the day after the crime was committed. The last thing I picked-up on is a powerful sub-system that allows the System Administrator to login to 'Equity' with multiple user ID's concurrently and communicate with anyone online with one or another of these alias handles."

"Thank you Miss Gilford."

"This will be our last two witnesses, your Honor. The State calls Mr. Terrence O'Leary to the stand."

Mrs. Sprong waits for the Bailiff to do his job, and once seated, asks the witness to identify himself and define his job title.

"My name is Terence O'Leary and I am the Chief Operations Analyst at Western New Jersey Telephone."

"You were asked by the State to extract any information packets going to Ms. Rossinski's residence on Saturday, 7 March 1992. Did you find anything, and if so, comment on as many attributes of the packets found?"

"There was an outgoing telephone call from Ms. Rossinski to Ohio; another incoming on the Saturday in question at five o'clock. It was from Mr. Headley's line; and a DSL packet that I had barely and variably parsed, back and forth between Ms. Rossinski and Mr. Headley and one with Mr. L'Italian. That occurred shortly after the call from Mr. Headley to Ms. Rossinski."

"Thank you Mr. O'Leary.

"Finally, the State calls on Mrs. Annie L'Italian to the stand."

Luke is quite surprised, and so is his attorney, even though the entire case laid out by the State was a surprise. Ms. Vincenzo stands ready to call out to the Judge.

"Your Honor, this witness is not on our copy of the State's witness List, and is on the Defense's witness list."

"State…what say you?"

"Your Honor this is a new witness that we spoke to just yesterday evening. I did not have the time to get a new copy of our list published and distributed. May we call her a 'surprise' witness?"

"She may offer testimony for both sides. Proceed!"

"Would your husband, the defendant, have the time and wherewithal to conduct in an illicit affair with the deceased Ms. Rossinski?"

"Absolutely not…He was always either home with me, or working with or without me there. She worked full time and had two other jobs on the side. Beside all that, I know Kat! I am sorry…I knew Ms. Rossinski quite well, very well. She would never do such a thing."

"Finally, all that is stated and understood by the State and this court, can you think of anytime at all when Mr. L'Italian would have the opportunity to gain entrance into Ms. Rossinski's home without her knowledge?"

"Yes, I suppose he could have…anytime when she and I were both away our homes for any extended period of time…sure. She and I traded house keys and agreed to watch over each other's homes while away."

"Thank you very much Mrs. L'Italian."

"Your Honor…The State rests its case."

*

"The court calls for an overnight recess. The Defense will present their case at nine tomorrow morning. The Court is adjourned for the evening!"

"All rise!"

The judge walks into his chamber, and the courtroom slowly empties. Before the officers come for Luke to return him to jail, Ms. Vincenzo whispers to Luke, "We have to talk. I will be right over."

Ms. Vincenzo is close to livid, as she has ever been. She believed Luke from the start, but after hearing and seeing the prosecution's case, she is clearly not sure, at all. Moreover, Luke lied to her.

"Well, Mr. L'Italian," the attorney for the defense begins. "Are you as surprised as I am?"

"Yes, I am."

"Let's get something straight. I recall a lyric written by Bob Dylan, which is, 'To be an outlaw, one must be honest.' Now talk to me, damn it."

"What do we have to counter with, Ms. Vincenzo?"

"Gee, Mr. L'Italian, I don't know. They have it all tied up in an ugly little package!"

"You are my attorney. Aren't you supposed to handle these things?"

"Sure Luke, I can *handle* it…but I cannot spin together a pack of lies on your behalf: I am sorry."

"I will tell you why it happened without going through all their witness's testimonies."

"Tell me, please. I am eager to know. Do not bullshit around with me…Understand?"

"The affair I had with Kat was an online affair using the private messaging, or chat messaging functionality within 'Equity.' We both wanted to follow that lead we shared with each other. I knew who she was, of course, but she did not know it was me at the other end. She believed she was carrying-on with a doctor from New York City. She finally invited me over to her house so we could meet in person. That is how serious this thing was. I went over with every intention of talking through the reason I had to remain anonymous, and try, and hope that she would understand. So, I followed-through and went next door and knocked. We both acted surprised that she was she, and I was I, we hugged and she kissed me on the cheek. We walked down the hall and into her dining room. Almost immediately, Headley came around the corner from Kat's living room to the entrance to the dining room. Kat told me off, slapped me across the face and Headley pulled her toward him and put his arm around her. It was no secret to me that he secretly pined for her…for a long time. Nevertheless, he never made a move on her. I did…and there I am, standing there thinking all would work-out, until he enters the room, and snidely, gruffly asks, 'So L'Italian, how much does 'Equity' mean to you, because I have you by the balls, I promise you.' My head explodes, and in a knee-jerk action, I pull out the gun and shoot."

"Jesus Christ Luke!" Vincenzo exclaims.

"I cleaned-up, carried them down the cellar steps, wrapped them up, and buried them in the freezer. I then went back home and immediately set forth on the cover-up and the frame-up of Stone. That is pretty much it."

"So I am supposed to go back in tomorrow and insist they have the wrong man; that they should have arrested Mr. Rossinski? That is absurd after all the evidence they have. They have physical, forensic, and eye witnesses, Luke!"

"Well either tell a story about a threat

to me and my livelihood that made me snap, or come up with reasons why Stone is more guilty than I."

"We have no one who has testimony to dispute most of what they presented, Luke. I will do my best to iron something reasonable to close-out with."

"Please do…I'm sorry I did not just tell you all of this in the first place."

"You ought to be, Mr. L'Italian!"

"Ms. Vincenzo?"

"Yes, Mr. L'Italian…"

"I have severe behavioral and physical disorders."

"Oh this keeps getting better by the minute! I will find them; just quickly give me some names."

She goes back to her office and notifies the court that she needs an extension of the recess to work on the defense, given some of the testimony given by the State. Although Luke did not mention the introduction of medical-related evidence, she calls in emergency subpoenas for Luke's Behavioral Health Doctors. He has a Psychotherapist, a Psychiatrist and a Neurologist. She then pours through the State's case looking for any potential holes that she can put into question, or reasonable doubt. Finally, she must make a decision of how to sway the jury away from Second-Degree Murder, to a reduced charge of the non-premeditated kind. She considers the two choices, goes home and tries like hell to get to sleep. All she can think of is mistrial…

*

Luke sits in the eight by ten cell trembling, eyes wide half the night. He finally lies down and falls asleep only to be haunted with nightmares until waking up for breakfast at seven in the morning. He forces it down, feeling as if he could throw-up at any given time. In short, he feels like shit…for all the right reasons. He lays there until eight-thirty wondering what Ms. Vincenzo came-up with overnight.

The court approves a two-day extension to the recess. The court notifies all parties involved, including Luke. Perhaps he can believe…as though there exists…even a glimmer of hope. He hears nothing from Ms. Vincenzo until the evening before the scheduled day the trial resumes. She does not enter his cell; she beckons him to the window in the cell door. She simply states to him "Do not be, or appear to be surprised at anything I present. I want you to sit with your head down, holding it in your hands if you want, but remain in that posture throughout my case and closing. Do you understand?"

"Yes…alright Ms. Vincenzo."

He and his attorney sleep a little better now that she has a conceivable, believable case to present. If she can win sympathy from the jurors, he might…just might be looking at a reduced sentence, charges and hospitalization instead of hard jail time. Luke tries to psych-up for anything and hopes for the best.

The trial begins in an hour. Luke lost all sense of time since court went to recess. He jumps when he hears the commands from the escort court police officers. He sits at the defense table with his head in his hands. He is on the edge of falling back asleep. Then, the Bailiff bellows his cry, "All rise. The High Court of Warren County in the state of New Jersey, Case NU812 is now back in session, the Honorable Judge Charles Dellaur presiding."

All rise except for Luke, who is snoring into his hands, head down and nodding. Vincenzo grabs his shoulder and pulls upward. He comes out of it, hard and slow. The Bailiff repeats the order, just for him. "Will the defendant please rise!"

Luke finally stands-up. He is in a haze and can only manage to gaze straight-ahead, as the judge enters and sits. Ms. Vincenzo says, "Sit down now Mr. L'Italian."

Luke's attorney stands and addresses the judge. "May it please the court; the defense thanks the court for approving the extended recess. It is much appreciated."

"And what did that buy you Ms. Vincenzo? Something well-worth it, I would hope."

"I believe so, your Honor."

"Well then, let us begin. We would all like to hear the defendant's case, now. Go on a head, please, Ms. Vincenzo."

"Yes, your honor."

Right away, the State objects to the introduction of new witnesses that did not appear on the latest case documents.

"Overruled! The State presented a surprise: I must approve of the Defense to take advantage of the same judgment I made for you. The defense may continue."

"The Defense calls Ms. Annie L'Italian to the stand."

Annie does appear on both sides' witness list, no matter how odd it may seem to her. With no objections, the Defense asks her, "Ms.

L'Italian, I have noted that your testimony did not quite pass in presenting 'beyond a reasonable doubt.' Considering this, can you tell me in no unspecific terms, if and how you know for a fact your husband Mr. L'Italian and Ms. Rossinski in no way had a relationship, be it platonic or sexual in nature?"

"Well, I just know that's all. I was there. I know."

"I see…not nearly fit for the prosecution, in my humble opinion. Before we go on, take this opportunity to further detail your knowledge of the answer to the questions at hand."

"I have answered to the best of my feelings, then, how is that?"

"Oh, I see…your *feelings*, okay."

"Are you aware of or witnessed any odd behavior or habits regarding your husband? It is my intention to present the request for clarification and an open question. It represents a chance to get a closer look at my client in the eyes of one who may know."

"He enjoys sexual fantasy. He regularly masturbates with thoughts of the Television personality 'Martha,' as well as Kat… or… sorry, Ms. Rossinski."

"That is hardly uncommon for a vital man,

perhaps neglected his needs in more mainstream circumstances, as within the confines and boundaries between a husband and wife."

"I think he is a sex-addict."

Ms. Vincenzo asks that last comment be struck from the court records.

"Sustained," growls a rather impatient Judge Dellaur.

"I have one more question for you, Mrs. L'Italian. Are you or have you ever been aware of the behavioral disorders your husband suffers?"

She bursts out, sobbing, and Ms. Vincenzo, in a soft voice says, "It is alright, take your time, and then answer the question when you are able."

It takes Annie about three minutes to speak clearly enough so the attorney understands her. "I made a vow to my husband I would never disclose any part of his health to anyone…"

The judge immediately interjects, "May I remind you that you are under oath in the court of law? You must voice your answers contributing to this case, whether asked by the prosecution or defense. We do not want to hold anyone in contempt of my court, Mrs. L'Italian. Is that understood?"

"Yes, your Honor."

"The witness shall answer the question."

Annie looks at Luke and then back at his attorney, and says, "My husband suffers with some physical disorders…but moreover, deep behavioral issues, as well."

"I see. Thank you Mrs. L'Italian: That is all I have for you."

Before calling the next witness, Ms. Vincenzo presents an over-head projection for the court to see.

"Ladies and gentleman of the jury, I ask you to take this information in carefully, in depth and breadth, as it is important factual matter in the Defense's case."

"I have already instructed the jurors, Ms. Vincenzo, no need to schoolmarm them."

"I apologize, your Honor. It was my intention to imply that the facts the Defense is about to present may be confusing.

I am going to keep the over-head up throughout my case and closing. If it please the court, I will get the presentation up on the projector right now."

"…Go on then…" The judge seems quite sensitive.

"Thank you, your Honor."

Ms. Vincenzo walks to her table, picks-up the transparency, and places it on the overhead projector.

1. <u>Hyperkalemia – Potassium Level High</u> –

   a. Dr. Allen, Hackettstown Regional Hospital

2. <u>DIABETIC NEPHROPATHY– RENAL KIDNEY FAILURE</u> –

   a. Dr. Allen, Hackettstown Regional Hospital

3. **Stage 3 Kidney Disease**

4. **Diverticulitis** – Hackettstown Urgent Care Center

5. **Ulcerative Colitis** – Hackettstown Urgent Care Center

6. **Diabetes** –

   a. Hackettstown Urgent Care Center

7. <u>CORTICOBASAL DEGENERATION</u> –

   a. Dr. J. Taylor, Hackettstown Regional Hospital

8. <u>70% Hearing Loss</u> –

   a. Prograssivley worse – various audiologists in several locations

9. <u>Post-Traumatic Arthritis right side was all fractured from shoulder to ankle – Broken hip -</u>

    a. Hackettstown Urgent Care Center

10. <u>Bursitis – in both shoulders -</u>

    a. Dr Paul Raczinski, Phillipsburg, NJ

11. <u>Spinal Stenosis-High pain spinal cord and spine lumbar -</u>

    a. Hackettstown Urgent Care Center, Hackettstown, NJ

12. <u>Gout- influx of uric acids -</u>

    a. Dr. Miller, Rheumatology Associates, Hackettstown, NJ

13. <u>Hypothyroidism- low thyroid -</u>

    a. Dr. Allen, Hackettstown Memorial Hospital, Hackettstown, NJ

14. <u>Hypertension -</u>

    a. Dr. Allen, Hackettstown Memorial Hospital, Hackettstown, NJ

15. <u>MANIC-BIPOLAR DEPRESSION -</u>

    a. Several Psychiatrists, recently Dr. Mitchell Pulver, Hackettstown, NJ (one of several to diagnose this reaching back over twenty years)

> i.  SOCIAL ANXIETY DISORDER-PEOPLE SCAREMR. L'ITALIEN
>
> ii. HE SOBS OFTEN
>
> iii. AGORAPHOBIA- HAS A HARD TIME LEAVING THE HOUSE
>
> iv. ANXIETY-MANIC AND NERVOUS THROUGHOUT THE DAY

16. <u>**INSOMNIA-I CAN'T FALL ASLEEP OR NATURALLY STAY ASLEEP**</u> –

    a. Several Psychiatrists, recently Dr. Mitchell Pulver, Hackettstown, NJ

17. <u>**Schizophrenia**</u> –

    a. Several Psychiatrists, most recently Dr. Mitchell Pulver, Hackettstown, NJ

18. <u>**G.E.R.D. - Gastro esophageal reflux disease**</u> –

    a. Lifelong Issue – PCP, Dr. Allen, Hackettstown, NJ

19. <u>**Vertigo/Labrynthitis**</u> –

    a. Several Doctors throughout the years (life-long: intermittent), PCP, Dr. Allen, Hackettstown, NJ

"Okay everyone: Thank you very much. Defense calls Dr. Mitchell Pulver to the stand."

The doctor walks in through the courtroom double doors, and takes the stand.

"Doctor Pulver, please take a moment to review the Behavioral Health Disorders displayed on the projector."

The doctor takes a couple minutes to study the chart, and then states, "Okay, I am ready."

"Doctor, referring to the behavioral health issues, specifically diagnosed for Mr. L'Italian, is the chart accurate?"

"Yes, it is accurate, but not quite complete in the way of Mr. L'Italian's symptoms and multiple crises' I have seen him through."

"Will you please share for the sake of a legal matter in the court of law, what is missing, or anything misrepresented?"

"Stressing the factoids numbers twelve, thirteen and fourteen, Mr. L'Italian has suffered with suicidal tendencies for the past twenty years. Under my care, to date, that I am aware-of, he has attempted suicide on ten occurrences under crises. He was housed each time in a Behavioral Health facility"

"Have you reviewed Mr. L'Italian's records from his previous provider, or providers?"

"Yes, I have. Mr. L'Italian, due to his

Manic Bipolar-Depression, Insomnia and Schizophrenia, has survived a lifetime of ill behavioral health."

"So, that means clearly, he is in fact, so bad-off that he is a suicidal risk, is that a fair statement?"

"Yes, it is."

"Has Mr. L'Italian ever, as far as you can be certain, ever, *ever*, had thoughts or displayed or complained of homicidal thoughts or tendencies?"

"No sir. He never has. Never…"

"Is it conceivable to you that he would ever commit homicide?"

"I have to say, no. The caveat being that anyone as ill as Mr. L'Italian, are prone to poor judgment, skewed circumstances, as he views them and making extremely irrational choices be it verbally or physically. He must call-up a tremendous amount of thought and concentration to endure the days as they come and go."

"In the briefing for this case, doctor, if Mr. L'Italian is being considered guilty of murder, and in his case, NOT pre-meditated, would he be a better candidate for imprisonment or rehabilitation or psychological care in an

Institution…In your professional opinion and your work with Mr. L'Italian?"

"He is a troubled, very ill and diseased man, but not a criminal. I would advise Institutionalization for an undetermined length of time, for acute and consistent treatment, evaluation, and rehabilitation. As I stated, I must stress to you that I know Mr. L'Italian from the inside out, so I repeat he is not your common criminal, but is sick enough to have literally snapped into taking the action he is accused of, without realizing what he is doing, until it happens to come to him."

"Is there anything else you can educate us about your diagnosis and analysis of Mr. L'Italian?"

"I would like to remind you all not to down-play the severity of effect that comes with number twelve-A, one, two, and three, and also number thirteen: Those illnesses and symptoms are enough to drive anyone into crises. Mr. L'Italian is the strongest man I have ever known and treated."

"Thank you Doctor. That's all for now."

"Cross-Examination, please, your honor…"

"Proceed…"

"Doctor Pulver what makes you sure beside

his manner when with you that he could or would never consider homicide?"

"Sir, I know what this man has been through: He has been accosted with guns, knives and hammers…all within the past seven years alone. He has suffered verbal abuse most of his life, as well. He has always had the means to strike back to the highest essence of that phrase, but he never did, even though he chose to arm himself many years ago. He has faced many hard times where it would almost drive even a completely healthy man to kill, but Mr. L'Italian never did."

"Thank you Doctor."

The Judge says, "You may step down, Doctor."

The Defense calls Dr. David Breer to the stand."

"Dr. Breer you were instructed to sit inside for Doctor Pulver's testimony. Do you concur with his statements and diagnosis about and for Mr. L'Italian?"

"Yes, I do."

"Is there anything you care to comment, besides Doctor Pulver's testimony?"

"No…He covered Mr. L'Italian's case extremely well and accurately.

"Thank you."

"Cross?"

"No, thank you your honor."

"The witness may step down."

"The Defense calls Dr. Herman Stegeman to the stand."

"Dr. Stegeman, you were instructed to sit inside for Doctor Pulver's testimony. Do you concur with his statements and diagnosis about and for Mr. L'Italian?"

"Yes, I do."

"Is there anything you care to comment, besides Doctor Pulver's testimony?"

"No…He covered Mr. L'Italian's case extremely well and accurately.

"Thank you."

"Cross?"

"No, your Honor."

"The Defense calls Doctor John Taylor to the stand."

"Doctor Taylor, please expound upon corticobasal degeneration for the court."

"Corticobasal Degeneration is a rare disorder that causes shrinkage to the brain."

"Please speak to the court about how this

affects the ill, and tell us how Mr. L'Italian contracted this disorder."

"The sadness of this disease is obviously very disturbing, given the explanation I just submitted to you, but particularly, it causes a slow yet sure disengagement to all senses and receptors in the brain. It eventually renders the patient nearly unable to simply think and concentrate through the days – everyday. In my interviews with Mr. L'Italian, I learned that Mr. L'Italian's father was killed when Luke was just twelve years of age. Six weeks later, while on holiday with a family friend, also a priest, the clergyman repeatedly raped Mr. L'Italian, before delivering him back to his home. Mr. L'Italian, in an acute state of shock, developed a severe case of double pneumonia, then shortly after diagnosed with Post Traumatic Stress Disorder. One year later, Mr. L'Italian puts the common reaction called 'masking' into play. That is, he went undiagnosed as his PTSD turned to an acute case of emotional diseases, well explained by Doctor Pulver, earlier. Mr. L'Italian fell-into and kept-up this skewed method of soothing his emotional stress and anxiety for nearly twenty years. The use of cocaine – a major player in his self-medication, or masking – for that extended period is what caused the disease in his case. His brain has lost five millimeters of mass so far. We do not know if the illness will continue, or become dormant, now that he is clean and sober."

"Thank you, Doctor Taylor. That is all I have your Honor."

Virtually everyone, from the judge down to the jurors and nonprofessionals observers sit in total dismay. Some people are crying.

The judge asks Mrs. Sprong, "Cross Examination?"

"No, your Honor."

"The Defense rests its case, your honor." Ms. Vincenzo walks slowly back to her seat at the defense's table.

"Let us hear each side's closing arguments before we break for lunch," Judge Dellaur instructs. "Will the State please offer your closing argument at this time?"

"Yes, your Honor, we are prepared to deliver our Closing Arguments. Ladies and gentlemen of the jury, we brought this case to trial with the burden of proof, beyond a reasonable doubt, that the defendant, Mr. Luke L'Italian, caused the death of the two victims, Ms. Kat Rossinski and Mr. Thomas Headley. I believe, by virtue of the complete story of the crime from the evidence and witness testimonies, as I would expect you to do, that we successfully did that for you.

The defendant is guilty of Second Degree Murder, and the State believes that it is reasonable to consider those charges. The State rests its Closing Argument."

The plaintiff's closing argument is no longer than five minutes. The defense presents its closing.

"Ladies and gentlemen of the jury, I will not address or try to disprove the State's representation of what they believe are facts. I would simply ask you to please, take *ALL* delivered to you close to your deliberations, in mind, in heart and in soul. The defense introduced the wholly and reasonable case that Mr. L'Italian is clearly *not guilty as charged*. We believe, by virtue of the professional medical and behavioral witness's testimonies, clearly introduces reasonable doubt considering all things, that is all things, the Defense's case as well as the State's charges, he is *not guilty* of murder to any degree. I ask that you keep the Defense's case testimony in the forefront of your mind as you deliberate. Thank you very much, ladies and gentlemen of the jury."

The plaintiff, because it has the burden of proof, has up to two minutes to present its rebuttal closing, if they wish. They do not.

The Judge's Charge to the Jury reminds them of the Instructions and the set of legal rules that jurors ought to follow when deciding a case. The jury instructor usually reads the same rules and instructions aloud to the jury initially just prior to the trial time of day. They are often the subject of discussion of the case, how they will decide who is guilty. The judge reads aloud in the court of trial, in order to make sure all interests remain represented and that they say nothing prejudicial.

After rounding-out the Instructions, and the Jury replies that they understand them, the judge orders Juror Deliberation. Directly after hearing the judge's instruction to deliberate, the jury leaves the courtroom and meets in their assigned jury room to decide on a verdict. This jury is made-up of seven females and five males. Jury members first select a foreperson that will lead their discussions and facilitate the process. They vote and elect a man, a common person from the Borough. The jury reviews the evidence and votes on a verdict. Although the U.S. Supreme Court has ruled that unanimous verdicts of guilty or not guilty are not mandatory in all criminal cases, almost every state, including New Jersey still requires them.

Several votes are necessary before they arrive at a unanimous verdict. If after a reasonable time, the jurors cannot reach a unanimous verdict, they become a 'hung jury.'

The foreperson will report this fact to the judge. If the judge believes that further jury deliberations are futile, the judge will declare a mistrial. The prosecutor will then have to either request another trial with a new jury, or drop the charges against the defendant. If the jury returns a unanimous verdict of not guilty, the defendant goes free. When the jury unanimously finds the defendant guilty, the judge sets a date for a sentencing hearing.

*

A sealed verdict is a verdict that the Jury Foreman puts in a sealed envelope. There is a delay in court activity outside of deliberation, so there is a delay in announcing the result. The jury foreman sends a note to the judge that they believe they have come to a unanimous decision…verdict. While waiting for the judge, the parties and the attorneys to come back to court, the verdict remains with the jury foreman in the sealed envelope until court reconvenes. When all parties return, the judge asks the jury foreperson if they have come to a unanimous decision and verdict.

"Yes, your Honor, we have…"

"Bailiff, please hand the sealed verdict it to me."

The judge silently reads the verdicts of each charge, poker-faced. He then hands the verdict to the court Floor-person.

"Floor-person…please read aloud the verdict for the court."

It is a Judge Not Withstanding Verdict. JNWV is the practice in American courts whereby the presiding judge in a civil, county or state jury trial may overrule the decision of a jury and reverse or amend their verdict.

"We, the jury find the defendant Mr. Luke L'Italian not guilty as charged in the indictment, Case NU812. The verdict is signed by Edward F. Kratzke, Foreman, and the eleven other jurors."

There comes a loud gasp from everybody in the courtroom. The Judge calls for order, hammering his gavel repeatedly. He considers amending the verdict, but instead offers a strong suggestion to Ms. Vincenzo.

"Ms. Vincenzo, I hereby charge you to assign guidance, by way of your office or a designee, facility, or treatment center, etc., to Mr. L'Italian in choosing a facility in-charge of custody, rehabilitation and treatment, given his behavioral health, which obviously played-into the verdict."

"Yes your Honor. I will do so. Thank you, your Honor."

Judge Dellaur speaks to the jurors.

"Thank you ladies and gentlemen. I wish I were eloquent enough to express my appreciation to you for your service in this case, as it was also difficult to try. I know you had a great responsibility also. I express to you in behalf of everybody concerned our deep and appreciative thanks for your service."

"You are now excused. Prosecution and Defense please remain in the courtroom. Everyone else, please exit the courtroom at this time."

Everyone remains seated, most of them dismayed, as the jury files out of the courtroom.

"Ladies and gentlemen, I was tempted to amend the verdict, or augment it as a Mistrial. However, I received a note for my eyes only that represented a short cover letter, delivered with the verdict, composed by the jury members. Listen carefully. The State filed the wrong charge: We have reasonable doubt. The Defense entered a plea, yet not one that is more precisely the case – Not Guilty, due to Insanity – be it terminal or temporary. Therefore, our stress points in this note are summed-up and constituted by three words...GUILTY AS CHARGED.

The court excuses you at this time. Think about it! If this happens again from either side in my courtroom, I *will* call a Mistrial!"

Luke hugs his attorney, his right hand caressing her lower back, dangerously close to her buttocks.

THE END